the cliff-top killer

BOOK EIGHT OF THE SYDNEY HARBOUR HOSPITAL SERIES

CHRIS TAYLOR

LCT Productions Pty Ltd
18364 Kamilaroi Highway, Narrabri NSW 2390

ISBN. 978-1-925119-39-8 (Paperback)

Published in the United States of America.

BOOKS BY CHRIS TAYLOR

THE MUNRO FAMILY SERIES
(In order)

The Profiler
The Investigator
The Predator
The Betrayal
The Deception
The Negotiator
The Christmas Vigil
The Ransom
The Defendant
The Shooting
The Maker
(Available in Audio)

THE SYDNEY HARBOUR HOSPITAL SERIES
(in order)

The Perfect Husband
The Body Thief
The Baby Snatchers
The Final Bullet
The Debt Collector
The Lab Test
The Stolen Identity
The Cliff-top Killer
The Likeable Fraudster

THE SYDNEY LEGAL SERIES
(in order)

An Accidental Murderer
At the Hand of her Father
A Woman Scorned
Lies and Deception
Ordinary Evil
The Perfect Crime
Malicious Love
Toxic Inheritance

THE BARRINGTON FAMILY SERIES
(in order)

Broken Lives
Broken Promises
Broken Bonds
Broken Spirits
Broken Vows
Broken Minds
Broken Dreams
Broken Hearts
Broken Homes

THE CRAIGDON FAMILY SERIES
(in order)

Callum
Joel
Isabella
Nicholas
Sophia
Flynn
Noah
Logan
Elizabeth

Get a FREE book when you sign up for Chris Taylor's
newsletter at: www.christaylorauthor.com.au

Love Audiobooks? Check out Chris Taylor Books on audio
on Audible.com, Amazon.com and the iBooks store.

Join Chris Taylor's Facebook reader group/fan page and be
among the first to receive news of book releases, read and
review books prior to release and other amazing offers. Join
Now at: www.facebook.com/groups/1758023621144744/

Find out more about all of Chris Taylor's books, by visiting her
website at: www.christaylorauthor.com.au/about/books

DEDICATION

This book is dedicated to Pat Thomas, editor extraordinaire. Nineteen books and counting and you still get a thrill out of my stories. Thank you.

And as always, to my rock: my husband, Linden. I love you.

ACKNOWLEDGMENTS

As usual, no book comes into being without a lot of help and support by my friends and family. A world of thanks must go to my wonderful editor, Pat Thomas. Thank you for everything that you do to make my stories even more amazing than I could ever dare to dream. To Detective Superintendent Michael Kilfoyle, thank you for lending my story credibility. Any mistakes are wholly my own.

To Alisha Moore and all of the staff at damonza.com, thank you for yet another fantastic cover. To my sister, Nicole Guihot and to my friend, Ally Thomson, thank you for your excellent editorial comments, proof reading skills and suggestions. I hope you like the final result.

To Amy Atwell and her dedicated staff at Author EMS who are so much more than book formatters. Amy, once again, thank you for your magic.

To the fantastic writer organizations such as Romance Writers of Australia, Romance Writers of

America and Romance Writers of New Zealand for all the help, support and encouragement they offer new and aspiring writers, including me.

To my readers, thank you for your support and love for my stories. Your encouragement and enjoyment make this journey all worthwhile.

And lastly, to my friends and family, especially my husband and children. Thank you for putting up with late dinners and even later conversations as I've emerged day after day from the sometimes scary but always enthralling world I've created on my computer.

PROLOGUE

Dear Diary,

I went down there last night, after the house was silent and still. I shouldn't have gone. It's not like I didn't know what I would find. But I couldn't help it. It's as if I was trying to punish myself. All it did was make me angry, so angry I could barely breathe. My pulse raced. It was like an elephant sat on my chest. I thought I was going to have a heart attack. Keel over, dead, right there on the floor of our basement. Imagine that?

Of course, I didn't. With an effort, I got my fury under control, until its white-hot heat had settled into an icy block of contempt, way down low in my stomach. As I returned to my usual state of calmness, everything became clear, like morning sunlight flooding a room on a glorious summer day. I knew what I had to do...

CHAPTER 1

Three months later

With an impatient sound in the back of her throat, Shelby Gianopoulos pushed a wayward strand of hair out of her eyes and ploughed her way through the crowd of early morning commuters departing the train station. Again she cursed the alarm that had failed to go off at the prescribed hour. She was going to be late for her first shift at the Sydney Harbour Hospital.

"Excuse me," she murmured, pushing past a woman dressed in a smart business suit and carrying a briefcase that looked like it cost more than Shelby earned in a month.

The woman threw her a stern look, her red lips pursed in a frown, but thankfully she moved out of the way. Shelby hurried forward a more few feet and then came up short behind two student types with backpacks slung over their shoulders. They strode casually in front of her, blocking her path.

"Please, I'm running late. Do you mind?" she

said to their backs, raising her voice above the din of several hundred people, all intent on reaching their destination.

One of the young men glanced at her over his shoulder and then continued on his way. His pace remained slow and measured. Shelby gritted her teeth and tried again.

"Look, boys, I understand that you have all day to get to your lecture hall, but some of us have to work for a living. I'm late for the first day of my new job. That's not your fault, but I'd appreciate it if you'd step aside and let me through. Please, I really need to get to work."

This time, the men stopped and turned to face her. The one who'd dismissed her, shot her a lop-sided, self-assured grin that immediately reminded her of her youngest brother. John was eighteen and every bit as good looking—and just as cocky as these two.

"What do you do?" the man asked, giving her a quick once-over.

Shelby suppressed a grin. She was close to a decade older than the guy and yet, his dark brown eyes shone with interest.

"I'm a midwife," she supplied. "I work at the Sydney Harbour Hospital. At least, I will if I manage to get there without being fired for being late on my first day." She softened her words with a smile.

The boy who'd spoken glanced at his mate and then grinned at her again. "Well, we can't have that, can we?"

Without warning, he let out an ear piercing whistle that sent commuters scurrying in all directions.

"Hey!" he yelled to no one in particular. "Move aside, this lady needs to get through. She has an emergency to attend."

Like Moses at the Red Sea, the crowds ahead of them parted. Shelby shook her head in amazement. She looked at the man responsible for the miracle.

"Thank you." She laughed. "I wasn't expecting you to do that, but I really appreciate it."

He shot her a wink and she couldn't help the way her belly did a little somersault. If only he were ten years older... Swallowing a sigh and with a brief wave of farewell, she surged forward through the gap in the pedestrian traffic and continued on her way.

The entrance to the Sydney Harbour Hospital, with its wide, double glass doors, was just as impressive as the sixteen-story sandstone building that towered before her. Butterflies churned in her stomach and she breathed deeply, hoping to calm her sudden rush of nerves. Adjusting her shoulder bag, she made her way down the cobblestoned path that led to the front doors.

Stepping inside, she breathed in the familiar hospital scent. It was the same in hospitals everywhere. A unique combination of disinfectant and other cleaning solutions. Uniformed staff members brushed past her, chatting to each other as they made their way to work. A surge of excitement went through her like it always did when she was in a hospital. There was nothing she didn't love about being a nurse.

Not far past the main foyer, she spied an

information desk. It was manned by a white-haired woman with the word 'volunteer' printed on a tag she wore. Shelby fumbled inside her bag and retrieved the crumpled letter she'd received from the hospital's HR department a fortnight earlier, confirming her acceptance for the position. She smiled at the woman behind the counter.

"Hello, I was wondering if you could tell me how to get to level seven of E Block?"

The woman's eyes twinkled with pleasure. "Good morning, and welcome to the Sydney Harbour Hospital. You're looking for one of our maternity wards. I take it you're new?"

Shelby nodded. "Yes. I'm Shelby Gianopoulos. This is my first day."

"Pleased to meet you, Shelby. What a lovely name!"

Shelby blushed. "Thank you. I was named after Julia Robert's character in the movie *Steel Magnolias*. My mom watched it not long before I was born and sobbed all the way home from the theater. My dad protested because he wanted a traditional Greek name, like all the other girls in his family, but Mom would have none of that."

The woman smiled. "Well, I'm glad your mom held out. I'm Marjorie Campbell, by the way. You can find me most mornings right here at the information desk. I share it with Dottie Featherdale. Between the two of us, there's nothing we don't know about this place." She winked and Shelby couldn't help but chuckle even though she was anxious to get on her way.

"That's good to know, Marjorie and it's nice to

meet you. I'd love to stay and chat some more, but I'm in a bit of a hurry. Do you mind telling me where I can find the maternity ward? If I don't get a move on, I'm going to be late."

"Of course, honey." She pointed down the corridor. "You're already in E Block. Keep heading in that direction. You'll go past the coffee shop and a florist. Keep going until you come to a bank of elevators. Take one up to level seven. The ward's on the left off the elevator."

"Thanks so much, Marjorie. I appreciate your help." She shot the woman a smile.

"You're more than welcome, Shelby. I look forward to seeing you around. You have a nice day, won't you?"

Turning away, Shelby stuffed the letter back into her bag and took off toward the elevators. She glanced at her watch and cursed under her breath. She had less than three minutes.

Half-running, she once again ducked and wove her way through people who were hurrying to work. The woman in front of her came to a sudden halt and it was all Shelby could do not to collide with her. With a quick sidestep, she avoided the collision, but ran into something solid.

"Oh!" A gasp fell from her mouth.

She looked up in time to see a large brown stain spreading over the crisp white coat of the man who stood beside her. In his hand was an almost empty jumbo-sized Styrofoam coffee cup. Realization suddenly hit her: She was responsible for the damage to his coat.

"Oh, my goodness! I'm so sorry! I didn't mean to

run into you. I was just trying to..." She shook her head, helpless to explain. He regarded her calmly. Heat burst across her cheeks.

He shot her a reassuring smile. "Don't worry about it. It was an accident."

Embarrassment continued to wash over her. "I'm sorry. Give me your details. I'll pay for the dry cleaning."

His smile morphed into a chuckle. "Don't be silly. I have plenty of coats. Besides, it's just a coffee stain. It'll wash out."

"But... But it's only early. You'll be walking around like that all day," she protested.

The man shrugged and smiled again. "I'm sure I've walked around in worse. In fact, I know I have."

Shelby's face grew warm again and it had nothing to do with embarrassment. Belatedly, she noticed how attractive he was as he casually brushed away her concerns with grace and charm. Her stomach somersaulted with a different kind of nerves. All of a sudden, she was eager to get away from him.

"Well, if you're sure. I guess... I guess I'd better get to work. I don't want to be late."

"No, you don't." He gave her a wink.

With another blush burning a path across her cheeks, she turned and fled.

———————

Doctor Samuel Munro stared in appreciation at the woman's departing back. Her long, dark hair danced around her head with every stride that took her away from him. His gaze roved over her tidy figure. Even under her nurse's uniform, it was obvious she was soft and curvy in all the right places. He wondered who she was.

He'd been employed as an obstetrician at the hospital for more than three years and had been a resident there for some years before that. He was sure he hadn't seen her before. Of course, it was possible she worked in a different building. The hospital was spread over nearly two hectares and employed more than a thousand staff. There were many employees he'd never met.

But this woman was in his building and had headed in the direction of the elevators. She'd said she was on her way to work. *Perhaps she was new on staff?* All of a sudden, he was eager to find out.

"Samuel, my man! What are you up to this fine and sunny day?"

Samuel turned and greeted his friend and colleague with a smile. "Fancy seeing you here so early, Ian. The way you were knocking back those tequilas last night, I was sure you were rostered on a late shift."

Doctor Ian Broderick grabbed Samuel around the neck in a friendly tussle. "Ha! What are you talking about? Do I look like a guy who lets the thought of a little hangover stop him from having a good time?" Releasing his grip, Ian stood back and then frowned. "What the hell happened to your coat? Didn't your parents teach you how to drink from a cup?"

Samuel glanced down at the coffee stain marking his jacket and grimaced. "Ha, ha. Aren't we the comedian today?"

Ian made a move toward Samuel's chest with a clenched fist and Samuel deftly sidestepped the mock punch. "So, how'd it go with that girl you were chatting up?" he asked in an effort to deflect Ian's attention. "You looked pretty friendly when I left."

Ian grin turned sour. "Oh, yeah! We got friendly all right. Right up until the moment I tried to kiss her. Then she suddenly remembered she had to get up early the next morning for some important meeting. Didn't want to oversleep."

Samuel shook his head in commiseration. Ian tried so hard to get on with the ladies. *Too* hard, in Samuel's opinion, but Ian would hear none of it. Samuel had stopped giving him advice as far as his love life went. Ian was an adult. He'd eventually figure it out. Samuel only hoped it would happen soon. Ian's whining about how the girls flocked to Samuel without any effort was getting tiresome.

"Hey, what are you doing Friday night?" Ian asked, dragging Samuel's attention back to his colleague.

"I don't know. I'm working until six. I guess we could do something after that."

"Great. I'm not rostered on until midnight. We can go out beforehand. I'll make some calls. I'm betting the Martin twins will be eager to hang out with us again. We had fun the other night, didn't we? Christina was all over you, pushing those big tits in your face. Did you get lucky?"

Samuel stared at his friend in disgust. "Don't talk about her like that, Ian. She's a nice girl. We had a good time."

Ian immediately looked contrite. "Sorry, mate. I didn't mean anything by it. Just guy talk, you know. Her sister was just as hot. Maybe we can get the two of them to double date again. What do you think?"

Samuel thought about Ian's suggestion. It was true. Christina and Catherine Martin had been fun. Tall, blond and busty, they'd surprised him with their humor. They both worked in the fashion industry and though they probably couldn't tell him who the current prime minister was, it was easy enough to spend a Friday evening with them. They were just the kind of girls he liked to spend his time with. Fun and flirty, with no strings attached.

He gave Ian a nod. "Sure, why not?"

Ian's face immediately broke out into a wide smile. "Great. I'll call them. See you round."

"Yeah, have a good day."

Samuel looked down at the stain on his coat and silently debated whether he should detour via his locker and get a clean one. He checked his watch. If he didn't get moving, he'd be late for the ward round. Geraldine Walker was the Nursing Unit Manager of the maternity ward on level seven and she wasn't a woman to be messed with.

He'd been employed at the hospital barely six months when she cornered him in her office and invited him out to dinner. Whilst he'd been flattered, she was at least a decade older than him and though she was an attractive woman, he wasn't interested. As tactfully as he could, he'd turned her down. It hadn't gone over well and ever since, she'd made it her business to chew his ass at any opportunity.

With his mind made up, he ducked into the nearest bathroom and took off his coat. Turning on the water, he held it under the flow and gave it a quick scrub. The stain lightened marginally. It now looked more like newborn baby poo. Too bad he worked on the delivery ward. People might jump to the wrong conclusion. Still, he was out of time. It would have to do.

Shelby smiled a nervous greeting to the nurse beside her and hastily stowed her bag in the locker inside the tearoom like she'd been told. Despite her best efforts, she'd been a couple of minutes late to the ward and had been confronted by a none-too-happy boss. Geraldine Walker had introduced herself in clipped tones and had then told her in no uncertain terms never to be late for a shift again.

"You're new, right?" someone said from behind her.

Startled out of her thoughts, Shelby blinked and turned. The sparkle in the other nurse's friendly brown eyes eased some of the tension that held Shelby taut.

"Y-yes. I started this morning."

"Ally Beckwith." The nurse held out her hand.

Shelby shook it. "Shelby Gianopoulos," she replied.

Ally's eyes twinkled. "That's a bit of a mouthful."

Shelby laughed. "Yes, it's Greek."

Ally nodded in understanding. "I guess that accounts for your coloring and great skin. I'd kill to have skin like that." Ally touched her mousy brown hair self-consciously.

"Thanks." Shelby smiled, but was a little embarrassed by the other girl's praise.

"Have you ever worked on a delivery ward?" Ally asked, closing the door to her locker.

"Yes, of course. I've been a midwife for nearly three years. I've been working at the Prince of Wales Hospital in the eastern suburbs. It's close to where my parents live in Bondi."

"So, what made you take a job across town? It's a fair commute from Bondi."

Shelby nodded. "You're right. I moved out of home a few weeks ago, right after my twenty-seventh birthday. I figured it was probably time to get a place of my own."

Ally smiled. "And did you?"

Shelby chuckled. "Kind of. I moved into a house with three of my siblings."

Ally shook her head in disbelief and her eyes glinted with laughter. "Oh yeah, I'd say that was a pretty big move. Did you even move out of Bondi?"

"Of course!" Shelby exclaimed in mock outrage. "What sort of twenty-seven-year-old, trying to stand on her own two feet, do you think I am?"

Ally's grin widened. "How far did you go?"

"I'll have you know, I moved all the way over to North Sydney."

Ally's expression was filled with mock surprise. "All the way to North Sydney? Wow! That's like, almost an hour away from your parents!"

"Probably more like forty minutes," Shelby murmured cheekily.

"Ah, but that doesn't take into account traffic snarls."

"You're right," Shelby agreed. "I did move an *incredibly* long way away."

"Just as well you still have family close by." Ally winked.

"Exactly!" Shelby said. "I knew there was a reason I decided to move in with my brother and two sisters."

"You must be close," Ally said, her expression wistful.

"Yes, we are. When we're not trying to kill each other. My brother, Dimitri can be—"

"If you ladies are finished gossiping in here, perhaps you'd like to join us for the ward round. Doctor Munro has arrived. We're about to begin."

Shelby took in the stern visage of her boss and clamped her mouth shut. Hurriedly closing the door to her locker, she picked up her pen and notepad and followed Ally from the room.

CHAPTER 2

Samuel scanned the patient list and waited for the nursing staff to gather. It was customary to begin the day with a ward round wherein he would be given an update on the progress of each of his patients and he would thereafter dispense orders. It also gave him a chance to speak with his patients before and after the exciting arrival of their newborn. He was able to reassure those who'd come in for a planned induction or who were in the early stages of labor, as well as congratulate, once again, those mothers who'd given birth.

The Nursing Unit Manager came to a halt beside him. "We're ready when you are, Doctor," she said, her voice all business.

"Thank you, Geraldine."

Only minutes earlier, he'd been forced to jog the final few yards to the ward and had rounded the corner slightly out of breath. Geraldine was seated behind the desk at the nurses' station and stood when he entered. Her gaze had zeroed in on the stain on his white coat and her lips had tightened when she frowned, but she'd remained silent about the questionable state of his attire and he'd been spared from providing any further explanation.

He waited for her to precede him and then fell into step beside her. A small gathering of nurses followed behind them. They entered the first room. According to Samuel's list, the woman due to give birth had a long history of hypertension and had been admitted for a planned induction. He smiled at the patient in greeting.

"Caroline, you're looking great. How are you feeling?"

The woman winced and rubbed her swollen stomach. "Much better after I deliver this one," she replied. A soft smile played around her lips.

"Well, don't worry about that. Hopefully your baby will be here before the day is out." He turned to Geraldine. "Let's get that IV started. The sooner, the better."

"Yes, Doctor." The woman turned to the group of nurses who'd gathered behind her. "Shelby Gianopoulos, this patient is yours. Make sure the IV is up and going right away."

The nurse who'd been spoken to nodded and turned to look in Samuel's direction. He started in surprise. It was the woman who'd spilled his coffee. She was every bit as attractive as he remembered from his fleeting encounter with her downstairs. Her gaze found his and widened and he could tell she'd also made the connection. A faint blush stained her cheeks and he suppressed a smile. She was adorable. He made a mental note to seek her out after the ward round.

———

Shelby tried hard to ignore her embarrassment. Of all the people to run into... He could have worked on any other ward in the hospital and yet, here he was, on the maternity ward. With her. *Great.*

Surreptitiously, she peeked at him through her lashes and noticed the coffee stain was now a yellowish-brown. The area looked damp, like someone had made an attempt to launder it. A fresh wave of embarrassment washed over her and she bit her lip against a groan. She could only hope he wouldn't say anything in front of her colleagues. It was her first day. She couldn't bear the thought.

To top it off, he was drop-dead gorgeous. From the moment she'd stared into his baby blues, her pulse rate had taken flight. His thick blond hair was sun bleached, like he spent a lot of time outdoors. With his tanned skin and white, even teeth, he looked the typical Australian surfer poster boy.

He turned to speak with one of the other nurses who blushed and tittered under his regard. Shelby could well understand the girl's reaction. Her own stomach felt like mush. Her glance slid to his large tanned hands and she noticed his ring finger was bare. Her heart skipped a beat.

Of course, he might be one of those married

men who preferred not to wear their wedding ring to work. After all, he specialized in delivering babies. Sometimes it got dirty.

And then he was nodding a farewell to the patient in the bed and heading out of the room. Shelby's boss and the other nurses followed suit. Shelby trailed behind them, trying hard to get her equilibrium back under control. *So what if he was sexy as all get out?* She'd met good-looking men before. *What was so special about this one?* She didn't know, but what she did know was that this was her first day on the ward as a new staff member. It was important she impress and she couldn't do that with her head in a spin about one of the doctors who worked there.

With a determined shake of her head, she forced all thoughts of the delectable Doctor Munro from her mind and steadfastly got on with her job.

———————

Samuel saw the nurse coming toward him and hurriedly stepped into her path. "Nurse Gianopoulos, do you have a minute?"

Her eyes widened at the sight of him—or was it because he'd pronounced her last name so easily? From the look of surprise and pleasure on her face, he was pleased he'd paid attention.

He'd been shooting glances in her direction all morning but apart from their earlier exchange she'd staunchly ignored him. *Perhaps he was the only one who felt the undeniable connection?* The thought sobered him, but he refused to let it put him off. Despite the fact he usually went for fun and flirty blonds, she intrigued him and something urged him to get to know her better.

"Yes, Doctor?"

He saw the grip on her pen and notepad tighten and noticed a pulse beating in her neck. He was filled with a surge of satisfaction. She wasn't as oblivious to him as she pretended.

"Shelby, isn't it?" he asked.

She nodded and glanced away. "Yes."

"I was wondering if you'd like to go out to dinner."

If his forthrightness surprised her, she didn't show it. Her expression was neither shocked nor unamused. Instead, she peered up at him from beneath impossibly long lashes and offered him a slow smile. "Dinner? Why would I want to do that? I barely know you."

"True," he conceded and shot her his most beguiling smile, "but there's only one way we're going to fix that. How about Lucifer's? My treat."

Her eyes flared wide with curiosity at the mention of the expensive Italian restaurant situated on the waterfront at Circular Quay. "Really?" she murmured, her lips curving into a wider smile.

What the hell was he doing? He didn't even know the girl! Surely a drink at his local watering hole would suffice? But something inside him refused to listen to the thoughts inside his head. Instead, he heard himself saying, "Why not? They serve great food, the atmosphere's always good and the service is excellent. What more could you want?"

"I take it you dine there often?"

He shrugged and told the truth. "Often enough. I like Italian food. Don't you?"

She laughed. "Yes, of course. Pizza, pasta, tiramisu. What's not to like? But just so you know, I'm Greek. Not Italian."

He chuckled, slightly embarrassed. From her coloring, he'd guessed she had Mediterranean heritage. He hadn't been sure which country her ancestors originated from. "Greek, Italian, Lebanese. Who cares? It makes no difference to me."

"I guess that's one way of looking at it."

"So you'll come?" he persisted, still uncertain as to why he felt so drawn to her,

She appeared to mull over his question. "I'm not sure I get it. I spilled coffee over *you*. *I'm* the one who should be offering some sort of reparation. Why are you the one asking me to dinner?"

"Does it matter?"

She looked at him with her dark-chocolate eyes and he waited for her answer. He could hardly believe his luck when she nodded.

"All right. Dinner it is. But *I'm* the one buying."

He opened his mouth on an instinctive protest. He'd been raised to act chivalrously and that meant paying the bill.

"My treat, or I'm not coming," she said, her jaw set in a stubborn line.

He stared at her in surprise and then at last, slowly shook his head. She'd just become even more intriguing. "Okay, have it your way. I'll pick you up at seven."

Once again, she appeared unsurprised by his boldness. After exchanging details, she gave him a quick smile of farewell and continued on her way. A surge of anticipation went through him at the thought of the evening to come. He couldn't remember the last time he'd so looked forward to a date. He'd agreed to meet up with the Martin twins later in the week, but spending time with those girls paled to insignificance at the thought of an evening sitting across the dinner table from the exotic Shelby Gianopoulos—and that was altogether unsettling. *What the hell was he doing?*

Shelby checked her appearance in the mirror for the tenth time and patted an errant strand of curly dark hair into place. It sprang forward again and she frowned.

"You'll get wrinkles doing that," her sister Athena stated, walking unannounced through the doorway of their shared bathroom.

Shelby poked her tongue out and resumed her efforts to tame her hair. It was at times like this she wished she'd been blessed with the kind of silky golden locks she saw on the shampoo models on TV. Hair that always looked perfect and shiny and never out of control. Hair that she could never inherit from her Greek parents. Athena's hair was the same.

"Here, let me have a go."

Shelby threw her younger sister a look of gratitude. Athena had a knack with hair. Somehow, she was able to make her thick, wavy mass behave itself, regardless of the time of day or the weather.

"Thanks, sis. I'd really appreciate it."

Athena took hold of the brush Shelby had abandoned on the vanity and began to work it through her hair.

"So, who's this guy you're going out with?" Athena's eyes gleamed with curiosity.

Shelby shrugged. It was a first date. She wasn't going to make a big deal of it. "Just a guy from work."

"What's his name?"

"Samuel."

"*Mm*, that's a nice name. What does he do?"

Shelby debated whether to answer. She knew how her sister would react if she did. But what did she have to hide? It was a first date. It didn't mean anything.

"He's a... He's a doctor," she murmured, keeping her voice casual.

Athena pounced. "A *doctor!* How interesting." She flicked Shelby a glance and continued working on her hair.

Shelby caught the calculating gleam in her sister's eyes and ground her teeth together. She should have kept her mouth shut. "Yes, Athena. He's a doctor. I work at a hospital. Most of the eligible men I come across are doctors. It's no big deal."

"Who said it was a big deal?"

Shelby wasn't fooled by her sister's insouciant tone. Athena's next words confirmed her suspicions.

"I mean, this is the first guy you've dated for like, a year or more. It's been at least that long since Kostas dumped you. We'd almost given up on you ever dating again."

Shelby opened her mouth on a protest and then closed it. Nothing she said would change her sister's opinion of Shelby's dismal love life. Besides, it was true; she hadn't been out with anyone since her very public breakup with the man she'd once been head-over-heels in love with. She'd dreamed about his proposal, the over-the-top wedding that only a large Greek family could pull off; the tidy house in the suburbs with the over-sized backyard for their five or six children to play in.

Looking back, she realized she'd had a lucky escape. She would never have been happy with Kostas. He'd been looking for a trophy wife, a wife who nodded and smiled and agreed with everything he said. A wife who looked good on his arm, and was able to give birth to his children and run the household like a well-oiled machine. A wife who would only bother him with serious matters such as the household finances and the purchase of the family car. She couldn't think of anything worse than living like that.

When Kostas eventually realized she wasn't

going to be as malleable as he'd first thought and that she was a little too opinionated for his liking, he'd taken decisive action. Upset at his error in judgement, he'd gone out of his way to humiliate her by breaking up with her in front of her entire family. It had happened at the christening of the baby of one of her cousins. Shelby still shuddered at the memory.

Aunty Maria, Aunty Sophia and Aunty Irene along with Uncle Theo had looked at her sadly with identical expressions of pity filling their old, wrinkled faces. It was all Shelby could do to stand there with a smile fixed to her face, pretending she'd known all along about the imminent breakup and praying desperately for the agony to be over.

"So, where are you off to?" Athena asked around a mouthful of hairpins.

"Lucifer's."

"Wow! That's my kind of date." Athena grinned and twisted Shelby's now-tamed mane into a chic knot at the base of her neck. "And I have just given you the perfect hairstyle for such a swish place."

After the style had been secured with hairpins, Shelby turned back to face the mirror and was both pleased and relieved to see that Athena had managed to work a miracle. Shelby looked stylish and elegant and the simple black dress she'd chosen to wear only enhanced the effect.

"You look gorgeous, Shelbs."

Shelby gave her sister a hug. "Thanks, sis. You've done wonders."

Athena pulled a face and dismissed Shelby's compliment with a wave of her hand. "All the necessary ingredients were already there. I just added some pizazz."

"More than pizazz. You worked a miracle."

Athena opened her mouth to protest again and Shelby held a finger up to her lips. "Don't say another word. You have an amazing talent and I'm beyond jealous and will be grateful forever. Now, where are my shoes?"

Striding out of the bathroom, Shelby padded down the carpeted hallway and returned to her bedroom. Athena trailed behind her.

"What time is he stopping by?" her little sister asked as she wandered into Shelby's bedroom.

Shelby opened the door to her closet, searching for her shoes. "Seven," she tossed over her shoulder.

"You'd better get a move on, then. If he's on time, he'll be here in ten minutes."

Shelby's heart skipped a beat at Athena's announcement and she was flooded with a sudden rush of nerves. She'd made some discreet inquires among the nursing staff. Doctor Samuel Munro was considered to be one of the Sydney Harbour Hospital's most eligible bachelors. According to the rumor mill, he was regularly seen squiring one glamorous woman after another out on the town. She still couldn't believe he'd asked her out. She—plain old Shelby Gianopoulos—was going out with a much-sought-after Adonis.

"There they are!" At last, she put her hands on the five-inch, open-toed sandals and slipped them on her bare feet. She was grateful she'd taken the time to paint her toenails the weekend before. The shiny, hot pink color peeking out from under the gold leather still looked fresh.

Hurrying back to the bathroom, she rifled in her makeup bag for her lipstick and swiped a matching pink color across her lips. With a last look at her appearance, she sucked in her belly, patted her hair and left.

CHAPTER 3

The evening was warm and balmy. A faint breeze drifted across the water. Samuel had called ahead to the restaurant with a promise to make it worth the maître d's while if he secured them a waterfront table. The promise and the hundred-dollar bill he'd slipped into the man's hand on their arrival had worked.

They were seated at a table for two only ten yards from the water and had already given their order. The breeze wafted in and lifted tiny tendrils of Shelby's hair, curling the strands like a lover's finger might. She looked even more beautiful than she had on the ward and he'd been trying hard all evening not to stare.

She wasn't beautiful in the classical sense and wasn't anything like the blond, blue-eyed women he usually dated, but her dark chocolate, almond-shaped eyes, coupled with her coloring gave her an air of the exotic that he found strangely disorientating and incredibly exciting. His body was as taut as a guitar string.

"So, tell me about yourself," he said, in an effort to relieve some of the nervous tension that had settled in his gut. He reached over and picked up a piece of garlic bread and forced himself to take a bite.

She looked across at him and smiled. Her glossy, pink lipstick shimmered in the candlelight. A surge of desire, hot and immediate, flooded through him and he clenched his jaw. *This was their first date, for Christ's sake.* He needed to take things slow, get to know her, charm her with his wit and intelligence, show her a good time like he usually did with his dates. Not toss her over his shoulder and drag her over to the bushes—no matter how much his body demanded it.

Swallowing the bread, he picked up his wine glass and took a sip. He threw her an encouraging smile. A faint blush increased the color in her cheeks. She cleared her throat, as if she was also finding it difficult to remain focused on their conversation.

"Well, like I told you, my parents are Greek. They were both born in Akrata, a little coastal village a couple of hours' drive west of Athens on the Peloponnesus. They emigrated less than a year after they were married. They've been here more than thirty years."

"Do you have any brothers and sisters?"

She chuckled and the humor lit up her eyes. "I'm Greek. Do you know of any small Greek families?"

He laughed and took another sip of his wine, enjoying the camaraderie. Some of the nervous tension in his gut eased.

"I have three sisters and five brothers," she continued, taking a bite from a piece of garlic bread. "And there're only eleven years between the nine of us," she added.

Samuel frowned. He wondered if she'd experienced the same downfalls he had being part of a large family. Pushing the depressing thought from his mind, he forced a smile.

"I can go even better than that. There are eleven children in my family, with only ten years between them." He waited for the light of comprehension to dawn in her eyes. It didn't take long.

"Twins?"

"Yes. My brothers, Byron and Jasper, are fraternal twins. They're twenty-nine."

She smiled in delight. "How wonderful! I can't believe I've met someone with a family bigger than mine! Are you sure you're not Greek?"

Despite the negativity that often surrounded him whenever he thought of his large family laughter burst out of him. She was beyond adorable. "With hair this color?" He made a show of pulling at his hair then shook his head. "I don't think so."

She shrugged. "Well, there are some fair-haired Greeks in the north. So what's your background? You're dark enough for me to guess you have something other than English blood running through your veins. Unless you're sporting a spray tan." Her eyes twinkled with mischief and he found himself smiling back.

"No, no spray tans. I'm afraid this is courtesy of the good old Australian sun. I'm a sucker for the

Bondi surf. That, and the fact my father's a full-blood Aboriginal. My mother also has some aboriginal heritage, but most people wouldn't know that."

"Wow! How amazing! Do your siblings take after you?"

He nodded. "Yeah, I guess so. I haven't really thought about it. We're not all quite as blond as me, but none of us are dark. My cousins are the same."

"On your dad's side?"

"Yes, but Mom's side, too. Aboriginal babies tend to throw lighter as the generations go on. I think we're the only race in the world that doesn't throw back darker."

Shelby shook her head slowly in wonder. "Wow, that's so fascinating," she breathed.

Samuel's heart skipped a beat at the frank admiration in her gaze. Things were moving fast. Earlier that morning, he'd been lining up another date with the fun and flirty Martin twins, no commitment necessary. Here he was, hours later enthralled with a girl who he instinctively knew played for keeps. They'd only just met and yet he felt an indefinable connection. He couldn't explain it, but it was like he'd met his soul mate, his perfect match. He wanted to talk to her all night. The knowledge frightened the hell out of him.

———————

Shelby reached for her wineglass with a hand

that was less than steady. She couldn't believe how easy it was to converse with the man who sat across from her looking good enough to eat. It was like they'd known each other all their lives. And yet, her belly was a bundle of nerves and her heart still pounded a mile a minute. It felt like her chest might explode. He was charming and personable and good looking and came from a family even bigger than hers. She hadn't been lying when she'd told him how surprised she was about that.

"Tell me more about your family," he asked. "Are you the oldest?"

She shook her head and grinned. "No, but close. I have an older brother, Dimitri, who's twenty-nine."

"So that makes you twenty...?"

"Seven." She laughed. "My youngest brother is eighteen. Like I said, there are only eleven years between us. Mom and Dad didn't waste any time."

He lifted his hands in cheerful surrender. "Hey, I'm hearing you. It's almost embarrassing to tell people how close in age me and my brothers and sisters are. It's like having to admit my parents couldn't drag themselves out of the bedroom."

He'd said it lightly, but Shelby's belly clenched on a sudden surge of need. Her gaze locked on his, and the restaurant, the diners, the wait staff... All of that melted away. His blue eyes darkened with some unspoken emotion and she felt an answering tug in her belly. He was totally and utterly gorgeous. There was no other way to describe him.

And then he cleared his throat and the spell between them was broken. She blinked and looked up in time to see the waitress bearing down on them.

"Here we are," the young woman announced, her hungry gaze fixed on Samuel. She leaned forward and set his plate before him, exposing a decent amount of cleavage as she did so.

Shelby frowned and was barely able to murmur her thanks when the girl came around her side of the table. The flash of jealously was both irritating and unwelcome. Samuel Munro was sexy enough to attract the attention of any woman under the age of ninety with halfway passable eyesight. It was silly of her to take offense.

He couldn't help the way he looked and he certainly hadn't done anything to encourage the waitress' attention. He'd barely glanced at her despite the fact she stood close enough that with the slightest encouragement, she could have tumbled into his lap. Shelby was sure the girl had brushed her breast up against his arm on purpose, and yet he appeared not to notice. *Good for him.* Her estimation of him went up another notch.

The waitress shot Samuel another heated gaze. When his attention remained fixed on the food in front of him she turned away with a huff.

"*Mm.* This fettucine is to die for," he murmured a few moments later, twisting a couple strands around his fork with expert precision and putting them in his mouth.

"I'm glad to hear it's standing up to its

reputation," she replied and dug into her lasagna and salad. "I've heard Lucifer's is one of the best Italian restaurants in town."

He looked up at her, surprised. "You haven't been here before?"

"No. It's..." She blushed, but forced herself to continue. "It's a little out of my price range."

He nodded in understanding, but mischief twinkled in his eyes. "And yet, you offered to treat me. Just so you know, I intend to stuff myself silly and just before I burst, I'll squeeze in dessert. Seeing as you're the one buying."

Shelby shook her head and shot him a wry grin. She almost cringed at the memory of how she'd insisted this was her treat. The whole coffee-spilling incident seemed like a world away and arguing over who was going to foot the bill now seemed childish. She'd honor her promise, even if it broke her. There was always her credit card to fall back on.

The rest of the meal passed amid comfortable conversation and laughter. They discovered both of them held passionate views on politics—even though they stood on opposite sides—and a mutual interest in country music had them regaling each other with amusing stories of attending the Tamworth Country Music Festival over the years.

Shelby learned his cousins were born and bred in the New South Wales north coast city of Grafton and that his uncle was a retired district court judge. He also told her that one of his cousins was also a doctor at the Sydney Harbour Hospital.

"Her name's Chanel Munro," he said. "She's a general surgical resident."

"The name sounds familiar," Shelby replied, "but I don't think we've met."

"She married a cop by the name of Bryce Sutcliffe. They have a set of identical triplets. Zoe, Charlotte and Ginny. Those girls are the cutest kids."

Shelby smiled in surprise. "I have a sister named Zoe, although I'm guessing she's a fair bit older than your cousin's daughters. I take it multiple births run in Chanel's side of the family, too."

"Yes. She has twin brothers. Clayton and Riley. They're fraternal, like my brothers."

"What do they do?"

"They're also in law enforcement. In fact, there are seven kids in Chanel's family and her five brothers are all cops."

Shelby leaned forward on the table and clasped her hands in front of her. "Wow! Your family sounds fascinating. I love hearing about them."

Samuel gazed at her and his smile faded. "Yeah, I wish I could say it was always fun growing up with so many siblings."

She sobered at the serious expression on his face. Shadows flickered in his eyes. She wondered what had happened in the past to cause it. She had nothing but fond memories of living in a household filled with people. Her idea of a family was at least five or six kids. She was totally out of step with her generation but she didn't care. She couldn't help the way she felt. It was a little disconcerting to discover that Samuel might not share her outlook.

"What do you mean?" she asked quietly, almost too scared to ask. Their date had been going so well. *Was it about to go horribly off track?*

"I'm not sure this is the kind of stuff to talk about on a first date." He laughed, but it sounded forced.

Shelby held his gaze. All of a sudden, it was important to find out how he felt, regardless of the fallout. If they weren't on the same page... Well, she couldn't say it would be a deal breaker, but it'd certainly take the shine off things.

"Tell me. I can handle it. First dates are all about getting to know each other. For me, family is incredibly important. They mean everything to me."

He looked at her with something akin to admiration. She spied yearning in his eyes.

"Then you had it good during your childhood," he murmured. It was a statement of fact.

"Yes," she said. "I did. My family have been lucky. They've never wanted for much. Dad's a very successful lawyer. Mom stayed home and looked after the kids. I guess my parents had their arguments, but they've made it work for thirty-two years. There's still plenty of love and respect between them. I admire them. One day, I hope I can say the same about my spouse."

Samuel stared at her. A wistful expression filled his face. "It sounds like your childhood was idyllic. You're very lucky."

She nodded. "Yes, I am." She could tell from the tone of his voice that he meant it and that his own upbringing hadn't been quite the same. All of a sudden she was beset with nerves.

What was she thinking? They were on their first date, a date that had been going so well. Did she really want to ruin it by asking him to dredge up unhappy memories? *And was she ready to hear them?* It would probably spoil the evening and she knew with sudden certainty, she didn't want that to happen. It was a long time since she'd felt so good in a man's company. She should just forget about his comments and enjoy the night. After all, she might never get another chance with the delectable Doctor Munro.

With her mind made up, she ignored the voice in her head that told her she was a coward, and cleared her throat.

"Let's forget about our families, for now. The good, the bad and the ugly. Tell me more about you. Who is Samuel Munro?"

He lifted his hands palm upward and shot her a disarming smile. "What do you want to know?"

"Okay, where did you go to school?"

"The Scots College in Bellevue Hill. Only the best for the Munro boys."

"University?"

"Sydney. I topped my class."

"First kiss?" Shelby tried hard not to blush.

A grin lifted the corners of Samuel's mouth. "That would be Melissa Stanford. We were in the third grade."

She ignored the flutter in her pulse. "You had your first kiss in the third grade? What took you so long?"

He laughed and the joyous sound of it did interesting things to her insides. She gulped a breath and did her best to slow her racing pulse, unable to look away.

The expression in his eyes intensified and Shelby's breath halted. He leaned back in his chair and stretched out his legs. His boot touched the side of her ankle beneath the table. Only a glancing stroke, but her skin burned from the contact. As if aware of the heat pulsing through her, the cobalt of his eyes darkened imperceptibly and her heart skipped a beat. Her gaze lowered to the strong, tanned column of his neck and then lower still, to skim over his broad, muscular chest, the outline of which was visible through the fine cotton of his white dinner shirt. She'd never been the kind of girl who slept with a man on the first date, or even the second or third, but right at that moment, all she could think about was pressing herself against all that taut, tanned skin and kissing him.

The thought stuck in her mind and refused to go away. Desire kindled through her veins and settled as liquid heat in her core. Her breathing quickened. Her lips parted. Samuel reached across the table and stroked her hand. A tingle of warmth and electricity shivered up her arm. She stared at him, unable to speak, barely able to form a coherent thought. She'd read about love at first sight in romance novels and seen it in chick flicks at the movies, but she'd never given it much credence, let alone experienced anything close.

And yet, every fiber of her being screamed out

for him to touch her and to let her touch him. He leaned forward and his spicy expensive cologne teased her nostrils. She could almost taste him on her lips. Her heart pounded. The fire inside her grew hotter...

"Would you like to see the dessert menu?"

The spell was broken. The young waitress was back and her lips gleamed with a coat of freshly applied red lipstick. She stood between the two of them, but she had eyes only for Samuel. Once again, he didn't appear to notice.

Blinking rapidly, he looked just as disorientated as Shelby felt. *What was happening between the two of them...?* She was impatient to find out.

"I... I think we're both good to skip dessert," she said, surprising herself with her boldness. She barely knew her dinner date and here she was making decisions for him. The realization was both nerve wracking and exhilarating. She peeked at him from under her lashes and was gratified to see an answering mischievous gleam in his eyes. He turned to the waitress.

"As much as I'd love to sample the chocolate gelato sandwiches, I think my date is right. It was a delicious meal. All we need is the bill."

The girl compressed her lips and nodded then abruptly turned away. Shelby hunted under the table for her evening bag.

"It's my treat, remember?" she said, eyeing him balefully.

He shrugged innocently. "Of course. I was only moving things along. I thought you were as eager to leave as I am."

Shelby blushed and nodded. "Yes, it's been lovely. It's a shame to see it end."

"How about a stroll along the pier?"

She smiled. "That sounds perfect."

———

Samuel watched Shelby tuck her credit card back inside her wallet and inwardly shook his head. She was stubborn, he'd give her that. The meal easily cost half her week's wages and yet she'd insisted on paying the bill, even after he'd offered again. He'd given in only to spare her pride. It was obvious it was important for her to repay him, even if it meant she'd be scrimping until the next pay check. He frowned at the thought, but then forced himself to let it go. She was a big girl. She'd done what she wanted to do. He refused to let anything spoil the wonder of their evening.

Reaching for her hand, they strolled along the wharf that led away from the restaurant and meandered its way to the Opera House. The night had settled in around them and the gentle spring breeze had turned cool. Shelby shivered in her sleeveless dress and Samuel put his arm around her. After a moment's hesitation, she relaxed against him and he smiled. She felt like she belonged there, tucked up against his side. He'd never felt more content. The knowledge troubled him.

"It's a lovely evening, isn't it?" she murmured, oblivious to his thoughts.

He gazed down at her and nodded, unwilling to ruin the moment. "Yes, it is."

"Thank you for asking me to dinner," she said.

He forced himself to regain his good humor and winked. "Thank you for paying."

She smiled ruefully and he pulled her even closer. His body burned with the need to kiss her, but he reminded himself it was their first date. His reservations had everything to do with the fact Shelby Gianopoulos was nothing like the girls he usually dated and the knowledge had him in a spin. He sensed this could be something very special and he didn't want to screw things up. He wanted to take things slowly and savor every moment; accept that his life was about to change forever, if he'd let it.

A buzzing noise coming from the direction of her evening bag interrupted his thoughts. She fumbled with the clasp and finally pulled out her phone. Glancing at the screen, she grimaced.

"I'm sorry, it's my mother and I've just noticed I've missed her last three calls. I'd better take it."

"Of course. Please, go ahead."

He moved a little way away to give her privacy and she threw him a grateful glance. With his hands in his pockets, he stared out at the water, watching the lights from the harbor side restaurants dancing patterns in the waves. He vacillated between joyous elation and panic. It felt like he was in a dream.

Had he met the woman of his dreams, or were they doomed to failure? There was so much about him she didn't know. How would she feel when she finally found out his secrets? Refusing to dwell on all that a moment longer, he thrust the troubled thoughts aside, determined not to spoil their night. In silence, he waited for Shelby to finish.

Shelby answered the phone and pitched her voice low. "Momma, what's the matter? Why have you called me four times?"

"Shelby Anna Gianopoulos! I've been trying to talk to you for hours! Why don't you answer your phone?"

A surge of foreboding flooded through Shelby's veins at the exasperation in her mother's voice.

"What is it, Momma? What's wrong?"

"Nothing's wrong, honey. Athena called me. She told me about your date. With the doctor." Her voice was full of innuendo. "I wanted to call and offer you some advice."

"Momma! Athena shouldn't have said anything. I don't need any advice. I know how to handle myself on a date."

"*Tut, tut, tut.* Of course you do, but I wanted to give you a few pointers. You haven't been out with anyone since Kostas and I know he broke your heart. You're not as young as you used to be. Time's marching on. If you want to get married and have babies, you'd better get a move on."

Shelby cringed with embarrassment. She was so not having this conversation with her mom at this moment. It was bad enough when her aunts got involved with their 'you don't want to be left on the shelf' lectures. She was only twenty-seven. It wasn't exactly ancient.

"It's fine, Momma and *I'm* fine. I can deal with this on my own. I'm having dinner with a nice guy. That's all it is."

"Yes, honey, but a *doctor*. You don't want to mess that up."

Shelby gritted her teeth and suppressed a groan. Samuel stood a short distance away with his back to her, hands in his pockets, facing out to the harbor. She wondered how much he could hear. With a surge of impatience she cut her mother short.

"Listen, Momma, I appreciate your concern, but I have to go. Samuel's waiting for me. I—"

"*Samuel*. That's a nice name. Is he Greek? It doesn't sound Greek."

"No, Momma. He isn't Greek. In fact, his parents are aboriginal."

"*Mm,*" came the non-committal reply. Shelby suppressed a grin. Her mother didn't have anything against other cultures, but she was determined to find good Greek boys for her girls.

"Anyway, Momma, like I said, I have to go."

"All right, honey. Don't forget about Elena's wedding next Saturday. It starts at three o'clock. The whole family will be there." Her mother's tone turned sly. "Perhaps you could bring Samuel...?"

Shelby groaned under her breath. She'd forgotten about her cousin's wedding. Twenty-three-year-old Elena was marrying her childhood sweetheart. Michael was a nice Greek boy from a nice Greek family. It was a perfect match.

Shelby thought of the deluge of relatives who'd descend upon her once again. 'Poor Shelby, desperate and dateless.' She didn't know if she could stand listening to another well-meaning 'don't get left on the shelf' lecture. They were exhausting and embarrassing and took all the fun out of any celebration. She'd be tense the whole night.

Her gaze fell on Samuel and without conscious thought, her mother's suggestion took hold. With Samuel as her wedding date, her aunts would have nothing to say. Well, they'd have plenty to say, but not about her getting stuck on the shelf, or other similar, completely unhelpful platitudes. With vague promises to get back to her mother later, Shelby ended the call and tossed her phone back in her bag. She wandered over to Samuel.

"Everything all right?" he asked. The twinkle of amusement in his eyes warned her that he'd heard more than he should.

"Yes, it was just my mom calling to remind me of a family celebration I'm meant to be attending on the weekend. My cousin's getting married. It's kind of a big deal."

Samuel smiled. "Of course it is. Wedding's are always a big deal. I can only imagine what they're like in a large Greek family."

She offered him a rueful grin. "Oh, yes, there's nothing like a big Greek wedding."

"Is it anything like what they showed in that movie, or was that only for Hollywood?"

Laughter spilled over. "Oh, no, Hollywood got it right that time. That's pretty much what it's like. In fact, my family will probably go even further."

Samuel's eyes sparkled with humor. "Really? It sounds like fun."

"Would you like to come?" she blurted out and then promptly clamped her mouth shut.

His face flooded with surprise. "Really? You want me to come?"

She blushed and looked away, grateful for the dimness that hid her embarrassment. *Was she being too forward?* After all, they'd only just met. Despite her desire to ward off her well-meaning aunts, to take him to a family wedding as her date could have serious consequences. Her relatives would immediately make assumptions and would hound him with questions until both of them wanted to scream, not the least being how he felt about their beautiful niece/cousin/sister/daughter and when he would be putting a ring on it. Shelby shuddered with horror at the thought.

"Actually, you know, on second thought, it might not be such a good idea," she said hurriedly. "You barely know me. It's way too presumptuous to think you might want to accompany me to a wedding— and a big Greek wedding, at that. My family are kind of...pushy. They'll never leave you alone. They'll presume there's something more between us than there is. You'll feel—"

"Honored that you asked me and very pleased to attend," he interjected softly and reached up to cup her cheek.

The breath left Shelby's body in a rush. Her heart thudded double time. Samuel's warm hand slid from her cheek to her chin and he tilted her face up to his. He bent his head and his mouth skimmed across her lips, soft, fleeting and full of promise.

The evening melted away. She was oblivious to the sound of lapping water, the screech of the gulls, the people walking by. There was nothing and no one but Samuel and then he kissed her again.

His lips were warm and curious as he sought out the taste and feel of her mouth. Magical kisses, whisper soft, glanced off her lips. She reached up and clung to his shoulders, feeling the warm strength of him through his clothes. His muscles bunched beneath her fingers and she was flooded with heat.

He felt every bit as good as he looked and she burned to pull him close, skin to skin, lips to lips, together as one, forever. Her mind spun with her ridiculous thoughts, but still, she wanted more. Holding his head in place, she kissed him back.

This time, his mouth opened under hers and her tongue snuck into its warmth. He tasted faintly of wine and garlic and something indefinably his own. She came up on her toes and pressed herself fully against him.

The feel of his erection hard against her stomach sent a thrill of excitement coursing through her. She couldn't believe this was happening, that she was making out with Samuel Munro. And then he was setting her away from him and she was gasping to catch her breath. She stared up at him in confusion.

"Please don't look at me like that, Shelby," he murmured, his voice hoarse.

"W-why...?" She could barely form a coherent thought.

"It's not because I don't want to," he assured her. "I want to very much."

"Then...?" She shook her head, her thoughts still in a muddle.

"This is our first date. I want more from you than a one-night stand. I... I want to take things slow."

She stared at him in confusion. "Slow? Who does slow anymore?"

He laughed and hugged her to him. "Not enough people, that's for sure. But I'd like to, if you're willing. We might have only met earlier today, but I can tell you're special. Let's not rush. I want to savor every moment."

Shelby continued to stare at him, hardly daring to believe what he said. She had no idea men like him still existed. *Could he be any more perfect?*

"Sure," she finally managed and then gave him a tremulous smile. "I'd like that. I'd like that very much."

He grinned and hugged her tightly to him before setting her away. Taking hold of her hand again, they continued to walk.

"So, you're bringing me to your cousin's *big fat Greek wedding*, right?" His wink was accompanied by a smile so soft and tender, it stole her breath away.

She smiled back at him. All of a sudden, the stars gleamed brighter and she swore she heard music in the air. It was just like in the movies... It was perfect.

CHAPTER 4

Dear Diary,

I'm surrounded by beautiful things. I live in a beautiful home. I have a caring spouse, good-looking, successful children, everything I could want or need. And yet, I'm filled with discontent. I've been that way for most of my life. There is beauty all around, but all I see is black. The blackness of deceit, of lies kept hidden for far too long. I don't know how much longer I can keep my secrets... Or even if I want to. Only time will tell...

It was just as I imagined it. I watched the procession of men who came and went from that secret place of abomination for several weekends. When I made up my mind to take action, I lay in wait for hours. I knew someone would come along. A Friday night in Bondi. The beach is never short of a crowd or people looking for a good time. Music pumped from the bars nearby. I could hear its throbbing beat all the way up on the hill. It was good. The music helped to camouflage his terrified cries for help.

It had been that way the first time. Oh, I can still hear his desperate pleas. They soothed my soul, helped me focus as I brought the tire wrench down. Over and over, my blows connected, until my arm ached and I gasped for breath. Only then did I cease.

He was barely recognizable when at last I stopped. I stared down at him, bleeding, bruised, broken...dead. The cap he wore had been lost in the bushes. With the aid of the flashlight on my phone, I found it and tucked it inside the waistband of my pants. A sense of calm exhilaration overcame me. Life was good. Some people might judge me harshly, but I'd do it again in a heartbeat...

———

Detective Sergeant Jared Buchanan stared at the battered remains of the young adult male and wondered, not for the first time, what the hell he was doing working a city beat. He'd moved from his hometown of Armidale only a month earlier in search of the excitement and exhilaration the city lights promised. He hadn't counted on coming face to face with three homicides, all in the space of four weeks, two of which had occurred right there, along the cliffs of Bondi. It was taking some getting used to.

"Do we have an ID?" he asked the junior detective who'd accompanied him to the crime scene.

The cool night air ruffled the young detective's longish hair, sending it into his eyes. Jared saw his lips move, but the sound of the surf crashing onto the rocks of Bondi Beach below muffled the man's words. Jared moved closer.

"I'm sorry, Greg. I didn't hear you."

"I found a driver's license in the pocket of his jeans," Greg replied. "The license belongs to someone by the name of Simon McLean. Though it's hard to be sure after the beating he's taken, he bears some resemblance to his photo."

Jared compressed his lips and nodded. The crime scene wasn't for the fainthearted. Simon McLean—if in fact it was Simon McLean—had been beaten to death with a blunt object. Contusions on the back of his head suggested the first blow had come from behind. It had been followed by several others that had torn into the skin of his face. One of his eyes had been pulverized. The man lay on his side among the scrubby bushes along the cliffs of North Bondi, tucked up in a fetal position, his face a mask of agony.

It was a sickening scene and was eerily similar to one Jared had attended close by a few weeks earlier. Worse still, as yet, they had no motive. The man's wallet had been found on his person. Two fifty-dollar bills and a few smaller notes were still tucked inside. An expensive watch had survived the blows and was still around the deceased's wrist and a couple of gold chains hung around his neck. It was obvious robbery hadn't been the motive.

Jared looked around him. He'd have to order some more lights. Though the moon was three-quarters full, it wasn't supplying enough for their needs.

The last murder scene hadn't offered up any hints as to the identity of the killer. He refused to let another murder go unpunished. This time, he'd scour every inch of the surrounding bushland for any clue about what had happened and who was responsible. He sighed quietly. It was going to be a long night.

———————

Samuel checked his bow tie for the umpteenth time and wiped imaginary pieces of lint from his suit. The reality of what he was about to do suddenly hit him. He'd been dating Shelby Gianopoulos for a little over a week and still hadn't come clean to her about his family. The more he got to know her, the more he liked her and the harder it was to take the risk and tell her the truth.

What if she dumped him? It was obvious family was extremely important to her. What would she think of him when he told her his family was... *Was what?* He wasn't sure how he'd describe his branch of the Munro clan, but they sure as hell weren't playing happy families like hers.

Why the hell had he agreed to accompany her to a family wedding? And not just any wedding, but the wedding of all weddings where he'd be subjected to sly glances, open curiosity, and no doubt outright questions about his intentions toward their girl.

"I still don't get it," Ian Broderick said from his lounging position in the armchair that stood in the corner of Samuel's bedroom. "Who goes to a wedding with a girl they just met?"

"I like her, Ian. I like her a lot."

"You've known her for a week, Samuel! Have you lost your freaking mind? Yeah, she's sexy as hell with that cloud of hair and a body just ripe for fucking, but going to a wedding when you know what every guest on her side will be thinking..." Ian shook his head in disgust. "I don't get it."

Samuel's lips tightened at Ian's words. Despite his inner reservations, he wouldn't stand for anyone to speak about Shelby like that. He glared at his friend. "Don't talk about her like that, Ian. She's off limits. I like her and I'm going to go to this wedding and be damned with what everyone thinks."

Ian threw up his arms in a sign of surrender and stretched his legs out in front of him. He stacked his hands behind his head and stared up at the ceiling. Samuel adjusted his bow tie. Again.

"What's so special about her?" Ian mumbled. "It's not like she's the only good-looking chick in Sydney. And I had the twins lined up last week. I can't believe you blew them off. Christina was livid when I turned up without you. I was kind of hoping she'd go for a threesome, but she turned me down flat. Then her sister blew me off, too and I went home alone."

He sat up straighter in his chair and shot Samuel an accusatory look. "That was *your* fault, Munro. Make no mistake."

Samuel shrugged, barely listening. Nerves had been twisting his stomach into knots since he'd woken early that morning. It wasn't that he didn't want to go to the wedding with Shelby. It was just that they barely knew each other and he wasn't sure he was ready to undergo a family inquisition. Like Ian said, was he out of his mind?

He'd spoken the truth when he'd told Ian he liked Shelby a lot and he was quietly hopeful she'd understand the difficulties he had with his family and that their feelings would develop into something lasting, but having their shiny new relationship put under the microscope by hordes of well-meaning, but no doubt intimidating relatives was enough to cause anyone to break out in hives. Including him.

He winced at the thought and made a concerted effort to force the negativity from his mind. Men and women had been dating since time began. It was a normal, natural progression for single people. He had nothing to be scared of. Once he got the family thing out in the open and laid the closet bare, things would be sweet. As for the wedding, they were her relatives and only had her best interests at heart. *He could cope with that, couldn't he?* After all, it was only for a few hours and then he'd take Shelby back to his place and laugh about it as they sipped icy cold Coke. That's where he'd tell her about his family. She'd commiserate, offer him comfort, tell him she understood. They could make out in the dark like teenagers before he reluctantly drove her home. Yes, he could do this. He was sure of it.

Shelby sat in the passenger seat while Samuel

parked his gunmetal gray Aston Martin DB 9 in the parking lot beside the church. He hurried around to open her door. She was touched by his old-fashioned manners. He looked every bit the sexy bachelor with his sun-bleached hair tamed into submission to complement his formal attire. The black tuxedo fit him perfectly. She guessed it had been custom tailored. His snowy white dress shirt with pin tucks only heightened the tan of his skin. A black satin bow tie completed the ensemble but sat slightly askew. She reached up and straightened it.

The action brought her close against him and she reveled in the feel of his hard body, however fleeting the touch.

"Shelby, honey. Hello, there! You look beautiful."

Shelby turned and greeted her mother with a hug. "Thank you, Momma. So do you."

Helen Gianopoulos was an imposing woman. It was from her mother that Shelby got her height. At six feet tall in bare feet and with her body only slightly turned to fat, Helen was even more intimidating when she wore heels. Dressed from head to toe in figure-hugging, silver-spangled Dolce & Gabbana, with sparkly silver high heels to match, she looked every bit the proud matriarch. To Shelby's consternation, her mother's gaze gleamed with interest as she looked from Shelby to Samuel.

"And you must be Samuel," she announced with no small amount of fanfare.

Shelby suppressed a groan. *It had started already.* She held her breath and steeled herself against the embarrassment that was sure to come. Throwing Samuel a quick look, she was relieved to see that he didn't look at all put out. Even better, his normal, friendly smile was in place.

"Yes, I'm Samuel Munro. It's a pleasure to meet you, Mrs Gianopoulos."

"Please, call me Helen," Shelby's mother tittered and then blushed when Samuel shook her hand.

Samuel inclined his head in acknowledgement. "I'm honored. And thank you for inviting me to your niece's wedding." He glanced around at the numerous shiny, expensive motor vehicles parked outside the church as far as the eye could see, and the even more well-dressed guests and then his gaze returned to her mother. "And what a beautiful afternoon for what looks like a grand family affair."

Helen's smile was filled with pleasure and she patted Samuel on the arm. Shelby stood tense, waiting for the next embarrassing moment. She didn't have to wait long.

"Shelby's so lucky to have found you. We were so worried she'd never recover from that broken heart." Her mother leaned toward Samuel and lowered her voice to a conspiratorial whisper. "She thought she'd *marry* Kostas, you know. We all did. Such a *nice* Greek boy. And then he went and broke things off. She—"

"Momma! That's enough!" Shelby interrupted a little desperately. "Samuel has no interest in hearing about my ex. Please, let's go inside and enjoy the celebration. This day is about Elena and Michael, not me."

Her mother opened her mouth to speak again, but Shelby took Samuel firmly by the arm and led him away. It wouldn't be the last time he was accosted by her curious relatives, but she wanted to give him some breathing room before the next one pounced.

What on earth had possessed her to invite him? Feeling desperate, she glanced at him sideways and some of her tension eased. He looked so handsome and distinguished in his tailored tuxedo that emphasized his trim physique. Gold cufflinks peeked out from the cuffs of his snowy white shirt and she could see reflections in the sheen of his black RM Williams boots.

As if sensing her anxiety, he reached for her hand and squeezed it and shot her a sexy smile. "Am I holding up okay?" He winked.

Laughter gurgled out of her and she was flooded with sheer delight. This beautiful creature, this Adonis, was her willing date for the night. And many more nights after that, if she had anything to say about it. What had started out as a desperate act to stave off the usual sympathetic looks and conversations with her elderly relatives had become something so much more. The speed of the acceleration of her feelings was a little frightening, especially at her age, but she was determined to be strong and brave and see exactly where they led. If the past week was any indication, there were only good times ahead.

———————

The speeches had been made, the cake cut

and the band was in full swing when Shelby's brother came up behind her and startled her with a playful slap on her butt.

"I think you have something to tell me, little sister. Where have you been hiding *him?*"

Shelby lifted her wine glass to her lips and followed Dimitri's gaze. She smiled at the sight of Samuel surrounded by her three spinster aunts. No doubt they were doing their bit to ensure another man didn't escape her clutches. She felt a stab of sympathy for him, but if the expressions of pleasure and approval on her aunts' faces were anything to go by, he looked like he was holding his own.

"He's a doctor at the hospital. We work together," she murmured and smiled into her wine.

Dimitri shook his head. "You're a sly old dog, I'll give you that! Here we all thought you were still in mourning over Kostas and all along, you've had a bronzed surfer-type keeping you happy. How come you didn't say anything?"

Shelby ducked her head. "We only met a week ago."

"Okay, now I forgive you for not telling me earlier. The way Mom talked, I thought you'd been hiding him in your closet for some time. I must admit, I was a little dubious about her claims, given that I share a house with you. I thought I would have noticed an extra body around the place."

Shelby laughed. "Oh, dear! I can only imagine what other stories she's spreading around the room. I think she's kind of taken with him. I wasn't sure she'd be happy—seeing as he's not a nice

Greek boy and all, but she seems to have gotten over that little anomaly rather well."

"You think?" Dimitri deadpanned and Shelby laughed again.

"Too well, probably," Shelby admitted with a grimace.

Dimitri chuckled with amusement. Shelby was reminded how good looking her brother was. Dark haired and dark eyed, like the rest of her brothers and sisters, he'd also inherited their mother's height. A successful litigation lawyer in their father's city firm, there was talk he'd make junior partner before the year was out. Shelby was happy for him. Dimitri loved his job and most of the time, he was happy with his life. She only wished he had someone special to share it with.

"So, when do I get to meet him?"

Dimitri's question broke into her thoughts. She flashed him a smile. "How about now? I'm sure he'll be happy for the interruption."

Tugging her brother by the hand, she threaded her way through the crowd of wedding guests, avoiding the eye of her Uncle Theo as she did so. Samuel lifted his head and saw her coming. A relieved expression crossed his face. She swallowed a smile.

"Samuel, do you mind if I steal you away for a minute?" she murmured and then turned and smiled sweetly at her aunts. "I'm sorry, ladies. Do you mind?"

"Of course not, dearie," Aunty Irene replied. Aunty Maria and Aunty Sophia merely smiled their approval and nodded.

Taking hold of Samuel's arm, Shelby steered him away from the women and brought him over to where Dimitri waited.

"Samuel, I'd like you to meet my oldest brother. Dimitri, this is Samuel."

Samuel held out his hand and Dimitri gave it a friendly shake. "It's nice to meet you, Samuel. Looks to me like you've made a lucky escape." Dimitri indicated from exactly where, with a nod in the direction of the aunts, who had their heads together, talking.

Samuel grinned. "I'd say you're right."

He shot Shelby a soft look and her insides melted like toasted marshmallow. Right here, right now, she could fall in love with this man. The thought filled her with equal parts nerves and excitement.

"So, Shelby tells me you're a doctor," Dimitri said.

"Yes, and she's told me quite a lot about you, too. In fact, I think I know almost everything there is to know about the Gianopoulos siblings. You two live together, right?"

"That's right," Dimitri replied. "Along with two more sisters, Athena and Zoe, who are both younger than Shelby, but you probably already know that, too."

Samuel lifted the glass in his hand and took a sip from his drink. Dimitri did likewise.

"So, Dimitri," Samuel said, "you're a lawyer."

"Yes. I work for a firm in the city. Harton and Wentworth. You might have heard of it."

"I haven't had much to do with lawyers,

thankfully," Samuel replied, "but the name rings a bell. Do you have offices down near the Supreme Court?"

"Yes. In Martin Place. Dad's a senior partner there."

Samuel's expression filled with admiration. "I'm impressed. Working under your old man. That's got to be tough."

"What's got to be tough?"

Shelby jumped as the brash voice of her father boomed from somewhere behind them.

"H-hi, Daddy. This is Samuel. We were just talking about how difficult it is being a lawyer. The long hours, the trying cases. I'm sure you know what it's like."

Ignoring her, Alexei Gianopoulos drew to his full height. At six-foot-three, he was imposing. He stared down at the three of them then narrowed his gaze on Samuel. Shelby held her breath.

"I understand you're seeing my daughter," he stated.

To his credit, Samuel stood his ground and looked her father in the eye. Shelby's belly clenched with nerves. Her father was known to be overprotective where his daughters were concerned.

"Yes, sir. I am."

Alexei's stare didn't waver. "What are your intentions?"

Heat crept up Shelby's cheeks. She didn't dare look at Samuel.

"I have the most honorable of intentions, Mr Gianopoulos."

"Are you sleeping with her?" Alexei demanded.

Mortification spread like flames across Shelby's face. "Daddy! This isn't the nineteenth century! That's none of your business!"

Unperturbed, her father's gaze remained fixed on Samuel. "Well, are you?"

She noticed a tic in Samuel's cheek. His jaw clenched. "No, sir. I'm not."

"Why not? Isn't she good enough for you?"

Shelby gasped, but Samuel remained composed.

"It has nothing to do with that, sir. It comes down to respect."

Her father looked unconvinced and turned to his son. "Dimitri, are they sleeping together? You share a house. You should know."

"Daddy!" Shelby protested again.

Her brother spoke over her. "You're behaving badly, Dad. What Shelby does is her business. She's a grown woman, not your little girl. And for the record, this is the first time I've even seen Samuel."

Her father looked unrepentant. Once again, he lasered Samuel with his gaze. "How long have you been dating my daughter?"

"A week and a half, sir."

"And you haven't slept with her?"

Samuel's jaw tightened again. Anger glinted in his eyes. "I think we've been over this, Mr Gianopoulos and I would thank you not to disrespect both me and your daughter that way."

Shelby's father moved closer. She was sure it was in an effort to intimidate her date. Impatience surged through her. She'd had enough. Dimitri was right. She was no longer a child. She stepped forward in an effort to insinuate herself between the two men.

"Dad—"

Her father spoke over her head. "I've read about men like you. Are you sure you're not using my daughter to cover up for the fact you're gay?"

Chapter 5

"Daddy!" Shelby exclaimed, shocked.

"Dad, that's enough." Dimitri's tone was cold.

Shelby burned with anger and mortification. She hardly dared to look at Samuel. When she did, she swallowed a gasp. He glared at her father. His eyes burned blue steel.

"Not that it's any of your business," he bit out, "but no, sir, I'm not gay. Just because I like women, doesn't mean I sleep with every girl I go out with before the end of the second week. I have a few more scruples than that, but you wouldn't know that because you know nothing about me and it's also obvious you know nothing about your daughter."

Samuel's gaze narrowed and his voice lowered threateningly. "But be careful, Mr Gianopoulos. One of these days, you might find yourself having to apologize for your rudeness and I get the feeling saying sorry isn't something that comes easily to you."

The two men faced off with each other, their breaths coming fast. A moment later, Shelby's father relaxed his stance and let out a chuckle.

"Guys, hey, lighten up! You're taking this way too seriously! I can't help it if I'm protective of my little girl. I'm her father. It's my job to protect her. She's already had her heart broken by that no-good, gutless Kostas. I want to make sure her choice of companion is worthy of her this time. Is that too much to ask?" He spread his arms wide, his face a picture of innocence. Shelby wasn't about to let him off the hook quite so easily.

"You were incredibly rude to Samuel *and* me, Daddy. It's uncalled for. Samuel's my guest. You have no right to treat him like that."

To her surprise, her father nodded. "You're right, honey." He turned to Samuel. "I'm sorry for my rudeness. Protective or not, there was no excuse. I know better."

To Samuel's credit, he graciously accepted her father's apology. "No harm done, Mr Gianopoulos. I understand."

Her father smiled and the tension between them eased. "You'll understand even more when you're in my shoes. Just wait until you have daughters. You'll be every bit as protective as I am." He gave Samuel a wink and all four of them chuckled. Shelby sighed quietly in relief.

The band chose that moment to start a new set and Shelby grabbed Samuel by the hand. "Come on! I love this song! Let's dance."

They strode hand in hand to the dance floor and Samuel took her in his arms. The music was slow and sensual. She clasped her fingers together around his neck. He moved with confidence, his feet sure and graceful.

"You dance well," she murmured.

"My mother thought it would be a good idea for her children to be given dance lessons—ballroom dance lessons, I might add. I was a surly teenager at the time and couldn't for the life of me think why I'd need such a skill. Now I'm glad she insisted."

Shelby smiled. Samuel tightened his hold on her and then twirled her around. She gasped and laughed and was filled with happiness. There was still so much she didn't know about him, but she knew the important stuff. He was good and kind and intelligent. He was polite and funny and generous. Not to mention drop-dead gorgeous. He was the complete package. She was the luckiest girl in the world.

It was the early hours of the morning when she and Samuel finally left the wedding reception and climbed into his car. Traffic was quiet through the city and they made it across the harbor in good time. Country music, turned down low, was playing on the radio.

Shelby's limbs felt heavy. She'd consumed more than her fair share of wine at the wedding and she looked forward to climbing into bed. She looked across at Samuel. His profile was in shadow, but every now and then, it was illuminated by the streetlights they passed.

He had a strong jawline, firm lips, a high forehead. His blond hair was slightly long, like he was overdue for a haircut. It curled over his ears. She itched to trace its path with her finger, to slide over the whorls and valleys and ridges, learning every inch of his skin.

The music came to an end and she vaguely registered the news had come on. In a somber voice, the newsreader announced there had been another murder the night before along the cliff tops of North Bondi.

Shelby came alert with a start. It was the second murder in that area in less than a month. When she'd learned about the first one, she'd been stunned. The scene of the crime wasn't far from her parents' home. It was shocking to realize someone had been murdered so near to where her mom and dad slept in their beds. Now another young man had been killed.

"Did you hear that?" she murmured.

"Yes. It's terrible, isn't it? There was another one a few weeks ago. It happened not far from where I live."

She turned to look at him, flooding with surprise. "Really? You live in Bondi?"

"Yes. It's probably a little further away from the hospital than is convenient, but what can I say? I love to surf. It's worth the pain of having to get out of bed that extra bit earlier."

He grinned and his teeth shone white in the streetlight. She was reminded once again of how good-looking he was. A shaft of desire tingled through her veins. The Aston purred to a stop outside her house. She glanced up at the windows that fronted the harbor. The place was quiet and dark. Samuel switched off the ignition and turned to face her. Shelby was beset with a rush of nerves.

"I-I'm sorry again about my dad. He was totally out of line. He—"

"Apologized, Shelby, and that couldn't have been easy for him. I accepted his apology and that's the end of the matter, as far as I'm concerned. Now," his fingers grasped her chin and he turned her face toward him, "let's not talk anymore about your family. I'd much rather spend time doing this."

His lips came down on hers and moved over them with fluid warmth. Desire, hot and immediate, catapulted through her body. She relaxed into his hold and returned the pressure of his mouth. Reaching up, she cupped his cheek, her nails scraping across the shadow of whiskers that had appeared as the night wore on. He adjusted his position and pulled her closer.

"Ouch," she squeaked and looked down at the gearshift where it dug into her hip.

Samuel cursed lightheartedly at the offending instrument and then chuckled. "The good old gearshift-in-the-hip trick," he said in a fair Maxwell Smart imitation.

"It will do it every time," she grinned. Silence fell between them. She broke it with a nervous clearing of her throat. "Would you… Would you like to come in? The rest of my family are staying at the reception center tonight. We have the place to ourselves."

She blushed as she said it and was grateful for

the dimness. She was no longer a virgin, but she was far from promiscuous and she hadn't had sex since her break-up with Kostas. It had taken her awhile to get over the fact the man she thought she'd marry wasn't that man at all. Sharing a house with three of her siblings was another deterrent to bringing men home.

But sleeping with Samuel seemed so natural and right. They might have only known each other a little over a week, but it felt like so much longer. She yearned to see him naked, to touch him, skin to skin. She was sure he'd look as beautiful without clothes as he did with them on. Butterflies swarmed in her stomach while she waited for his answer.

"I'm sorry, Shelby. I'd love to, but...I think we should wait."

For a moment, she thought she'd misheard him. She frowned and replayed his words in her head. "Did you just say you didn't want to come inside?"

He shook his head. "It's not that I don't want to, Shelby," he said gently. "It's just that, I meant what I said. Let's get to know each other better. There's no rush. After all, we have the rest of our lives..."

His voice had lowered to a husky whisper and her stomach somersaulted with anticipation. But still, he was turning down her offer to sleep with him. *What kind of guy did that?* And then she suddenly cottoned on to the truth.

"Does this have anything to do with my father?" she demanded. "Is that why you're reluctant to come inside? He's put you off your game, hasn't he? Despite everything, my dad's won. I want to drag you up the stairs and into my bed and you're offering me a couple of kisses and then bidding me a chaste goodnight." She laughed without humor and shook her head, increasingly convinced she was right.

Samuel stared at her, his expression somber. "It doesn't have anything to do with your father, Shelby, despite what you might think." He took her hands in his. "What we have together is special. You know it and so do I. Let's wait for the right time, for when it will be the culmination of our love. And just so you know, I'm falling hard and fast, Shelby Gianopoulos. I hope you are, too."

She trembled at the emotion that shone in his eyes and all of a sudden, she wanted to wait, too. She wanted their first time to be everything he imagined it could be: memorable, loving, lingering, sublime. She'd never had that before and was unlikely to at two in the morning. Samuel was right. She was sure it was worth waiting for.

———————

Shelby glanced at her watch and cursed under her breath. Once again, she was late for work, this time courtesy of a delayed train. She hurried through the entryway, tossing a wave in Marjorie's direction. The elderly woman gave her a huge grin and waved back to her from the information booth. She was way too cheery for so early on a Monday morning.

"Shelby Gianopoulos?"

Shelby heard her name coming from somewhere behind her and half-turned to glance over her shoulder. A man about her age, wearing a white doctor's coat and a stethoscope casually around his neck, half-jogged to catch up with her.

"Shelby Gianopoulos?" he asked again.

Shelby frowned, but nodded and continued her rapid path toward the elevators. "Yes. Do I know you?"

"No, but I've heard a lot about you."

The innuendo in his voice pulled her up short. She stopped and turned to face him. "Excuse me?"

"Oh, I'm sorry," the man said, sounding far from apologetic. "I forgot to introduce myself. "I'm Doctor Ian Broderick. I'm a friend of Samuel's."

"Oh," Shelby replied, still feeling a little confused. *Why would Samuel be discussing her with his friend?* Disquiet stirred in her belly.

"So, after all I'd heard about you, I just had to meet you. You've been monopolizing my buddy's attention to the point I barely see him anymore. I decided I had to meet this Shelby Gianopoulos, who seems to have stolen all of his spare time and maybe even his heart."

Shelby stared at him, feeling at a distinct disadvantage. She'd never even heard about this man before and yet he seemed to know all about her. What was more, he implied he knew far more intimate details about her than she'd ever care to discuss.

"Look, Ian. I'm sorry Samuel hasn't had the time for you that he normally does. I'm not sure that's my fault. In fact, I'm certain it isn't. Samuel's a big boy. He can make his own decisions. He gets to choose where and with whom he spends his time. If you have a problem with that, I suggest you take it up with him."

"Whoa!" Ian laughed, holding up his hands in surrender. "I can see what Samuel's all hot and bothered about. You're a feisty one, aren't you?"

He moved closer and ran a finger slowly down Shelby's arm. She stared at him, shocked, and a moment later moved out of the way. She shivered in distaste. Ian merely chuckled and shot her a knowing smile.

"Did I tell you I was an orthopedic surgeon?" he asked in a casual tone.

Shelby blinked and did her best to keep up with the sudden change in conversation. "Excuse me?"

"Yes, Samuel and I attended university together, but we chose different specialties. There's something about all those hammers and chisels that gets my blood flowing. Sometimes I even get aroused. Of course," he lowered his voice conspiratorially, "it would be pretty cool doing what Samuel does every day. All those half-naked women, begging for his help."

Shelby's anger hit overdrive. Fury heated her cheeks. "You're disgusting," she growled. "You're a disgrace to your position, this hospital and every other doctor in this state. I have no idea what Samuel sees in you, but nothing would please me more than never setting eyes on you again. Now, if you don't mind, I'm running late. There are half-naked women who need *me* and I'm not going to let them down." Her breath came fast and her heart beat hard. He stared at her in surprise.

"Hey, calm down. I didn't mean to make you mad. I was joking! A little joke! That's all it was."

His accompanying smile looked forced and only served to grate further on her nerves. She made a move toward the elevators and then once again, his voice stopped her in her tracks.

"He's gay, you know."

She spun around on her heel and stalked back to him. "What did you say?"

Ian eyed her innocently. "I said, he's gay. Samuel. Not many people know about it, but I've been friends with him for years. Like I said, we went to college together. A lot of things went on there." His smile was sleazy. His tone was filled with innuendo.

Shelby frowned in confusion, her mind in a spin. *Samuel, gay?* It couldn't be true. She shook her head with increasing certainty.

"You're lying," she said, grateful her voice remained sure and steady. "There's no way Samuel's gay."

Ian stared at her pityingly and then shrugged. "Suit yourself. You're entitled to believe whatever you want to believe, but I know the truth. He tries hard to hide it. I've seen it happen over and over again. He goes out with girls in an effort to get over it, like it's some kind of temporary illness that can be treated." Ian grimaced. "Poor sod. He's only deluding himself, but what can I do? He won't listen to me. He needs to work it out on his own." He sighed heavily. "I guess he'll get there one day."

Shelby stared at him a moment longer and then wrenched herself away. She refused to listen to such garbage an instant longer. Stumbling toward the elevators, she tried hard to slow her confused thoughts. It couldn't be true. *Could* it?

Ian had seemed so sure. *Was her father onto something? Had he sensed something Shelby hadn't? Was that the real reason Samuel hadn't slept with her?* She'd as much as thrown herself at him the other night.

But what about the passion they'd shared? The mutual desire? She'd felt his arousal on more than one occasion. *How could all that have been an act?*

No, it couldn't have been an act. She was sure of it. She prided herself on being an astute judge of character. She couldn't have been that far off. It just wasn't possible.

She'd discuss his friend's accusations with Samuel as soon as she could, hopefully later that day. He was rostered on the afternoon shift. She'd corner him somewhere and demand to know the truth. If he *were* gay, she wanted to know sooner rather than later. She didn't have anything against gay men, but there was no point wasting time with someone who was never going to work out.

CHAPTER 6

Dear Diary,

He thinks he's so discreet, but I know his every move. I see his friends come and go and then come back again. I saw the argument with his latest companion. It spilled out on the streets. They spoke to each other in the harshest of words. He didn't know I was listening. He doesn't know about a lot of things. Unlike him, I know how to be discreet, how to wait in the shadows in silence. How to seize my moment and never let go, like an avenging angel.

Jared Buchanan eyeballed the suspect who sat across from him in the confined space of the Bondi Police Station interview room. Surrounded by the bare gray walls, a solitary desk, two chairs and a wall mounted camera, the man Jared believed was responsible for the murder of Simon

McLean couldn't seem to control his fidgeting.

"Simon McLean's buddies told me you left the Oxford Street Bar with him a little after nine the night he was murdered. CCTV footage from the bar clearly shows you and Simon leaving the building and crossing the street. That was the last time he was seen alive." Jared leaned forward and glared at his suspect. "Now, if you don't want me to charge you with murder, I suggest you start talking."

Peter Browning swiped the back of his hand across his forehead. A fine sheen of sweat glistened on his upper lip. He glanced at Jared and just as quickly looked away, focusing instead on his fingernails. They were clean and well-manicured.

According to Jared's inquires, Peter Browning was employed at a call center for a local cell phone provider. In his early twenties, he rented an apartment with a couple of other friends and caught the bus from his home in North Bondi to the call center in the city. On paper, he appeared to be everything he said he was, but Jared was more interested in the fact this kid was last seen with the most recent cliff-top victim. A victim who'd been savagely beaten to death.

The man remained silent. Jared tried another tack. "You met Simon at the Oxford Street Bar, is that correct?"

"Yes. I was there with a couple of friends last Friday night. We were having a drink. Simon's group was nearby, watching cricket on the big screen. We got to talking. I like cricket, too. We bought each other a couple of drinks. By nine o'clock, I suggested we go back to my place."

Jared's gaze remained steady on his suspect. "Mr Browning, the Oxford Street Bar is a well-known hangout for homosexual men. Are you gay?"

The man nodded. "Yes, I am."

"How often do you pick up men for sex?"

The young man blushed and picked at a hangnail. "I like to go out on the weekend. I'm a social kind of guy. If I meet someone I click with and they feel the same, we spend the night together. So what?" His gaze met Jared's. "There's nothing illegal about it."

Ignoring the young man's comment, Jared continued: "When you said you suggested to Simon that he go home with you, I take it that you intended to have sex with him. Is that correct?"

Browning compressed his lips and stared down at his hands, but he answered with a nod.

"I'm sorry, Mr Browning, but for the purposes of the audio, I need a verbal response."

"Yes, we were going home to have sex."

"How did you know Simon McLean was gay?"

"For a start, he was in a gay bar, Detective. Not many straight guys hang out in that kind of place. Secondly, I got to talking to him. You get a sense for these kinds of things. When I invited him home, he was happy to leave with me. He wasn't stupid. He knew we were going to have sex."

"What happened after you left the bar?"

"We caught a bus home to North Bondi."

"Do you know what time it was then?"

The man shrugged. "It took awhile for a bus to come along. I guess it might have been nine-thirty by then."

Jared made a note on the paper in front of him. Many city buses were equipped with security cameras. He'd get someone to check the footage and verify Browning's statement.

"So, you caught a bus back to North Bondi. What happened next?"

"I only live a few blocks from the bus stop. We got off the bus and walked home."

"Was anyone else there?"

The man shrugged again. "Maybe. I share with two other mates. I didn't see or hear anyone, but they might have been asleep. I didn't check their rooms. As soon as we got there, Simon and I went straight to my room."

"Where you had sex," Jared stated.

"Yes."

"Except, you didn't."

Browning's head shot up in surprise. "Of course we did. It's like I told you earlier. I took him home, we had sex and then he left. I didn't see him again."

"There was no semen found on Simon's body," Jared said, watching his suspect closely.

"We used a condom. What do you think we are? Stupid?"

Jared's gaze didn't waver. "No, I don't think you're stupid. I think you're a liar."

Anger flooded Browning's face, coupled with a flash of panic. "I'm telling you the truth!"

Jared leaned back in his chair and propped his

foot up on his knee. "See, this is what I think happened. You met a guy; you seemed to click. You had a few drinks in the city and then you brought Simon back to North Bondi. You suggested he come home with you, but he didn't want to, so you suggested you go for a walk, instead. You headed along the boardwalk and then into the bushes along the cliffs. It's a well-known haunt for gay hook-ups. I'm guessing as a local, you know that. You were hoping to convince Simon to have sex with you after all, even though he'd been reluctant to go home with you. His continued reluctance pissed you off and it escalated into a fight. You picked up a tree branch or something similar and bludgeoned the poor guy to death."

Browning was shaking his head with increasing vehemence even before Jared came to a halt.

"No! No! No! You have it all wrong! It didn't happen anything like that! I didn't kill him! I swear. I was just as shocked as anyone when I heard it on the news."

"We have a bloody palm print taken from the scene," Jared informed him quietly. "It will go better for you in the long run if you cooperate with us."

The man's eyes got wilder. "I'm telling you, it wasn't me! I could never kill anyone!"

"But you've been involved in a number of serious assaults, haven't you, Peter?"

Jared's accusation was all the more deadly for its gentle delivery. Browning's jaw clamped shut. He stared at Jared with fear in his eyes.

"It's not the first time you've been up on charges, is it, Peter?" Jared flipped open a folder and read from Browning's criminal record.

"Two assaults in 2015, another one in January this year. In fact, this one involved a glassing, didn't it? You sliced a man's cheek in half."

"He came at me first! I swear he did! He called me a fag." Tears glinted in the young man's eyes and his bottom lip trembled. "What was I supposed to do?" he choked.

Jared had previously noted the penalty handed down by the court had been limited to a good behavior bond. For such a serious assault, he could only guess there was some substance to Browning's claim of self-defense.

Silent tears ran down Browning's cheeks and Jared suppressed a sigh. At five foot three and weighing less than one hundred pounds, the kid didn't look strong enough to beat Simon McLean to death, but it never ceased to amaze Jared what people were capable of in the throes of anger fueled by alcohol and possibly drugs.

"I want to call a lawyer," Browning muttered, swiping at his eyes.

"Of course. I'll bring you a phone. But you can make this easy on yourself and let us take your palm prints. If you're confident it wasn't you who left that bloody print at the scene, you shouldn't have any problems."

"I'm already in the system. You have my prints."

"We have your fingerprints. I need your palms." He stared hard at Browning and was surprised when the man offered a sigh of resignation.

"If I let you take my prints, will you leave me alone?"

"If they're not a match, you won't hear from us again," Jared promised.

"All right, I'll do it."

"Good. Let's go. The sooner we clear you as a suspect, the sooner you can leave." Jared pushed away from his seat. Browning did the same.

"Oh, by the way, Mr Browning, do you know anyone by the name of Howard King?"

Browning frowned and shook his head. "No, should I?"

"His body was found in the same vicinity about three weeks ago. He'd been viciously beaten to death. His family confirmed he was gay. We see a bit of a pattern forming. Let's hope for your sake your prints come back clean."

———

Shelby checked her watch for what must have been the hundredth time. Her shift was coming to an end. Any moment, she expected Samuel to appear. It was his practice to come by before the changeover and get an update on his patients from the nursing staff. It was also a way they could see each other on the days when their shifts didn't coincide. If he was rostered on a late shift, like he was today, he often wouldn't finish before midnight—long after Shelby had called it a day.

She finished the report she was writing and stood to return the file to its place in the rack behind the nurses' station. She caught movement from the corner of her eye. Turning her head, she saw Samuel stride onto the ward. He smiled the moment he saw her.

"Nurse Gianopoulos, how nice to see you."

Despite the fact there was no one else around, Shelby blushed. "Good afternoon, Doctor Munro. It's nice to see you, too."

Samuel halted beside the counter. "How was your day?"

"Not too bad. Lily Bradman's waters broke about two hours ago. She's in early stage one labor. Jacquie Nolan has just given birth. We anticipate there'll be five more women come in over the course of the evening." She offered him a smile. "It sounds like you might be in for a busy night."

"Too bad you won't be here to help me," he said and gave her a wink.

Shelby recalled her conversation with Ian and frowned. Samuel noticed.

"What is it?" he asked.

She bit her lip. This wasn't really the time. She was at work. Someone could come by any minute. Still, if she didn't say anything now, she'd spend the rest of the night worrying about it. She'd never get any sleep.

"I met your friend, Ian, this morning."

Samuel nodded. "Ah, Ian Broderick. Yes, we went to med school together."

"So he said. He seemed to know a lot about you—a lot about both of us."

Samuel's gaze remained steady. "I've mentioned you to him, of course. He and I often catch up after work. I've barely seen him since I met you. He was curious. Wanted to know what was keeping me so occupied."

She held his gaze, unwilling to stop until she had the answers she needed. "He seemed to insinuate he knew a whole lot more about me than I was comfortable with. What did you tell him?"

Samuel's expression grew somber. "What are you saying, Shelby?"

"I don't know, Samuel. What did you tell him?"

"Nothing personal, I assure you. I'm not the kind of guy who gets off on sharing that kind of thing with his mates. I told him how we'd met, that I liked you a lot and that I'd been spending time with you. Nothing more than that."

Shelby probed his gaze, seeking the truth. His expression remained serious. She wanted to believe him. But there was more.

"There's something else," she said and saw him tense.

"What is it?"

"He... He told me you were gay. That you have been since your college days. Is it true? Are you? Is that the reason you don't want to sleep with me?"

Shelby was sure the look of shock and disbelief that flooded Samuel's expression couldn't possibly be fake. He shook his head back and forth.

"*What the hell?* Of course I'm not! Why would Ian say something like that?"

A little of Shelby's tension eased. She shrugged. "I don't know. He's supposed to be your friend. Why do *you* think he'd say something like that?"

"Bloody hell," Samuel muttered. "I don't believe

it. I thought we were mates. What the hell's he thinking?"

Shelby relaxed her stance and moved a little closer. "So, you're not gay?"

"Of course I'm not gay! I thought I made that clear to your father."

"You did and I believed you. It's just that...Ian seemed so certain, and he *is* your college friend. I... I didn't want to believe him. I didn't know what to think."

Samuel blew out his breath on a sigh. "I don't know what the hell got into him or why he'd say such a thing. The only thing I can think of is that he's jealous of all the time I'm spending with you— time I used to spend with him. Why he'd come out and tell a lie like that though... I'll talk to him. Don't worry, he won't bother you again."

Relief rushed through her and she offered him a smile. "Good. I'm glad."

Samuel quirked an eyebrow. "What, that I'm not gay, or that Ian won't annoy you with stupid stories again?"

"Both." She laughed. "But mostly that you're not gay."

Samuel leaned over the counter and with the back of his hand, stroked her gently on the cheek. "I like women more than you could ever know. The only reason I haven't made love to you is because I want to wait and make it the best it can be. It's not that I don't want to or that I don't think about it all the time. If making love to you is what it takes to convince you of my heterosexuality, than I'm more than willing to oblige."

Shelby's breathing hitched and her heart skipped a beat. The blue of Samuel's eyes turned cobalt.

"I'll meet you in the treatment room," he growled huskily and turned on his heel.

Her pulse rate spiked and then took off at a gallop. Heat flooded her veins. With a casual air she walked around the end of the nurses' station and headed in the direction Samuel had taken. Checking the way was clear, she opened the door to the treatment room.

She'd barely cleared the entryway before Samuel dragged her inside. With a deft twist of his wrist, he locked the door and then pressed her back against it. Her lips parted on a gasp and he captured it in his mouth, stealing her breath.

Her world narrowed to the planes and valleys of his face. Soft and warm and tender, he kissed her gently on the mouth. She closed her eyes and relished the feel of it, tasting coffee on his lips.

His hand moved to cup the back of her head and his fingers buried themselves in her hair. Holding her head still, he kissed her again and this time, increased the pressure. Desire burned through her. She yearned to touch his skin. Moving closer, she pressed herself against him, mindless of the fact they were at work, albeit locked inside the treatment room. The sound of someone knocking on the door brought her back to reality with a jolt.

"Samuel!" she gasped in a panic.

He lifted his head and stared at her, his expression dazed. The knock came a second time and this time it was accompanied by an impatient twist of the door handle. Samuel blinked and finally the noise appeared to register somewhere in his brain.

"Just a minute," he called out and Shelby was amazed he could sound so calm. He looked anything but.

Straightening his coat, he patted down his hair and Shelby did the same. They looked at each other and grinned, feeling like children caught with their hands in the cookie jar.

"Ready?" Samuel mouthed.

Shelby nodded. Stepping out of the way, she watched him unlock the door and turn the knob. Geraldine Walker stood on the other side of the doorway, her face as dark as the sky right before a storm hit.

Shelby pulled away and stared guiltily at her boss. Of all the people to catch her kissing on the job, it had to be her. Geraldine's eyes shot fire and when she spoke, her voice was colder than ice.

"Doctor Munro, if you're done in here, we're ready to start the handover. Nurse Gianopoulos, I'll see you in my office."

Shelby's cheeks flamed and her heart thumped with something that had nothing to do with passion. She couldn't bring herself to look in Samuel's direction.

"Yes, of course, Geraldine. I was... I was just telling Doctor Munro about Lily Bradman and Jacquie Nolan and the other women expected to come in tonight."

Geraldine's hard expression didn't change.

"Don't take me for a fool, Nurse Gianopoulos. I suggest you stop talking before you're in even more trouble."

With nerves weighing down her every step, Shelby threw Samuel a quick, desperate look and headed for her boss' office as quickly as her rubber-soled shoes would allow. All the while, her heart filled with dread.

It seemed an eon before Geraldine entered her office and closed the door behind her. For every minute Shelby waited, her anxiety rose another notch. The Nursing Unit Manager's expression hadn't softened since their confrontation in the treatment room. Shelby swallowed another surge of nerves.

"Nurse Gianopoulos, not only are you stupid, you're also incredibly ill-advised. Samuel Munro is a charming, good-looking womanizer. Make no mistake, you're one in a very long line of women. I can only put your actions down to the fact you haven't been here very long. You haven't had time to listen to the rumor mill. Even so, fraternizing with a member of staff whilst on duty is severely frowned upon. You'll be lucky to retain your job."

Shelby froze. Geraldine's disclosure about Samuel's dating habits shocked her. She'd never imagined he'd been celibate all his adult life, but she didn't expect to discover he had that kind of reputation. Even more shocking, it hadn't occurred to her that her harmless tryst could jeopardize her much-coveted position at the Sydney Harbour Hospital. *What had she done?*

"I'm so sorry, Geraldine. I... I had no idea."

"Come, Nurse Gianopolous, you're not a silly teenager, although you're acting like one. What did you think would happen? Imagine if a patient or one of their relatives had walked past that door and seen you?"

"We-we had the door locked," she stammered, flushing. Geraldine's frown deepened. She glared at her and Shelby wished she'd kept her mouth shut.

"As this is a first offense, I'm not going to report it to my superior, but be warned, this sort of behavior won't be tolerated. I'll be putting a notation in your file. Any more missteps and your employment at this hospital will cease immediately." Her gaze narrowed. "Do you understand?"

"Y-yes, Geraldine. I'm-I'm so sorry. It won't happen again."

"See that it doesn't."

CHAPTER 7

Samuel climbed the stairs to his third-floor condominium. It would have been easier to take the elevator, and after the night he'd had birthing one baby after another, it would have been wiser. But he worked hard to stay fit and healthy and taking the stairs was an easy way to do it when he didn't have time for the gym. Still, he was bone tired and couldn't wait to crash.

Sliding the key into his door, he tossed his white coat and briefcase on his couch and headed straight for the shower. Standing beneath the hot spray, he let the heat and pressure work its magic on his sore muscles.

All five women who'd been expected to go into labor had done so and he'd been kept busy throughout the night. Two of the deliveries had turned into emergency C-sections, which had made the night even more eventful. Fortunately, all of the new mothers were resting comfortably and their babies were tucked up tight. It had been a good and satisfying night.

Lathering the soap across his chest, he scrubbed the night away. His thoughts wandered to Shelby and their tryst in the treatment room. He recalled the conversation that had triggered it. He still couldn't believe Ian had told her he was gay.

He'd left a message on Ian's voicemail, demanding to know what the hell he'd been thinking, but he hadn't heard back. Not that he expected to. They both knew Ian's little stunt was no more than a jealous prank. Samuel vowed to make it clear to his friend that Shelby was going to remain an important part of his life and Ian best get used to it. Samuel wouldn't tolerate any such nonsense again.

Despite the fact it was one-thirty in the morning, at the thought of Shelby, blood rushed to his groin. His cock hardened. He hadn't been lying when he'd told her he wanted her. The thought of burying his face between her breasts and loving her with his body had kept him sleepless on more nights than one. He couldn't believe she doubted his attraction and he was determined to make up for it. By the time he finished making love to her, she'd have no doubts about his sexuality.

Sliding his hand along his shaft, he worked it up and down. He imagined her naked and spread out before him. He'd kiss every inch of her, driving her wild and then the real fun would begin.

He'd tease her with his cock, rubbing it up and down her slit. She'd beg him for more, but he'd make her wait until he'd driven her mindless with need. He imagined all the different positions he'd take her. He saw her bending over, taking him in her mouth. From behind, on top, underneath. He didn't care which way. All he wanted was to have her, to claim her for his own.

He could even take her in the shower, slick and soapy and wet. He'd turn her around so she faced the tiles. He'd spread her cheeks and ease himself inside. It was good that they were about the same height. Things were easier, then. She wouldn't have to stand on tiptoe and he wouldn't have to bend his knees. They'd fit together beautifully and he'd fuck her all night long. She'd press back against him and he'd pump her hard and together, they would come.

The warm fluid spurted out of his cock and he couldn't suppress a groan. Despite his fatigue, he was now wide awake. He wished he could call her, but she'd be well and truly asleep and it wasn't fair to wake her. She was rostered to work in a few hours. Besides, she lived on the other side of the city. It wasn't like she could hop in her car and come over.

He wondered briefly about her confrontation with Geraldine. What they'd done was unprofessional, but it wasn't like any of the patients had caught wind of it. A little indiscretion behind closed doors wasn't exactly a sacking offense. He was sure she'd be back on the ward, where she belonged.

With a sigh, he turned off the water and stepped out and toweled himself dry. Padding naked down the hallway, he collapsed back on his bed. Within moments, he was asleep.

Shelby entered the room of one of her patients and greeted the expectant mother with a smile.

"Good morning, Vivian. How are you doing?"

The thirty-five-year-old, about-to-be fourth-time mother grinned ruefully and indicated her swollen stomach. "I'll be better after I get this one out."

"Yes. I'll do my best to help you there. Let's hope your baby's going to cooperate." Shelby picked up the chart that hung on the end of the bed and checked her patient's vital signs that had been recorded by the night staff the evening before. All were within normal limits.

"Will the doctor induce me this morning?" Vivian asked, a hopeful expression on her face.

"Yes. As soon as you've finished breakfast, I'm going to put up the drip. The IV will contain oxytocin and it will hopefully give things a kick start. Given this is baby number four, with a bit of luck, you might even have your little one by the end of the day."

"It can't come too soon for me." Vivian laughed.

Shelby returned the chart to the end of the bed. "Everything looks good, Vivian. I'll leave you to enjoy your breakfast and I'll be back soon."

Vivian smiled. "Bring it on."

Shelby left the room and headed toward the next

patient on her list. It was another one of Samuel's patients. At the thought of him, she recalled Geraldine's words of wisdom and frowned.

What was this thing between her and the sexy doctor? Was it even real? She was neither blind nor stupid. Most of the female nurses flirted madly with him at every turn. He didn't seem to mind. In fact, he often responded in kind. Secure in her knowledge they had something special, his behavior hadn't fazed her, but perhaps she was too trusting, too naïve? Was it like her boss had warned her? Had she failed to see what was right before her eyes?

She didn't think of herself as gullible and she was far from a clueless teenager. She'd been around long enough to gain experience in not only men, but in the world in which they operated. She'd taken Samuel at his word when he'd told her they had something special, but was that just his charm talking or could she trust what he said?

The buzz of her phone indicating a new text message broke into her troubled thoughts. Tugging it out of her pocket, she checked the screen.

Samuel.

Her heart skipped a beat. It was like he knew she was thinking about him. Eagerly, she read the text.

R u free 2 night?

Despite her thoughts of a few moments ago, anticipation surged through her. She shot off a reply.

Yes.

A moment later, his response zinged into her phone.

Pick u up at 7. Wear something nice.

Shelby's heart took off at a gallop. *Would this be the night she and Samuel would make love?* What was she going to do about Geraldine's warnings? Ignore them? No, that would never work. She'd always believed in being upfront and honest and dealing with problems head-on. Like she had with Ian's accusations, she'd discuss them with Samuel and give him the benefit of the doubt.

Even though it hadn't been quite a fortnight since their first date, they'd already shared so much personal information. He knew she was allergic to peanuts. She knew he'd been bullied as a kid. He told her about his nightmarish school days when he'd worn glasses from the time he was in kindergarten until he was halfway through his teens. But still, there was a lot she didn't know about him and his family. He was easy to talk to. She just had to open her mouth.

She'd tell him about Geraldine's comments tonight, after dinner. That way, they could clear the air and focus on what was really important: Making love for the very first time. Her phone buzzed again and she smiled in anticipation before glancing at the screen

Where r u? I need 2 talk 2 u. Call me. Dimitri.

Her smile faded and was replaced with a frown. Dimitri's text sounded urgent. A sudden shiver of foreboding ran down her spine. She sent a silent prayer heavenwards that everyone in her family was all right and then sent off a reply.

At work. What's the matter?

Before she could return the phone to her pocket, another message came in.

Not over the phone. What time will u b home?

She forced herself to type the words.

Is it about Mom and Dad?

She breathed a sigh of relief when he replied.

No, nothing like that. I just need 2 talk.

Out of all of her siblings, she was probably the closest to Dimitri. He was only a couple of years older than her and they'd always had a lot in common. They shared a similar sense of humor and both of them were mad about football. She sent off another reply.

Would love 2 Dimi, but I'm going out 2 night. Can we do it tomorrow?

A moment later, she received a reply.

I really need 2 talk 2 u.

She stared at the words and her heart sank. No matter how much she wanted to see Samuel, her brother needed her more. She slowly typed her reply.

OK. C u 2 night.

Dimitri sent her an emoji of two smiley faces and a thumbs-up. Shelby grinned. With a deep breath, she composed another text. This one was to Samuel.

Something's come up. Can we make it 4 later?

Her phone buzzed a few moments later and she read his response.

Sure. How about 9? Is that too late?

A fresh surge of anticipation went through her and she hurriedly typed her reply.

Sounds great. I don't have 2 work tomorrow.
His final response made her smile.
Neither do I.

Jared Buchanan stared at the crime scene photos displayed on his desk and looked for something he might have missed. Three weeks had passed since the first murder on the cliffs of North Bondi and he was no closer to solving either of them.

He was sure the deaths were related. There were far too many similarities. Both victims were white males, both in their early twenties. Both were gay men who were known to frequent gay bars. Both had been found brutally murdered, suffering from blunt force trauma. Both had been found along the scrub that bordered the cliff tops of North Bondi, a well-known haunt frequented by gay men looking for sex.

He'd run Peter Browning's palm print through the system and had cursed aloud when he discovered they weren't a match. Browning was their only suspect and he was now off the list. Unless they could find some other evidence linking him to the scene, he was free to go.

Jared had put together a press release which included a photo of Simon McLean and a request for information from anyone who had seen him that night. The print and television media had run with it for the first couple days, but then they'd moved on to other stories and the few leads that had trickled in had amounted to nothing. It was the same with the first victim, Howard King.

Both men seemed to have only a small number of family and friends, but that probably wasn't so unusual. They were young, just starting out; both had moved to the city from the country. What was unusual was that nobody had seen or heard anything during the time the murders took place—at least, nobody who was coming forward.

Jared made his mind up to revisit the crime scenes. Bondi was a highly populated suburb. With a beautiful stretch of pristine beach, it attracted a lot of people. Bars and restaurants along the promenade were open very late. It wasn't inconceivable that someone might have been returning home after a night out at the same time either of the men were being brutally slain.

Like McLean, King had been struck first from behind. The blow had knocked him to the ground, where he'd suffered numerous other injuries. Either the perpetrator had come upon the victims by mistake and had simply lashed out, or he'd lain in wait, knowing that sooner or later, someone would come along. The second scenario was so much more chilling. It sent a shiver down Jared's spine.

Of course, the media were all over the gay angle and Jared couldn't blame them. Both victims were homosexual. It was hard not to draw a link. Still, he needed to keep an open mind or risk missing important clues. Right now, without a viable suspect, he couldn't afford to overlook anything.

———————

Shelby stepped out of the shower and toweled herself dry before pulling on her robe. Dimitri wasn't home when she'd arrived from work, so she decided to get a head start on her plans for the evening—an evening she hoped would end with her in Samuel's bed. The thought filled her with excitement.

She'd gone all out with her toilette: shampooing, exfoliating and shaving. Her skin felt soft and silky and the moisturizer she poured into her hand smelled divine. When she finished speaking with her brother, all she had to do was get dressed in something sexy and she'd be ready for her date. She couldn't wait.

Back in her room, she chose her underwear with care. The black lacy bra and panties had been bought for her cousin's wedding. She'd worn them on purpose on the off chance she'd end the night in Samuel's arms. Things hadn't worked out that way, but now she was being given another chance.

Pulling on a T-shirt and denim shorts, she ran a comb through her wet hair and worked her way through the knots. Twisting it into a simple bun at the nape of her neck, she surveyed herself in the mirror, mostly satisfied with the results. It would have to do. Athena was staying over at their parents' place for a few days while she studied for her bar exams. Apparently Shelby, Dimitri and Zoe were all too noisy and her sister couldn't concentrate. Anyway, for whatever the reason, Athena wouldn't be around to work her magic on Shelby's hair tonight.

Shelby heard the front door open and called out. "Is that you Dimi? I'm in my room. I won't be long."

Pushing a few more hairpins into her bun, she spritzed on her favorite Nina Ricci perfume and then left the room. Dimitri was already at the fridge, pulling out a beer.

"How was your day?" he asked before cracking open the can.

She smiled. "It was good. How was yours?"

"Shithouse. Like every other day I spend in that place."

Shelby gaped in surprise and alarm at the pain on her brother's face. She moved forward and reached out and put a comforting hand on his arm.

"Dimi! You've worked in that firm for nearly five years! How can it be that bad?"

Her brother stared at her with sad eyes and slowly shook his head. "You have no idea, Shelby. You have no idea what it's like to work for Dad. He's not even my supervising partner, but he seems to stick his nose into everything I do. The latest thing he has going is holding out the promise of a partnership."

Dimitri sneered and the bitterness that twisted his lips nearly broke Shelby's heart. *How long had*

Dimi been so unhappy? How long had her father been treating him like this? She wished she'd noticed sooner how miserable her brother was. She would have talked to him about it earlier.

Shaking off her arm, Dimitri left the kitchen and headed for the couch. Shelby followed him. Throwing himself down on the sofa, he took another swig from his beer and sighed.

"He wants me to get married, Shelby."

Shelby's mouth dropped open in surprise. "He *what?*"

Dimitri raised his gaze to hers. "He wants me to get married. He thinks it's way past time. I'm twenty-nine, after all. Old enough to have a wife and family of my own. At least, that's what Dad says. He's sweetened the deal by offering me a junior partnership in Harton and Wentworth, but only if I find myself a nice Greek girl and settle down. Pronto."

Shelby stared at her brother and shook her head in disbelief. "What has gotten into him? He didn't used to care about this kind of stuff."

Dimitri rubbed a hand wearily across his face. "I don't know, sis. Perhaps he's feeling his age. Perhaps he wants the opportunity to spend time with his grandkids before he dies."

"He's only just turned fifty-five," Shelby protested. "It's not exactly old."

Her brother shrugged. "Who knows? All I know is that as the oldest child, I'm getting heat for not wanting to settle down. A wife!" Dimitri shook his head in disbelief. "You have to be kidding!"

Shelby moved toward the couch and sat down

beside him. Studying him closely, she asked, "Would it be such a bad thing? Most of us settle down at some point in our lives. Is it too much to accept Dad might want to know his grandchildren?"

Dimitri scoffed. "Like you can talk. You're only a couple of years younger than me. Why do I have to be the one who settles down? There's nothing stopping you from getting married and carrying on the family line."

"You're right," she agreed. "And one day, I hope to do just that. At least I'm seeing someone. I can't remember the last time you brought a girl home."

Dimitri grimaced and the pain in his eyes nearly stole Shelby's breath. She moved closer to him on the couch and rested her hand on his arm.

"Dimi? What is it? What happened? Did some girl break your heart? Is that why you haven't been out with anyone since high school? Does it go that far back?"

Her brother closed his eyes. Drawing in a deep breath, he let the air out on a heavy sigh. "No, Shelby, it's nothing like that."

She watched him, becoming more and more concerned. "Then, what is it, Dimi?"

For a long time, he remained silent. Shelby heard the sound of passing trains outside the window. Dimitri tilted his beer up to his lips and drank until it was finished. Setting the empty can down on the coffee table, at last he turned to her.

"The thing is, Shelby, I don't want to marry a Greek girl. I don't want to marry any girl."

She stared at him in confusion. "You don't want to get married? Ever?"

"No, I want to get married. Just not to a girl."

As his words sunk in, her mouth gaped in disbelief. Shock ricocheted through her nerve endings.

"You mean... You mean, you're gay?"

His gaze was steady on hers. "Yes, Shelby. I'm gay."

She shook her head, her mind spinning. "How? When? Why didn't you tell me? Is this what you wanted to talk to me about?"

Dimitri lowered his gaze and stared at his hands that were clenched into fists in his lap. "Yes. I think I've always been gay. I dated a few girls in high school, but it was really only because all of my friends had girlfriends. It seemed like the right thing to do. I even kissed a few of them. I always wondered why it didn't feel more electrifying.

"Then, when I got to college, things weren't so clear cut. There was a blurring of the genders, if you like, of the genders and sexuality didn't seem so black and white. People were into experimentation and that seemed perfectly fine. I met a couple of gay students at a bar on campus. One night, after a few too many beers, I ended up in bed with one of them and all of a sudden I knew. I knew why kissing girls hadn't been exciting, why it hadn't turned me on. I was gay and I hadn't realized. The first night I spent with a guy was the happiest night of my life."

"Oh, Dimitri!" Shelby breathed, appalled that she hadn't known. He was her brother, her confidante. She should have seen, she should have known. She was filled with anguish that he'd carried such a secret for so long.

"Does anyone else know?" she asked.

Dimitri compressed his lips and shook his head. "No."

"You haven't told Momma and Daddy?"

"No."

"Do you think they suspect anything? Could that be the reason behind Daddy's push for you to marry? Does he think the promise of a partnership might be enough to bring you back to girls?" She drew in a quick breath and continued: "Daddy was all over Samuel at the wedding, accusing him of being gay. Although he was way off base, I wonder if the thought had been playing on his mind."

Dimitri offered her a slight smile. "We're talking about Dad, Shelby. I'm sure he doesn't have a clue. He was only grasping at straws, throwing things out there, trying to shock your date. You know how he is. It had nothing to do with him actually believing Samuel might be gay."

Shelby regarded him hopefully. "You think?"

Dimitri nodded. "Yes, I do. For all Dad's amazing intuition in the courtroom, his gaydar doesn't even come close. If he had any idea, he wouldn't keep going on about me finding a nice Greek girl. Hell, I think he'd be happy if I found *any* girl, Greek or otherwise. As for Mom, she doesn't have a clue. As far as she's concerned, her children are perfect and believe me, her idea of perfection doesn't include being gay."

Shelby mulled over his comments in silence. She didn't want to accept them, but she knew what he said was true. The same went for her brothers and sisters. If she hadn't realized Dimitri preferred men over women, she was sure her siblings were equally oblivious. She felt awful for not recognizing the signs earlier and being a support for him.

"I'm sorry for not realizing," she murmured and reached out and squeezed his hand.

Dimitri offered her a sad smile filled with resignation, but he returned the pressure. "Yeah, me too. It would have been nice to have someone I could talk to, someone I could trust to understand. But don't go beating yourself up about it. I worked hard at keeping it hidden."

She stared at him, feeling awful. "What are you going to do? You can't keep living a lie."

Her brother sighed. "I've been living a lie my entire life. What do another few years matter?"

Shelby shook her head, appalled. "You can't keep pretending you're something you're not—not about something as important as this! You're never going to be happy until you tell them. Come out of the closet, live your life the way you want to. It's not illegal, after all. You can't help the way you are...the way you feel."

She paused to draw breath and then another thought struck her. "Do you... Do you have a partner?"

Dimitri compressed his lips. "No. No one special. I hang out in the bars in Oxford Street every now and then. Occasionally I go home with someone."

Shelby was appalled all over again. "Dimitri

Gianopoulos! You can't live like that! Do you know how dangerous it is? You could be going home with anyone! And what about disease?"

Dimitri rolled his eyes and a smile tugged at his lips. "I'm careful, all right? Don't worry about me. And I don't go home with just anyone. We usually chat for at least an hour or two over a few drinks before making any advances of that nature."

She punched him in the arm. "You're being facetious. Haven't you been listening to the news? The media are calling the murders of those two gay guys hate crimes, like they were targeted because of their sexuality. There are a lot of people who can't stand the thought of homosexuality. All I'm saying is, watch out for yourself."

Dimitri's expression sobered. "You're right. It could be dangerous and I promise to be more careful. I'll make sure we talk for three hours at the minimum and even then, they'd better be football fanatics or they'll have no chance with me. As for going for a midnight walk across the cliff tops of North Bondi, next time I agree to it, I'll be sure to invite you along for protection."

Despite herself, Shelby laughed and then Dimitri joined in. She reached over and hugged him.

"Thank you for telling me, Dimi. I love you."

"I love you, too, Shelby.

It was nearly nine o'clock when Shelby's phone buzzed with a new message. Snatching her phone off the charger, she eagerly read the text. It was from Samuel.

U wouldn't believe it, I've been called in 2 work. Can we try again tomorrow?

Her shoulders slumped. She was flooded with disappointment. After all the events that had transpired, she'd been looking forward to spending time with him. With a sigh, she headed for her bedroom to change. The lingerie would have to wait. Again. She sent off a reply.

Sure. Call me.

CHAPTER 8

Dear Diary,

I've started on this high path of retribution and now there's no going back. Nor do I want to. I've struck back against the abomination burning up our shores. It will take a long time to rectify the imbalance, but we need to start somewhere. I don't intend to rest until it's done.

Alexei Gianopoulos leaned back against the leather recliner in his basement and swallowed a sigh. For so many years, his life had cruised along on an even plane. He'd worked his way up to senior partner, he had a wife who still turned heads and children who made him proud. He had nothing to complain about and yet, just recently, his life had begun to go off course.

First it was Helen who'd started grumbling,

complaining about the way he lived his life. They'd been married for thirty-two years. For almost all of that time, they'd never argued. Squabbled, maybe, over insignificant things he couldn't even remember, but not out-and-out arguments where neither of them would give in. It wasn't them and it never had been, but Alexei could feel a storm gathering on the horizon and he wasn't sure what to do about it. If there was one thing he avoided, it was confrontation—which was laughable given his chosen occupation. Still, it was different in the courtroom. *He* was different. It was his job, his profession. It didn't mean he wanted to endure conflict in his home.

Then there was Rodriguez. He'd started out with so much promise, so much allure in his midnight-dark eyes. Alexei had been immediately smitten. The man was young enough to be his son, but Alexei was drawn to him like he'd been drawn to no other. They'd met in a gay bar in the city. Alexei had spotted him from across the room. The music, the chatter of conversation, the hum of the traffic outside—all of it receded until there was nothing and no one, but him.

It sounded like some corny scene from a movie, but it was exactly the way it had been. Even from a distance, Alexei had felt a burning need. He had to have him.

And he had. With a little persuasion, Rodriguez had become his lover and Alexei had enjoyed delights like he'd never experienced before. For six wonderful months they'd been together, almost every night. It was heaven. Until it wasn't.

The sound of his cell phone ringing broke into his somber musings. Glancing at the screen, he bit back a curse, tempted to let the call go through to voicemail. But ignoring Rodriguez wouldn't solve anything. In fact, it was likely to make things worse. With a growl of impatience, he answered.

"Rodriguez, what do you want? I've told you, we're over. I don't want you calling me again."

"But, Alexei, I don't understand! What did I say? What did I do? You still haven't told me."

"I told you plenty of times, Rodriguez. You just haven't been prepared to listen. I have a wife and family. They're a big part of my life. You're too possessive, too needy. I can't afford to be caught in an indiscretion."

"But, Alexei, you love that about me! You told me my confidence was one of the things that attracted you in the first place. I can't help it if I want everyone to know you're mine."

With an effort, Alexei held onto his irritation. Rodriguez was right. As an ageing lawyer almost past his prime, Alexei had been flattered by Rodriguez's attention and had been eager for more. But that was before his lover had become so demanding, so insistent they tell the world he was his.

As much as he wanted to shout at Rodriguez that it was over, that whatever they'd had once was gone, he erred on the side of caution. Rodriguez was young and headstrong. Alexei needed to handle him carefully.

"It isn't that I don't want you, Rodriguez, or that I'm tired of your company. I simply have to protect my other interests, and that includes my family."

"So you're choosing that stuck-up wife over me? Is that it?"

Alexei compressed his lips over the churlishness in Rodriguez's tone. With a deliberate calmness, he offered a reply.

"I'm choosing to keep my life intact, like it's been for more years than you've had on this earth. Please try and understand."

"Understand? How can I understand? You're passing me over because you're a coward and let's not make any bones about it! If you had real guts, you'd tell the world who you really are and how happy you feel in my arms. I *love* you, Alexei! I'm not going to give you up without a fight!"

Rodriguez's voice caught on a sob and Alexei gritted his teeth. *Hell, just what he needed.* His lover blubbering like a baby all over the phone.

"This is not fair, Alexei! You can't do this to me! Say you're sorry! Say you didn't mean it! Say you'll take me back!"

"I'm sorry, Rodriguez. I really am, but this is the end for us. It's over. Finished. You and I will never be again."

"You asshole!" Rodriguez screamed and Alexei barely held on to his anger.

"I'll show you!" the man continued. "I'm going to throw myself off the cliff! I'll kill myself, or maybe I'll kill you? Or both of us! Yes, that's what I'll do! We'll go down together! By the end, the whole world will know."

Fear, thick and visceral and immediate flooded

through Alexei's veins. It had never occurred to him that Rodriguez might take their break-up so badly. They'd been together a matter of months. It wasn't like it had gone on for years... What the hell was the idiot going on about? Neither of them wanted to die.

Alexei was almost certain Rodriguez was too big a coward to go through with it. He was bluffing. It was another cry for attention. He was good at that. It was the threat to go public that had Alexei most concerned.

"Did you hear about those killings?" The abrupt change of subject and the slyness in Rodriguez's tone as he asked the question put Alexei on edge.

"What killings?" he asked.

"The ones up on the cliffs at North Bondi. You must have heard about them. It's been all over the news."

Alexei gave a non-committal response. He'd heard something about it, but the truth was, he'd been buried deep in a trial representing a man charged with supplying and manufacturing more than twenty pounds of methamphetamine. He had a little more on his mind than watching the news. In fact, his trial was about to *become* the news.

"What are you getting at, Rodriguez?" he asked, suddenly impatient to end the conversation.

"The media are calling them crimes of passion," Rodriguez continued in the same sly tone. "Both victims were gay. The police are still speculating if the murders were the result of lovers' quarrels or if something else was at play."

"What the hell does any of that have to do with

me, Rodriguez? Spit it out. I don't have time for this shit."

"That's how I could do it. A lovers' quarrel, up on the Bondi cliffs. You wouldn't even have to go far from home."

The man's chuckle on the other end of the phone sent a chill through Alexei's veins. His gaze drifted to the Melbourne Storm football cap that he'd spied on his bed earlier. He didn't know where it had come from or who had put it there. He'd barracked for the Cronulla Sharks all his life. Everyone knew that. Even Rodriguez.

"Did you get my gift?" Rodriguez murmured, interrupting Alexei's thoughts.

Once again, Alexei's gaze went to the football cap. It must have been Rodriguez. It was just like him to be so spiteful.

"Yeah, I got it." His tone was cold.

"I thought you'd like it," Rodriguez protested.

"Well, I don't and you shouldn't be surprised." A surge of impatience went through him. He'd had enough of this bullshit.

"Look, Rodriguez, we're over. It's finished. No more. I don't want your stupid gifts. I don't want your phone calls. In fact, I never want to see you again. Got it? And don't threaten me with suicide or murder or anything else you might come up with. I won't fall for it. Not now, not ever. It's time to move on."

Alexei held his breath, unsure whether his harsh words would push Rodriguez over the edge. He waited nervously. When Rodriguez started to cry quietly, Alexei swallowed a sigh of relief. Tears were fine. He could handle tears. "I'm sorry, Rodriguez," he said quietly and realized he meant it. He'd miss his Latin lover. There was no doubt about it.

"I... I love you, Alexei!" the man sobbed. "I'll love you until I die!"

"And I love you, too, Rodriguez. I wish there was some way we could be together, but there isn't. I'm sorry. I really am."

After a few more reassurances from Alexei that Rodriguez would be fine and would move on and find another man to love one day, he ended the call. Blowing out his breath on a heavy sigh, he prayed that was the end of it.

Samuel woke to the sun in his eyes and then sat up with a start. After the disappointment of not seeing Shelby the night before, he was eager to set things right. Barring another emergency, they both had the day off. He intended to make the most of it.

Following a quick shower, he threw on a polo shirt and shorts and strode into the kitchen. The sight of the Pacific Ocean outside the glass sliding doors that led out onto his balcony gave him pause. The sun sparkled bright and golden off the water in the distance. The tiny dark smudges on the horizon were container ships shifting freight down to the port.

Closer to shore, surfers rode the waves. A pang

went through him. It had been more than a fortnight since he'd been out there. Even the smell of sea salt had disappeared from his hair. Still, today he'd catch up with Shelby and he was hopeful the day would end with her in his bed. The thought made his gut clench with anticipation and excitement. They'd waited long enough.

Popping two pieces of toast in the toaster, he set the coffee machine to percolate and then poured a glass of juice. Reaching over the stack of medical journals piled high on his kitchen counter, he found the TV remote and switched it on. Flicking through the channels, he settled on the morning news.

"Police were called to the cliff tops of North Bondi last night after the discovery of yet another body. The man, who has yet to be identified, is believed to be in his late teens or early twenties. Early investigations lead police to believe the man was bludgeoned to death with a blunt weapon. This is the third murder in the area in less than a month. Residents are becoming increasingly concerned."

The picture of the newsreader switched to a reporter who was live on the scene. Samuel could see the boardwalk in the distance that ran parallel to the beach. He knew the area well. It was part of his neighborhood. In fact, if he walked down the street a bit, he'd probably see the news crews. The thought sobered him.

Bondi had always enjoyed an excellent reputation of being a safe, fun place to live. Locals and tourists alike flocked there to enjoy the beach and the trendy café vibe. Now there had been three murders. He didn't know what was going on. The feed came back to the news anchor. The man looked suitably serious.

"If anyone can provide the police with any information, you're asked to contact Detective Sergeant Jared Buchanan at the Bondi Police Station or call Crime Stoppers." The phone number scrolled along the bottom of the screen, over and over.

The toast popped up in the toaster and Samuel turned away. Refusing to allow the somber news to ruin his morning, he finished his breakfast and then reached for his phone. Smiling to himself, he composed a text to Shelby.

Morning, beautiful. R u awake yet?

Almost immediately, the phone beeped back at him.

Of course, I've been up 4 hours. I've eaten breakfast, cleaned the house, done 2 loads of washing. What r u up 2?

He grinned and shot off a reply.

Nothing quite so domesticated, although let me tell u, I'm impressed. Someone's trained u well. That's going 2 stand u in good stead in the future. A woman who's so highly skilled is great wife material.

He finished it with two smiley emoijis. A moment later, the phone beeped again.

Ha! Who's the comedian? Don't quit ur day job!

This time, he laughed out loud and then typed:
Can I come over?

He held his breath as he waited for her reply.

I'm sorry, my sister Zoe has a migraine. She's in bed with the curtains drawn. She's asked me 2 keep the noise down.

Samuel's cock stirred at the implications and then he told himself to forget it. Shelby's comment was innocent. There was no way she was referring to rowdy sex. He was the only one who couldn't stop thinking about all the ways he wanted to have her. Despite his misgivings about how she'd feel when he laid all his secrets bare, he was done with waiting. He wanted her in his arms, in his bed. In his life. He sent back a reply.

2 bad 4 Zoe. U could always come over here.

Once again, he waited with anticipation for her response.

All the way 2 Bondi? U know I live on the other side of the harbor.

He chuckled and texted back.

At least we won't disturb Zoe.

A few moments later, she replied.

LOL. There is that. OK, I think I can manage it. C u in a couple of hours. I have 1 more load of washing 2 go. (Just kidding!)

His heart soared.

Shelby checked the address Samuel had given her and then parked her BMW Roadster in a vacant space. The car had been a gift from her parents on her twenty-fifth birthday and she loved driving it. She was particularly grateful for their generosity seeing as she could never have afforded it on her wages.

Climbing out of the vehicle, she looked up at Samuel's building. It was one of the newer condominium complexes that had sprung up around Bondi over the past few years. The building was rendered in a modern, charcoal color with the trim painted a sparkling white. There looked to be four or five floors. Samuel had told her he was on the third. Even so, she'd bet he had a decent view of the ocean. Locking her car behind her, she drew in a deep breath to settle the sudden rush of nerves before heading inside.

Her thoughts centered on the conversation she'd had with her boss the previous afternoon and she wondered if she had the courage to discuss it with Samuel. She'd always known he was flirtatious and charming. He'd been that way when she'd met him. What she didn't know was if she could put any stock in his claim that he was falling in love with her. *Was it just his way of sweet-talking her, or did he really mean it?* There was only one way to find out.

The ride up in the elevator took less time than she needed to calm her jitters. She was about to enter Samuel's private domain. After their kiss at the hospital, she knew exactly what his invitation meant and what her acceptance of it would indicate. Despite Geraldine's warning that he was a player, the thought of loving him sent a shiver of anticipation through Shelby's veins.

They hadn't known each other long, but she

felt like she'd been waiting for him her whole life. She thought of Dimitri and vowed to take the happy ending that was within her grasp and hold on for dear life. Arriving outside Samuel's door, she smiled to herself and knocked without hesitation. Seconds later, it opened.

"Hi," she said, suddenly flooded with nerves. Heat rushed to her face. *So much for her being ready to grab the bull by the horns.*

"Good morning." Samuel grinned at her. A moment later, he dragged her into his arms.

His kiss started out warm and tender, but it quickly ignited a fire. Shelby put her arms around his neck and returned his passion. Without breaking contact, he walked them backwards into a bright, sunny living room. From the corner of her eye, she noticed expensive furnishings—dark wood bookshelves; a matching coffee table; a white leather couch. And just as she'd suspected, he had a terrific view.

The kiss came to an end and she broke away with a gasp. She was pleased to see Samuel was also breathing hard. She touched her lips and smiled. "Wow! That beats doing the wash any day."

He grinned and then his smile slowly faded. "I missed you," he said.

Her heart somersaulted. When she finally managed to speak, her voice was husky with need. "I missed you, too."

She set her handbag down on the coffee table and then turned back to face him. Hunger had replaced the tenderness in his eyes. Taking a step back, she cleared her throat.

"There's something I wanted to talk to you about."

He frowned. "What do you mean?"

Shelby looked around the room, trying to find the right words. "It's...about the other day. The kiss... When we were found by Geraldine."

Samuel looked more concerned. "She didn't fire you, did she?"

"No. But she did warn me off you."

Samuel's concern morphed into surprise. "She warned you off me? Why would she do that?"

Heat stole up Shelby's cheeks. She kept her gaze fixed on a picture that hung on the wall opposite. "She said... She said you were a womanizer and that I was only one in a long line of women. She implied that you'd tire of me soon enough and I'd be left with a broken heart."

Samuel shook his head in disbelief. A humorless smile played around his lips. "I can't believe she said that."

Shelby frowned. *Did he think she was making things up?* In clipped tones, she asked him as much.

"Good God, no!" Samuel explained. "I believe you when you tell me that's what she said. It's her I don't believe. The nerve of her!"

"What do you mean?"

Samuel held her gaze and then sighed and moved away to stare out the window. A moment later, he spoke: "I've been employed as a doctor at the Sydney Harbour Hospital for more than seven years. I'd been working on your ward for about six months before Geraldine approached me and invited me out on a date."

Shelby stared at him in surprise. Though attractive and sporting a body that looked like she was devoted to her gym, Geraldine Walker had to be at least a decade older than Samuel.

As if reading her mind, Samuel nodded. "Yes, she's good looking and great at her job. I admire her for her attitude toward her patients and her professionalism. But she's quite a lot older than the women I usually date. I wasn't attracted to her. I didn't see any reason to give her false hope. So, I turned her down."

"You said no?"

"Yes. I tried to do it tactfully, but even so, she was pissed. She was a confident, attractive woman who was at the top of her game. I don't think she expected me to decline."

"But that was years ago. Surely she still can't harbor a grudge?"

Samuel shrugged. "Who knows? But doesn't it seem spiteful to you that she catches us kissing and then tells you to keep your distance from me?"

Shelby pondered his comment. "You've been out with a lot of women. You're always a hot topic of discussion in the tea room. I've had to keep my mouth shut this past fortnight, listening to my colleagues deliberate about who is the lucky girl to have caught your interest this week. I got the distinct impression you switch your affections as often as you switch your sheets."

She said the words lightly, but tension coiled tightly in her stomach. She held her breath and waited for his response. Finally, he turned back to her and nodded.

"You're right. Up until I met you, I was a serial dater. Ask Ian. Ask anybody. I've lost count of the number of women I've taken to dinner. It was fun. I enjoyed being single and being in the company of beautiful women. Did I sleep with them all? No, not all of them, but enough. I've never proclaimed to be a saint. Does that matter to you?"

"Do you believe in monogamy?"

His gaze was steady on hers. "Yes. I never dated more than one girl at a time. I've only been in serious relationships a couple of times and those only lasted a few months. I didn't realize until I met you, that all that time, I was searching, searching for the right one." He moved closer. Shelby could see the earnestness in his eyes. "And now I've found her."

The light in his eyes burned brighter and her breath caught on a silent gasp. Her heart pounded at the heat in his gaze.

"I want you," he said simply.

"I want you, too," she whispered and just like that, all her reservations melted away.

One small step forward was all it took and she was in his arms once again. His lips found hers and they fused together, drinking each other in. He urged her closer and she moaned softly, relishing the feeling of being pressed up close against his chest. Hard muscles came into contact with her breasts. Even through the soft cotton of her blouse, her nipples tightened. She shivered from the impact.

Splaying her hands across his shirt front, she

savored the warmth and feel of him. Her fingers scraped across the hard little nubs of his nipples and he groaned against her mouth. Tingles of desire coursed through her and centered in her groin. She pressed herself against his erection and was rewarded with another moan.

"How about we head for the bedroom?" he muttered, kissing her eyes, her nose, her cheeks.

She nodded and let her hands fall away and then gasped when he picked her up in his arms.

"Samuel! Put me down! I'm too heavy."

"Nonsense!" he growled and bent his head to kiss her on the mouth again.

He carried her with ease down the carpeted hallway and into the room she assumed was his. The king-sized bed was neatly made and the room was clean and tidy. Gauzy, white curtains fluttered lazily in the light breeze swirling around open sliding glass doors that led out onto a balcony. Shelby had time to catch another glimpse of the ocean before Samuel lowered her onto the bed.

The mattress felt like she was floating on clouds. She had no idea there were beds like that. It was pure luxury. She'd never be satisfied with her plain old four-poster again.

"Your bed feels incredible," she murmured and watched him lower himself down.

He moved to lie next to her and nuzzled her neck. "That's not the only thing that feels incredible."

She turned her head, giving him greater access and reveled in the feelings he generated. His lips nibbled their way across her throat. Tugging the ends of her blouse out of her shorts, he slid his hand over her belly, pulling the shirt higher as he went. His mouth replaced his hand and he kissed his way up her chest.

When his mouth closed over her nipple, she gasped. White hot heat shot through her and centered between her thighs. He suckled her breast through the fabric of her bra until she was screaming inside for the feel of his mouth on her skin. Moving restlessly, she reached behind her and undid the clasp, sighing as her breasts were released.

"You have way too many clothes on," he mumbled between kisses.

"I agree," she said and sat up so she could work on her buttons. In her haste to undress, her fingers turned clumsy and she cursed softly under her breath. Samuel grinned.

"I love that you're eager to get naked, but there's no rush. We have all day, remember?"

She smiled back at him and lowered her hands. "You're right. How about you do it?"

His eyes flared with heat. She lay back against the pillows and waited for him to make his move. She didn't have to wait long. Moving so that he straddled her thighs, he shot her a sexy smile and then leaned over and started at the top. He worked his way slowly, methodically down her blouse, exposing her skin one button at a time. At last, he finished and she couldn't hold back a sigh.

He stared down at her, his eyes dark with desire. "You're so beautiful."

She gazed back at him. "Take off your shirt."

In silence, he pulled his T-shirt over his head. Underneath, he was just as firm and muscled as she'd imagined. His skin glowed golden—she guessed it was a combination of his aboriginal heritage and the hours he spent in the surf. She reached up and dragged her fingernail across the taut flesh. His muscles tensed beneath her touch.

She smiled. "You're beautiful, too."

Samuel shot her a wry smile and shook his head. "You have it all wrong. Guys aren't beautiful."

"Some are," she replied. "*You* are."

He bent low and captured her mouth with his. The soft fullness of his lips sent a renewed wave of desire pulsing through to her core. She reached up and framed his face with her hands, holding his head in place. Deepening the kiss, she traced the outline of his mouth with her tongue.

He groaned beneath her ministrations and lowered his weight until he was pressed full against her. His erection pressed into her belly, hard and insistent. She moved restlessly beneath him as the need inside her burned hotter. He rolled onto his side and she went with him and then kept going until she was sitting on his lap, straddling his hips.

"Now I have you where I want you," she teased, pressing herself against him.

"Good. Now you can get out of those shorts and while you're at it, you can get rid of mine."

Tossing him a teasing smile, she undid the button on her shorts and eased her zipper down. Lifting her bottom, she shucked the shorts over her hips and down her legs, taking her panties with them. Her gaze remained fixed on Samuel's face and she was pleased at the heat that flared in his eyes.

Still on her knees, she leaned forward, making sure her breasts grazed his chest. She reached for the button on his shorts and once again, slid the zipper down. His cock lay thick and hard beneath the satin of his boxers. Clearly outlined, she marveled at its size. Her fingers itched to touch him.

Giving in to the impulse, she put her hand inside his shorts and ran her fingers along the hard length of him. She smiled when he sucked in his breath. Squeezing rhythmically through the satin of his underwear, she was rewarded with another groan.

"You're a witch, Shelby Gianopoulos," he growled, but made no move to stop her.

She smiled, but didn't answer and continued to caress him with increasing boldness. Not until his cock glistened with need did she finally slide his shorts and boxers down. Samuel lifted his hips to assist her and within moments, the two of them were naked. Shelby moved until she lay spread-eagled on top of him, skin to skin.

"God, you feel so good," Samuel muttered. Stroking her back, his hands reached down and cupped her ass. He pressed her intimately against him.

With his cock lying thick and hard against her belly her need spiraled out of control. Desire pooled between her legs. Her breasts felt achy and heavy. Her nipples were pebbled. She moved until the tip of his cock slid up and down her slit and another wave of desire rushed through her.

With a hand firmly on her bottom, holding her in place, Samuel rolled slightly until he could reach into the drawer of the nightstand. He pulled out a condom and held it out to her.

"Would you like to do the honors?"

She took the condom from him and tore the packet open. Sitting back on her haunches, she rolled the condom over his cock. Returning to her original position, she took him in her hand and guided his shaft into her warmth.

Easing herself down onto his erection, she lost all thought of time and place. He stretched her wide, filling her, stealing her breath, blinding her senses. There was nothing and no one but Samuel and the way he made her feel.

"You feel amazing," she whispered.

As if he couldn't bear to remain still a moment longer, he thrust his hips upward and buried himself all the way in. The feel of him was like nothing she'd ever felt. She hadn't had many lovers, but she'd had enough to know there was something magical about their joining, something that had never been there before. She only hoped he felt the same way.

"Shelby!" he gasped and thrust into her again, his voice hoarse with need.

Responding to the tension in his body, she lifted herself up and down on his cock, setting up a rhythm that would ultimately lead to satisfaction. Moving beneath her, matching her movements, Samuel's breathing quickened.

With his eyes closed and his head thrust back

against the pillows, she'd never seen anything so sexy or so beautiful. His total absorption in their joining, the desire that stained his cheeks—it sent her spiraling out of control until her inner muscles clenched tightly around him.

"Oh!" she exclaimed, all of a sudden overwhelmed by the relief of her orgasm. Samuel opened his eyes and stared at her and a moment later, rolled them over.

With their positions reversed, his expression grew fierce and his thrusts became harder and faster. The tension around his mouth increased until she didn't know how he could stand it. Plunging into her over and over, she clung to his shoulders and rode out the waves of his passion. Minutes later, he stiffened and cried out and then finally collapsed against her as a second climax swept her along with him.

His breath was harsh in her ear, but she didn't mind a bit. Making love with him had been like nothing she'd ever experienced. It was partly because they'd taken time to get to know each other, but it was more than that. After all, she'd been with Kostas for more than three years and she'd always thought they'd known each other well. And yet, she'd never experienced a lovemaking session with Kostas remotely like the one she'd just shared with Samuel, or climaxed like that with any other partner. There was no other way to explain it. Samuel was the difference.

With a muffled apology, he seemed to recall that he was still lying with his weight on top of her. Rolling onto his side and taking her with him, he pulled her close against him. He pressed a kiss upon her hair and sighed quietly.

"I hope you agree with me when I say that was more than worth the wait."

She smiled and nodded and ducked her head. Even after all they'd done, she was still a little embarrassed. It was different when she was in the throes of passion. She didn't care about anything then, but now, after the event, she felt a little shy. Samuel looked down at her with a curious expression on his face.

"Don't tell me you're embarrassed?" he chided gently.

When she ducked her head even lower, he took hold of her chin and eased her head up until she had no choice but to look at him.

"You have nothing to be embarrassed about, Shelby," he said softly and then slowly shook his head. "You were amazing, incredible—it was indescribable. I've never felt like that with anyone before. I think it's the difference between having sex and actually making love. There was nothing about what we just shared that felt like sex. Sex doesn't even come close. Don't you agree?"

All of a sudden, he looked a little uncertain and the fact he wasn't sure how good it was for her filled her with tenderness. She reached up and cupped his cheek.

"You're right. What we just experienced doesn't come close to just having sex. It was beyond anything I could have imagined and it was all because of you. I'm falling in love with you, Samuel Munro."

His eyes lit up with tenderness and joy and he bent his head and kissed her softly on the mouth.

"I've been falling in love with you from almost the first moment I saw you, Shelby Gianopoulos. I'm so glad you feel the same way."

His arms tightened around her and he hugged her hard. Shelby was filled with wonder at finding her soul mate, the man she knew she could love all her life. It was a heady feeling. It almost felt too good to be true. She drifted off to sleep with a smile on her face.

CHAPTER 9

Athena Gianopoulos stared at the textbooks opened on the kitchen table in front of her. She'd been studying hard for the past three days and yet she still felt overwhelmed. She'd been an attorney for two years, working for various small firms around the city, doing everything from wills and probate to conveyancing. But what she really wanted was to be a barrister and to specialize in criminal law, like her father. Before she could do that, she needed to pass the bar exam and right now, she wasn't confident that was going to happen.

She'd come over to her parents' house in Bondi to escape the usual hubbub of the house she shared with her siblings. With her father spending long hours at his firm in the city, her mother busy with her various charitable engagements, and her two younger brothers at school most of the day, Athena had the place to herself. It should have been the perfect environment to memorize everything she needed to know, but she was restless and bored and suddenly wished she hadn't removed herself from the comings and goings of her normal life.

The sound of a door closing snagged her attention and she frowned. Pushing back the chair, she went to investigate. As far as she knew, she was the only one home. *Perhaps one of her siblings had stopped by to say hello?* The thought instantly revived her flagging spirits.

A moment later, her father appeared and started when he noticed her. "Oh, Athena. I'm sorry, I forgot you were here."

"Daddy! What are you doing here? I thought you were at work."

An embarrassed flush stained his cheeks. He looked away. "I am. I just had to come back and get...a file. I'd left it in the basement."

"Is that where you've been? I didn't even hear you come in."

"Yes, well, as I said, I forgot you were here. I snuck in the back entrance."

She laughed. "You *snuck*? Daddy, it's your house. You don't have to sneak anywhere."

Once again, he looked uncomfortable. She was suddenly intrigued. Her father's den in the basement had always been a no-go zone. For as long as she could remember, she'd understood the den was her father's private space. A place where he liked to go to unwind from his stressful days in the courtroom. A place where no kids were allowed. She couldn't even recall her mother venturing down the stairs, though Athena supposed she must have at some point.

"Yes, well, anyway, I'd better get going. I have a client coming in shortly. If I don't hurry, I won't make it back in time. See you later, Athena. Don't study too hard."

He turned and headed toward the front door, closing it softly as he left. A moment later, she heard the sound of his Mercedes rumbling down the drive. She moved toward the kitchen, intent on fixing a snack and then it hit her. Her father had left the house empty-handed. He'd told her he'd come back for a file. He must have forgotten it. She wondered how important it was and then grimaced. Of course it was important. He'd come all the way home from the city to retrieve it.

Knowing he'd already left, she picked up her phone and dialed his number. *Perhaps he could turn around again and come and fetch it?* The phone went straight to voicemail and she could only assume he was already on a call. Sometimes it felt like her father spent more time on the phone sorting out work problems than he did talking to his family.

She ended the call and blew out her breath on a sigh. She could probably get the file herself and take it to him in the city. He said it was in his den. She assumed it was somewhere easy to find. He'd probably put it down and forgotten to collect it. With her mind made up, she hurried over to the door that led down to the basement. Her father usually locked it, telling them he didn't want anyone touching his things. With nine rowdy children living under his roof at one time, she'd always understood his caution.

She turned the doorknob and was surprised when it turned under her hand. In his haste, he must have forgotten to lock it. Or perhaps he didn't bother doing that anymore? After all, only her two younger brothers lived at home and the youngest had turned eighteen. They were hardly going to disobey an order that had been in force for so many years.

Feeling around for a light switch, she found it and flicked it on. The carpeted stairwell was flooded with dim light. Making her way down the stairs, she rounded the corner and came up short.

Shelby flipped over onto her back and enjoyed the feeling of the sun on her skin. It was her second day off and the second day she'd spent with Samuel and she'd never felt more content. They'd agreed to spend the morning down at Bondi Beach, where Samuel intended to catch some waves while Shelby worked on her tan.

The warmth of the sun was making her drowsy. Closing her eyes, she relaxed against her towel. The sound of her phone startled her and she blinked and opened her eyes. Reaching across, she pulled it out of her beach bag and glanced at the screen.

Athena.

She was supposed to be studying, but Shelby bet her sister was bored out of her brain by now. She'd been at it for the past three days. No doubt she was looking for an excuse to take time out from her books. Shelby could understand that. She wasn't that old that she couldn't recall the drudgery of studying for exams. She didn't know anyone who enjoyed it. She answered the call with a cheery greeting.

"Hi, Athena. How are you this glorious day?"

"Where are you?"

Shelby frowned. There was an edge of panic to her sister's voice. "I'm at the beach," she replied.

"Bondi?"

"Yes."

"Oh, thank goodness!"

Shelby's frown deepened. "What's the matter? What's going on?"

"I can't talk about it over the phone. You need to come home. There's something you're not going to believe."

"What is it? Is it Momma or Daddy?"

"No, nothing like that."

"Then what?"

"Just get over here, quick."

Athena ended the call and Shelby stared down at her phone. Her sister sounded panicked, almost fearful. *What the hell was going on?*

She squinted through her sunglasses in the direction of the surf. The reflection of the sun on the water was almost blinding. She could barely see Samuel. He was a tiny dot in the distance. She had no way of knowing how long he'd stay out there. After all, they both had the day off and he'd only been gone ten minutes. He'd told her on their walk down to the beach from his condo that it had been more than a fortnight since he'd hit the waves. She imagined he'd take advantage of the beautiful weather and stay out for a decent amount of time.

She thought about Athena and the panic in her voice. Something was up. Athena wasn't the kind of girl who panicked for no reason. Shelby needed to go and see her and find out what was wrong. She was also curious about what Athena wanted to show her. Coming to a decision, she sent Samuel a text.

Gone 2 Momma and Daddy's. Athena has something 2 show me. Not sure how long I'll b, but call me when u get this.

Tossing her phone back into her beach bag, she collected her flip flops and with her towel draped over her shoulders, she made her way across the sand and back onto the boardwalk. Once on solid ground, she slipped on her footwear and headed up the hill, thankful that her parents didn't live far away. In fact, Samuel's condo was only a few blocks from her childhood home.

The thought brought a rueful smile to her lips. She'd been a regular visitor to his neighborhood and she hadn't even known it. It was like that movie, *Six Degrees of Separation*. She'd been way too young to watch it when it had first been released, but she'd since caught the movie on DVD. It still gave her goosebumps.

Her phone rang again and she dug around in her bag to answer it.

Athena.

"Okay, okay, I'm coming," she said by way of greeting.

"Hurry up, all right. I'm kind of freaking out."

Shelby felt a rush of impatience. "Why don't you just tell me?"

"No, I don't want to. It's not the kind of thing I can talk about. You need to come and see. How far away are you?"

"I'm halfway up the hill. I'll be there in less than five minutes."

"Okay, but get a move on."

"In case you hadn't noticed, Athena, it's a little hot out here. I'm walking as fast as I can."

"I'll come and get you."

"There's no need. I'll be home before you open the garage."

"Well, all right," Athena sighed. "Just hurry."

Shelby ended the call and tossed her phone back into her bag. Stuffing the towel in with it, she adjusted the bag on her shoulders and increased her pace. It was far too hot for jogging and her fitness level probably wouldn't allow her to do more than a fast walk anyway. She was heading up a very steep hill. Athena would just have to be patient.

Shelby had almost reached the front door of her parents' home when she remembered she'd left her house key in her handbag. She hadn't expected to go calling on her parents while she'd been making wild love to Samuel. Her fantasies of the day went something along the lines of endless mind-blowing orgasms followed by eating tubs of salted caramel ice cream in bed, with a little more loving to come. She hadn't planned on involving her family in any way.

The double oak doors opened before she could ring the bell and she guessed that Athena had been watching for her.

"There you are! You took long enough!" her sister complained.

Shelby chose to remain silent. There was a tension in Athena's eyes that seemed to be more than merely the stress of studying for exams. She followed her sister into the wide entryway and dropped her beach bag inside the door.

"So, what's so important I had to hightail it up the hill in this heat?" she asked with her hands on her hips.

Athena's lips tightened and her face lost a little more color. "Come with me."

Without waiting to see if Shelby was behind her, Athena strode down the hallway, past the display of family photographs and limited edition prints, across the wide expanse of white Italian marble tiles that covered the floor of the large open-concept living and dining room and finally came to a halt beside the basement door.

Athena twisted the door knob and Shelby frowned in confusion. "What are you doing?"

"Come with me."

"That's Daddy's den. You know we don't go in there."

Athena's gaze sharpened. She stared at Shelby. "Yes, and have you ever wondered *why*?"

Shelby shrugged. "Not really. It's Daddy's private domain. It's his hangout, a place where he can escape the world. What's so wrong with that?"

Athena's expression revealed nothing. Without another word, she opened the door that had been closed to them ever since Shelby could remember and proceeded down the stairs. A light switch had been turned on, illuminating their progress, but Shelby still felt a shiver of unease. She was entering a forbidden place and even though she was a grown woman and hardly likely to upset her father and his things, it still didn't feel right.

Still, she was curious about what the room looked like and why Athena was so worked up. *What could it be that she wanted to show her that she couldn't tell her about on the phone?*

Her sister rounded the corner ahead of her and stood back to wait. Shelby couldn't help but notice the renewed tension on Athena's face. More and more apprehensive, Shelby crept the final few steps. Rounding the corner, the room was laid bare to her gaze.

"What the hell?" she gasped in disbelief, hardly able to comprehend.

"Exactly," Athena declared solemnly. "You see why I told you to come quick."

Back upstairs, Shelby paced the kitchen in a daze, still unable to believe what she'd seen. Athena sat on a bar stool, hunched over the counter.

"I can't believe it," Shelby muttered. "I just can't believe it."

"I know. I didn't want to either. I saw what was down there and I didn't know what to think."

Her sister still sounded shocked and confused. Shelby went over to her and gave her a hug.

"Who else have you told?" she asked.

"No one," Athena replied, her voice dull.

Shelby thought for a moment and came to a decision. "I'm going to talk to Daddy."

"Shelby, no! You can't do that! Then he'll know we've been down there. What if he gets mad?"

"Getting mad at us is the last thing he'll do. Besides, we're not babies. It's not like we knew the real reason why he's kept the door to the basement locked all these years."

Athena frowned. "Do you think Momma knows?"

Shelby shook her head, bewildered. "I don't know. Maybe. Who knows? That's why I'm going to speak to Daddy. I want some answers."

"But what if he does get mad? What if he gets so mad he disowns you? What then?"

"He's not going to disown me, Athena."

"How can you be so sure?"

Shelby squared her shoulders. A surge of determination went through her. "Okay, I'm not sure, but I'm willing to take that chance."

Athena jumped down off the stool and threw her arms around her sister. Shelby hugged her back.

"Be careful," Athena whispered.

"Of course. Don't worry. I'm going to talk to

Daddy, remember? I'm sure he'll be fine. Surprised that we've discovered his secret, perhaps, but what's he going to do? Call the police? I don't think so."

Stepping away from Athena, Shelby walked back to the front door and collected her things. She thought fleetingly of Samuel, no doubt still soaking up the surf. She'd catch up with him later. There was nothing else she could do. She'd seen what was in the basement. The need to speak with her father took precedence. When Samuel found out what she'd discovered, she was sure he'd understand. With her mind made up, she let herself out of the house and headed for the bus stop.

———

"Mr Gianopoulos, I have your daughter out here. She's wondering if she can have a word?"

Alexei heard his secretary speak and started in surprise. "Which one, Jennifer?" he asked, curious.

"Shelby."

He smiled with genuine pleasure. *Ah, his eldest daughter.* Most of the time, they got on well. "Send her in."

Pushing away from his over-sized walnut-and-beech wood desk, he came around to greet her. The door opened a moment later and Jennifer ushered Shelby in.

"Shelby! What a surprise!" He leaned down to peck her on the cheek.

She turned her head slightly away and his kiss landed in her hair. He frowned in surprise. The tiniest frisson of fear tingled down his spine. *Had Rodriguez made good on his threat? Had he exposed their secret?* No, he wouldn't dare. Alexei was sure of it. With renewed confidence, he stood back and surveyed his daughter.

She was dressed in a short-sleeved, loose floral top and cotton shorts, their bright colors in stark contrast to the paleness of her face. Her long tanned legs were bare except for a pair of flip flops on her feet. Her hair was held loosely back with a hairband and looked a little wild—like she'd been sleeping on it and hadn't brushed it, or like she'd been caught out in the wind.

"What is it, honey? What brings you here?" he asked, forcing a casual tone.

Still, she remained silent. Crossing the room, she set her bag down on the floor next to a wingback chair. Richly upholstered in a deep blue fabric, the chair was one of a matching pair and faced a small, butter-yellow leather sofa.

He liked that the furniture formed a little nook away from his desk. It was a space he sometimes used for important clients when he needed to hash out the details of a deal. Cleverly hidden in a cavity in the wall behind the couch was a wet bar that also came in useful at such times.

At Shelby's continued silence, a frisson of unease danced along his spine. She stood stiffly, staring through the huge plate glass window that took up a large portion of the wall. The view looked out onto Hyde Park and the Sydney

Harbour Hospital. He enjoyed looking down upon the hustle and bustle of the city as people hurried along the paths that cut through the park, fed bread to the ducks who lived near the pond or lay on blankets on the soft grass, eating their sandwiches and soaking up the sunshine.

But right at that moment, with his daughter acting so strangely, blankets and sunshine were the last thing on his mind. Once again, he thought of Rodriguez.

"What's the matter, Shelby? You seem upset. Has something happened to your mother? Your brothers or sisters?" The thought momentarily filled him with concern.

She took a long time to respond. At last, she turned to face him. The devastation in her eyes sent fear racing through his veins.

"Shelby..." He took a step toward her and held out his hand. "Talk to me, honey. What's going on?"

She remained where she was, as if rooted to the spot. Her expression grew even more haggard.

"I know about your den, Daddy."

Shock arced through him. His mouth gaped open in disbelief. *Rodriguez. It had to be him. The son of a bitch.* First the football cap and now *this.* He was playing him.

Alexei's head spun with the enormity of Shelby's discovery. Fear of the repercussions gripped his gut like a vice. In the very next moment, he wondered what explanation he could give. He had to think of something. She was a smart girl.

She wouldn't be appeased with vague platitudes and flat-out untruths.

"Shelby…" He spread his arms wide in supplication. "Please, let me explain."

Her eyes turned to flint. "What's there to explain, Daddy? All these years, you've been living a double life." She shook her head in disgust and disbelief. "How could you have been married for three decades and yet be a closet homosexual?"

CHAPTER 10

Dear Diary,

For so many years I kept the secret, honored my promise to my spouse. I smiled and nodded and kissed and hugged. It was all an elaborate lie. I did what I had to do for my family and I'd probably do it all over again. That's the thing about family—they get to you, take over your heart, infiltrate your mind until every thought, every action is about them. Well, not anymore. I'm done with the deceit. It's time the world, and my family, knew the truth...

Alexei winced at the anger in Shelby's voice. The disillusionment that flooded her face pierced his heart. She was his little girl, his Shelby, and right now, she was looking at him like he was a monster who'd torn her life apart.

"Shelby, honey. Let's sit down. I... I want to explain."

There was a stubborn tilt to her jaw. She remained where she was. "Does Momma know?"

The words came out hoarse and low. He drew in a slow, deep breath and eased it out on a heavy sigh. His shoulders slumped. All of a sudden, he felt a hundred years old. It was time to come clean. Rodriguez had gotten to her. She knew about his den. There was nowhere left to hide.

Feeling like he carried the weight of the Harbour Bridge on his back, slowly and laboriously, he made his way over to the couch and sat down. He glanced at his daughter encouragingly, but still she didn't move. He cleared his throat and cast his mind back to a lifetime ago.

"I think I always knew deep down I was gay, even though I spent years in denial. I went out of my way to date girls in high school. I kissed them, fondled them, I even went all the way. It was pleasant, but I never felt the way the other boys did. They'd gather behind the sports shed and joke and brag about their experiences and how they felt like they were soaring to the moon and I'd wonder what they were talking about and why I didn't feel the same.

"Then, one weekend I was home alone, studying for my final exams. My parents and siblings had gone to a christening on another island. We had a boarder staying with us who was helping out on the farm. He came to me after dinner... It was then that I knew."

His voice drifted off as memories beset him. He'd spent the rest of the weekend in his lover's arms, coming up for air only to attend to the basic necessities. It was the most magical time of his life.

He glanced at his daughter and was relieved to discover some of the anger had faded from her face. She shook her head slowly back and forth. When she spoke, her voice was laced more with confusion than disgust.

"I don't understand, Daddy. Why did you get married?"

He compressed his lips and sighed and did his best to make her understand. "You have to remember, honey, it was the early eighties. I came from a very traditional Greek family. So did your mom. Though there was the occasional rumor about someone who was suspected of being gay, it was still very much frowned upon and for a young man living in a small Greek village, it just wasn't possible for me to shame and dishonor my family that way. And that's exactly what would have happened."

He shrugged. "So, I did what was expected of me. I did the only thing I could do. I found a nice girl in a neighboring village and I married her."

Shelby's eyes welled up with tears. Her face was filled with sadness. "I can't believe you've spent the past thirty-two years living a lie. In all that time, have you *ever* been happy?"

He heard the anguish in her voice and immediately rushed to reassure her. "Of course I have! And I love you and your brothers and sisters with all of my heart."

"What about Momma? Do you love her? Did you *ever* love her?"

"Yes, Shelby, I did and I still do. The truth is, I'm probably bisexual. I didn't know it at the time. I married because it was the acceptable thing and I managed to be intimate with your mother frequently enough that I thought we were doing fine. I still visited gay bars in secluded parts of the city and those illicit meetings with strangers in the dark of night helped to keep me sane."

Shelby stared at him. "Did Momma know?"

"Not in the beginning, although she must have suspected something wasn't right. There were many times over the years she came to me to talk about our relationship, but I always shut her down. I wasn't brave enough to say anything. I was terrified she'd hate me; that she'd take my children away."

He looked down to where his hands were clenched in his lap, remembering the agony of indecision. He'd hated to deceive his wife, but he had been even more frightened of the consequences if she were to discover his secret life.

"We'd been married for more than a decade when she found some magazines I had hidden in the basement," he said quietly. "They were gay porn magazines."

Heat rushed up his neck and swept across his cheeks. He stared at the carpet and willed his embarrassment away. He'd never dreamed he might one day be having this conversation with his daughter and the thought that the secret he'd lived with for so long was no longer a secret left him feeling vulnerable and exposed.

Who else had Rodriguez told? Did all of his children know? What would they say? Would they still love him, respect him, be proud to call him their dad?

"What happened then? Did Momma ask you to leave?"

He stared down at his hands and sighed. "No. Your mother is the kindest, most forgiving woman in the world. She confronted me with them and I finally broke down and told her the truth. She was relieved she'd finally worked out what was wrong with us, relieved that it had nothing to do with her. She understood she couldn't compete with my male lovers and I think it provided her a kind of closure.

"We had the nine of you by then and I was doing well in my career. I was almost guaranteed a partnership and with that, came a good deal more status and money. We agreed that as long as I remained discreet, she'd stand by me. And she has. To the world, we're a normal, loving couple."

Shelby's expression grew distant and he could tell she was trying hard to process everything she'd learned. It would take some time before the shock wore off. After that, it was anybody's guess how she'd react.

"Who else knows?" he forced himself to ask.

His daughter sighed heavily and slowly made her way over to the couch. Perching on the edge, her gaze remained fixed on the carpet. He didn't care that she couldn't look at him. It was enough that her disgust and anger had apparently eased and she was sitting there, beside him.

When she spoke, her voice was soft. "Athena."

Alexei cursed under his breath and anger swelled up inside him. "Damn, Rodriguez! Wait until I get hold of him! He had no right to approach either of you. He's—"

"Who's Rodriguez?"

Alexei blinked and focused on his daughter. Her forehead was creased in a frown. She looked confused. *Was it possible Rodriguez hadn't been the one to blow his secret? Had his daughters found out another way?*

Ignoring her question, he forced himself to ask. "How did you find out about the den, Shelby?"

She remained silent, as if gathering her thoughts. Again, she kept her gaze focused away from him while she spoke.

"It was Athena. She told me you'd come home looking for a file. She noticed you left empty-handed. She thought she'd help you out by going into your den and finding it. She was going to bring it to your office." Shelby grimaced before continuing.

"Instead, she found a stack of gay pornographic DVDs and magazines, a double bed with black satin sheets; handcuffs, whips, leather thongs and masks and expensive camera equipment."

She stared at him and her gaze turned accusatory. "You entertain men down there, don't you? Is Rodriguez one of the men you bring home for sex? Is that what's on the extensive DVD collection I found in the cabinet near the bed? I could see they were recorded discs. Do you feature on them, Daddy? Does this Rodriguez? Has it gone as far as that?"

Once again, Alexei stared at the floor and rode out another wave of shame, even as relief poured through him that his lover hadn't ratted him out. He wished he could issue an emphatic denial and erase the anger that was back on Shelby's face, but he couldn't. He'd spent hours and hours filming his bed partners, including Rodriguez, and the mutual pleasure Alexei offered and received. The DVDs were among his most prized possessions. He couldn't imagine not having them in times of need.

At his wife's request, he hadn't slept with her since the day he'd come clean about his sexuality. When he was in between lovers or was just taking a break, he liked to slip in one of his home movies. Watching a scene he could remember participating in never failed to relax him and it gave him mindless pleasure. Reliving the experience was almost as good as the real thing.

But having the daughter he loved look upon him with such horror and loathing was almost more than he could bear. It tore him up inside.

"I'm sorry, Shelby. I don't know what else you want me to say."

In the silence that followed, he could hear her breathing and how it hitched on the occasional quiet sob. He wished he could do something to ease her distress, but it was way too late for that.

She'd discovered a secret that he'd kept carefully hidden for most of his adult life. Now that she knew, there was no going back.

———

Shelby clenched her fingers together and tried hard to get a grip. Ever since she'd discovered her father's shocking secret, her emotions had been all over the place. She'd looked around the den, taking in the bed, the movies, the TV. Though her brain screamed that she was standing in some kind of weird sex room, she hadn't wanted to accept the truth.

But now, hearing her father talk about the double life he'd led for so many years, she had no choice. She listened to his explanation and though she was angry he'd deceived them, she also felt a reluctant sympathy for his plight.

She couldn't imagine how terrible it must have been to pretend he was something he wasn't and to marry because there was no other choice. She hadn't been born until the late eighties, but she knew enough about those times and about her Greek culture to understand where her father was coming from.

It didn't make the discovery that he was a closet bisexual any easier, but some of the heat went out of her anger and was replaced by sadness. She tried to imagine living a lie for decades, denying an instinctive need and want, and she couldn't. She thought of Dimitri and opened her mouth and then quickly closed it again. It wasn't for her to disclose his situation, to her daddy or to anyone, but she vowed silently to talk to Dimi and encourage him to come out. She was sure he'd find an ally in their father.

With another quiet sigh, she pushed away from the couch and prowled around the office. The familiar assortment of knickknacks and expensive collectibles lined the dark wood shelves. Law books she was sure no one ever read filled another wall, floor to ceiling. She wandered over to his desk and spied a photograph of her mother. She clenched her jaw against a wave of anger.

Further along the shelf, behind the desk, were several more family photographs. Shelby featured in at least three of them, along with her brothers and sisters. Laughing, smiling, happy times. They were a close and loving family. Despite her father's predilections, he and her mother had done a good job of raising their nine children and keeping them all together.

A Melbourne Storm Rugby League football cap sat on the shelf among the pictures. Shelby stared down at it and frowned. She turned slowly to face her father.

"I thought you were a Cronulla Sharks supporter, Daddy?"

He heaved himself to the edge of the couch and then stood and joined her on the other side of the room. "I am."

"Then why do you have a Storm's football cap?"

"A...client gave it to me," he said after a slight pause. "I didn't have the heart to tell him I go for the Sharks." He chuckled, but it sounded forced and the humor didn't reach his eyes. Shelby shrugged and moved away. She didn't care less where he'd gotten it from. The truth was, she had far more important things on her mind.

————————

The moment Shelby cleared her father's building, she called her sister. Athena answered on the first ring.

"Shelby! How did you do? Please, tell me Daddy had a reasonable explanation."

"I'm sorry, sis. I wish I had better news. It's as we suspected. He's bisexual. He's been leading a double life."

The shocked gasp on the other end of the phone was followed by a noisy bout of sobbing. Shelby bit her lip and waited it out. It was better to let her sister do what she needed to. If that meant letting it all out, then so be it.

If Shelby had her way, the discovery in the basement would remain a secret between them and would never be spoken of again. Her father had been relieved when she'd proposed the idea to him. She was hoping Athena would see it that way, too. After all, what good was there in exposing the dirty little secret to all and sundry? It wouldn't change anything. Her dad hadn't chosen to be attracted to men. Like her brother, he'd probably tried hard to fight it, ignore it, pretend it wasn't true. After all, he'd gone to the extent of marrying, had nine children and had managed to keep up the pretense that he was happy with his life.

She thought of his comment to Samuel and was filled with a surge of anger at the hypocrisy. Her father had the nerve to accuse Samuel of being gay, when all along, he was a closet bisexual. She felt like turning on her heel and storming back to his office, demanding to know why he'd insulted her boyfriend like that and then she forced herself to let it go. *What good would it do? What did it matter why he'd said it?* He'd apologized for his rudeness. It was best she leave it at that. After today, she never wanted to think about his secret life again and she'd make sure neither of them spoke about it.

As Athena's sobs quieted, Shelby murmured into the phone. "I understand how you're feeling, honey, but this is how it's going to be." In simple tones, she laid it out for her sister.

"But—"

"No buts," Shelby interrupted, her voice firm. "We aren't going to speak of this ever again. Momma knows and she's kept it secret all these long, long years. If she'd wanted us to know, she would have told us. It serves no purpose bringing it up now. We're going to keep this between the two of us. Nobody else in the family needs to know. Do you understand?"

"Y-yes, but does it really have to be like that?

I'm going to see those things in my nightmares. I might even need therapy."

"By all means, if you feel the need to talk to a professional, go ahead. Just don't go telling anyone who isn't bound by a confidentiality clause. Okay?"

"O-okay, Shelby."

Relieved that her sister was on board, Shelby shortly thereafter ended the call. She was about to return her phone to her bag when it chimed. Seeing Samuel's number on the screen, she thought fast and then plastered a smile on her face. Doing her best to sound normal, she answered the call.

"Samuel! How are you? I'm so sorry I had to rush off."

"No problem. I'm still at the beach. I hope everything's all right?"

"Yes, of course, it was just Athena. She was freaking out about her exams. I think she's fine now. I'll be back soon."

"Sure. That sounds good. How about I meet you back at my place? I've probably had enough of the salt and sand today."

Shelby ignored the stab of guilt and breathed a quiet sigh of relief. The last thing she felt like was to take up where she'd left off earlier that morning, sunning herself on the beach. It felt like a lifetime ago that she'd been there, relaxing on the sand, without a care in the world. It just went to show how life could turn on a dime. Her world would never be the same again. She just hoped she could pull off pretending everything was fine. She'd never been good at deceit.

Samuel pulled two Cokes out of the fridge and handed one to Shelby. Ever since she'd arrived back at his condo, she'd been quiet and withdrawn. It was almost like the girl who'd been filled with smiles and sunshine that morning had up and moved away. He wondered what had caused her sudden change in mood.

Wanting to get to the bottom of it, he took a seat beside her on the couch. Putting an arm around her, he drew her close and pressed a kiss against her hair.

"Are you all right?" he asked quietly.

She nodded and took a sip of Coke, but her eyes remained distant and he couldn't help but notice the death grip she had on her drink.

Setting both cans down on the coffee table, he turned to her and took her hands in his. "Shelby, look at me."

It took awhile, but eventually she lifted her gaze to his. Tears sparkled in her eyes. She looked sadder than he'd ever seen her. His heart clenched at the sight of her distress. He reached up and tenderly wiped the moisture from her cheeks.

"Honey, what's the matter? Talk to me. What happened?"

A sob escaped and she bit her bottom lip.

Without another thought, he pulled her into his arms and held her close.

"Shelby, honey, what's wrong?" he murmured and slowly stroked her back. The occasional tear erupted into a deluge of sobs until she was crying all over his shirt.

"*Shh*, honey, it's all right. Nothing's as bad as that."

"Oh, Samuel! You don't understand!" she cried, her voice muffled.

"Then talk to me, Shelby. Tell me what's wrong. I can't help you if I don't know what's going on."

"You can't h-help me anyway! No one can!" Her wail was met with a fresh round of sobs and the sound of them tore at his gut. *Was it only a handful of hours ago that they'd been loving each other, delirious with happiness?* The reality of those memories was now distant and fading, as if they'd never really been.

He tightened his arms about her and did his best to offer comfort. It was hard when he didn't know what had happened to upset her. "*Shh*, babe, *shh*. It's going to be all right."

She lifted a tear-stained face off his shoulder. "No, it isn't! It's never going to be right again! My father—" She broke off and stared at him.

He frowned in confusion. "What about your father? I thought you went over to see your sister?"

She compressed her lips. "Forget about it. I promised I wouldn't say anything. Here I was worried about Athena telling someone and I'm the one about to blab."

Samuel stared at her. "What are you talking about, Shelby? You're not making sense. Tell me what happened."

She looked up at him and he was taken aback by the bitterness in her eyes. "Nothing about this makes sense, Samuel. I wish I'd never seen it. I wish I could rewind the past hours, go back to when I woke this morning with you beside me, holding me in your arms. But I can't."

Her voice broke with emotion. He was no closer to working out what had gone wrong. A sense of foreboding settled, heavy and suffocating, in his chest.

"Shelby, tell me what happened. I can't stand seeing you so upset. Something terrible occurred while I was surfing. Please, talk to me."

She was silent for so long, he didn't think she was going to answer him. When she finally did, she drew in a ragged breath. "I told Athena not to say anything, but I didn't know how hard it was going to be to keep quiet. I don't want to have this burden. I didn't ask for it and neither did Athena. It's not fair that Daddy did this to us. It's totally screwed up everything. I can't—"

"Shelby! Listen to me!" Samuel's voice was harsher than he intended, but he needed to cut through her haze of confusion and doubt and work out what the hell was going on.

The stern order seemed to work. Shelby let out a shaky breath and some of the tension left her body. When she spoke, her words were more controlled.

"I was enjoying the sunshine on the beach,

working on my tan. You were out there on your board. I got a phone call from Athena. She was in a panic. She told me to get over to Momma and Daddy's place right away. She sounded scared, but she wouldn't tell me what was wrong, so I packed up my things and hightailed it to the house."

"Go on," Samuel urged, all the while dread trickling through his veins. He hoped he could cope with what she was about to reveal.

"For as long as I can remember, Daddy has had a den in the basement and it was always a place that was off limits to us kids," she said quietly. "Today, I found out why."

He squeezed her hand in silent encouragement, bracing himself for the discovery of what had affected her mood so drastically. She turned to stare at him, her eyes huge in her pale face. She bit her lip, as if still undecided what to tell him and then finally, she just said it.

"My dad's bisexual."

If she'd told him she'd had a sex change when she was a teenager, he couldn't have been more surprised. He shook his head, certain he'd misheard. *"Excuse me?"*

As if the act of making the shocking statement had given her courage, she lifted her head, straightened her shoulders and looked him directly in the eye.

"My dad likes men and women, although I believe he's pretty much stuck to men the past two decades or so."

Samuel tried hard not to let his shock show, but

it was a struggle. "O...kay." It was all he could manage.

She threw him a slight, wry smile. "It's all right, Samuel. You're allowed to be shocked after what he said to you at the wedding. I was."

He frowned, his mind still reeling. "How did you find out?"

Shelby leaned back against the couch and folded her arms across her lap. "Athena. For the first time in her life, my sister went into Daddy's den. She found a variety of sexual paraphernalia, including pornographic DVDs featuring men on the covers, sex toys and of course, there was a bed. She phoned me in a state of panic but wouldn't tell me why. I went over. I saw it all."

Samuel was shocked all over again. He couldn't imagine how he'd feel finding something like that in his parents' basement. He now understood the dramatic change in her mood.

"What did you do?" he asked quietly.

She surprised him again by saying, "I went to see him."

"Your dad?"

"Yes. I went to his office in the city."

"What did you say?"

"I told him I knew about the den. We talked."

She went on to tell Samuel about the conversation she'd had with Alexei. Samuel couldn't help but remember the night of the wedding, when Alexei had been boorish enough to ask him if he were gay. And all along, the man had been entertaining men in his basement. The hypocrisy was laughable. Anger stirred in his veins.

Shelby might be able to see things from her father's point of view and forgive him for his deceit, but Samuel didn't have the same family ties binding him. What Alexei was doing was plain wrong. He was deceiving the people who loved him the most and in such an awful way. The fact his wife condoned it didn't make it any more acceptable. Still, it wasn't Samuel's family and it wasn't his battle. If Shelby was prepared to forgive and forget, there was nothing he could do and in her current fragile state, he would refrain from even mentioning it.

"How did Athena take the news?" he wondered aloud.

"About as well as you could expect. I told her what Daddy said. She was still in shock. We agreed not to tell anyone, and never to speak of it again. And now I've blurted it all out. I'm ashamed of myself."

A fierce denial burst from Samuel's lips. "You're not the one with something to be ashamed of."

She cupped his cheek with her palm. "I'm grateful for you saying it, but I'm not blaming Daddy for deceiving us. Yes, he's lived a lie for all his married life, but he didn't have a choice. And it's not like Momma didn't know about it. She could have left him years ago. She chose not to. I admire her for sticking with her marriage in the circumstances, but it was still her choice to stay. Twenty years ago, there were services available to single mothers. We wouldn't have been as comfortable as we are now, but we would have gotten by. I think Momma was trying to save face as much as Daddy wanted to protect us. They did what they thought best—for them and for us. It's not my place to judge."

Samuel stared at her. "You're a lot more forgiving than I would be."

She shrugged. "That's what love is. If you truly love someone, you can forgive them anything. Besides, none of us know what we're capable of until we're tested."

He laughed without humor. He hadn't told her much about his family. Perhaps it was time for him to come clean. It would probably bring her comfort, knowing she wasn't the only one with skeletons in the closet. Then again, she had enough to deal with. Perhaps his revelations would make her head for the hills. But his feelings for her had deepened to the point where he wanted to take the chance. He wanted her to know everything there was to know about him, skeletons and all.

He shifted his weight until he was angled toward her. "While we're doing the family reveal, I guess I ought to tell you a little more about mine."

CHAPTER 11

Shelby felt a wave of curiosity. She didn't know much about Samuel's family. In the short time they'd known each other, they hadn't talked a lot about them. She knew his parents lived on the waterfront in the ritzy eastern suburb of Point Piper and he was the oldest of eleven children, but that was about the extent of it. She shot him a rueful smile. "They can't be any weirder than mine."

To her surprise, his answering grin failed to materialize. "I guess that depends on your viewpoint," he said somberly. "My parents are over-achieving, often emotionally distant workaholics. I blame them for the fact one of my younger brothers is a drug addict, living on the streets, with no greater ambition than to find his next fix."

Shelby gasped in shock. *Samuel had a brother who was an addict?* The image conjured up in her mind was so far removed from the suave, successful doctor she sat next to on the couch, it was almost unbelievable. And yet, he looked perfectly serious.

"What's your brother's name?" she asked, unable to think of anything else to say.

"Paul."

"How old is he?"

"He's three years younger than me. He's twenty-seven."

"Same age as me," she murmured and tried to imagine what might cause her to turn to drugs.

"How did his life go so far off course?" she asked.

Samuel sighed heavily. "Who knows what makes someone choose a certain path over another? One thing I do know is that my parents have to shoulder some of the blame."

She frowned. "But you turned out okay. Better than okay. They must have done something right."

"Perhaps I was just more determined to make a success of my life."

"What about the others? Your siblings? How did they fare?"

"They did okay. Some of them went to college, some pursued other career paths. Most of them still live in Sydney."

"So it's only Paul who went astray. Most people would think with that many kids to consider, having only one make a few wrong turns along the way is pretty good."

Samuel grimaced. "I guess if you look at it objectively, take all the emotion out. Real life's not like that. Paul's a flesh and blood man, not part of the odds."

"Tell me about your family," she said softly, sensing there was a lot he hadn't shared. He'd hinted at difficulties the night of their first date, but she hadn't been brave enough to push for more information. Things were different now. Knowing about his family was important. She needed to know if there was anything that could come between them; anything that could jeopardize the future she was starting to believe in.

He leaned forward. Resting his elbows on his knees, he stared out through the sliding glass doors at the gathering evening. Shelby remained silent, giving him the time he needed to gather his thoughts. After taking a couple of mouthfuls of Coke, he spoke again.

"My parents are wealthy people. Dad's a hotshot stockbroker. Mom's the CEO of a bank. Growing up, the eleven of us wanted for nothing. At least, in the material sense. As far as emotional riches went, let's just say my parents were close to being bankrupt. From the earliest I can remember, we had nannies seeing to our needs. More often than not, my parents were at work. They were gone before we got out of bed and didn't arrive home until well after we went to sleep. It was like that for years, until we got old enough to fend for ourselves. Then the nannies disappeared and it was just my siblings and me."

Shelby tried to imagine the life he described and couldn't. Rarely had she come home from school without finding her mother in the kitchen, preparing dinner, baking treats, mending clothes. She assumed her parents had agreed early on in their marriage that her mother would stay home and raise the kids while her father went out to work. It was that way for a lot of her friends, although she did know some kids who went home to an empty house. For those kids, their parents both worked, but she'd figured, most did that out of necessity. In those instances, two incomes were needed just to keep the roof over their heads. There was no choice. She'd always felt sorry for them.

From what Samuel said, things were different in his household. Both his parents chose to go to work rather than be there for their children. Money was the sole motivating factor. Accumulating as much wealth as possible had been put above everything else, including the needs of their children. The thought saddened her. Reaching across, she squeezed his bicep in silent encouragement for him to continue.

"As the oldest, I took on responsibility for my brothers and sisters. Some of them made it easier than others. Paul was one of the challenges. I did my best to keep him focused and out of trouble, but I was serious about my school work. I didn't have a lot of spare time. I was good at school and from about the age of thirteen, I knew I wanted to be a doctor. Everyone told me how hard I'd have to work to get there and I was determined to do whatever was necessary to succeed.

"Paul was bright, too, but he couldn't have been less interested. It didn't seem to matter what I said to him—neither threats nor cajoling worked—he didn't care about school, exam marks or anything else to do with learning and getting ahead."

"What about your other brothers and sisters? Didn't any of them try to persuade him?"

"I guess they did. I don't remember. All I remember was the feeling that as the oldest, he was my responsibility. I tried to talk to my parents, to insist they needed to be there for him, to take more of an interest in him but I got the same old response. They wanted to help, but they were busy. There were interstate trips and overseas conferences, staff to manage, deadlines to meet. They offered to pay for a therapist. Mom even set up an appointment. Paul refused to attend."

Samuel paused, as if remembering the past. When he continued, his voice took on a distant tone.

"Paul was about fourteen when he fell in with a bad crowd. He used to meet up with them in the city. Drugs were in ample supply and he had access to plenty of money. I remember pleading with him not to be so stupid, that he was throwing his life away but he wouldn't listen. He got more and more involved with them and I was scared he was going to get arrested or something equally bad. Once again, I turned to Mom and Dad."

"What did they say?" Shelby asked, although she hardly dare listen to the answer. Her hands clenched into fists. She hid them beneath her thighs.

"They were concerned, of course, and expressed all the normal platitudes. We had a family meeting and they demanded that Paul stop using drugs. They threatened to cut off his allowance. They made him agree to attend therapy. At one stage, they even got him into an exclusive rehab clinic. I didn't see him for six weeks.

"But every time he got out of those places, he'd end up right back where he'd been before. The terrible cycle repeated itself over and over again. It was like he couldn't help it; like the drugs had taken hold of his soul."

Samuel grimaced and Shelby saw the shadow of pain in his eyes. "Of course, Mom and Dad were at a loss about what to do. They thought they'd tried everything."

"Problems with drugs and addictions happen in good families with stay-at-home moms, too, Samuel," she said gently. "You can't blame everything on them and the choices they made."

His gaze hardened. "I get that, but Paul needed them! He needed to feel he was worthy of their time; that for even a moment, they'd recognize his importance in their lives."

"Paul probably wasn't the only one of you feeling like that," Shelby said quietly. Her heart ached for the eleven Munro children who'd grown up with everything money could buy, material possessions lavished on them by their hard-working parents, but given so little of their parents' time.

Samuel nodded, a sad expression on his face. "You're right, we all suffered from emotional neglect. It was so different in my cousins' household. There are only seven of them. We used to visit them during vacations. It was always such a fun time. My aunt and uncle would join in the games and arrange exciting outings. They were hands-on in the fullest sense. My cousins were so lucky."

His voice was so full of wistfulness, tears pricked Shelby's eyes. For all her parents' failings, they'd always been there for their children. She was definitely one of the lucky ones.

Samuel spoke again, his voice as distant as his gaze. "My parents didn't get it. They still don't get it. I've tried to tell them over and over, but nothing's ever changed. It's like they're defined by their wealth and when it failed to solve the problems with Paul, they were at a loss about what to do. So, they did what they always did: They went back to work, stayed away for longer and longer hours. As soon as I finished college, I moved out. I rented an apartment with some buddies until I could buy a place of my own."

"Do your parents visit?"

Samuel made a noise of disbelief. "Visit? You have to be kidding. They don't have time for that. Mom sent me a suitably expensive housewarming gift and wished me the best of luck. It was like I was an employee or something. Dad sent me a ten thousand dollar check."

"What about Paul? Do you see him at all?" Shelby asked softly.

"I haven't seen him for a long time. To tell you the truth, I'm not sure where he is."

He paused, his breathing harsh in the stillness. Shelby wanted to comfort him, but he seemed distant, lost in his thoughts, and then he spoke again.

"He used to call me sometimes to ask me for money. The last time he called I couldn't do it, Shelby. I couldn't give it to him. I didn't want to enable him to feed his habit. I knew if I refused, he'd get it some other way—most likely from my parents—and I had to accept that. It was their money, their decision, if they decided to give him more. They knew as well as I did what he needed it for. But at least my conscience was clear. Now I live in dread that one day he'll be brought in by ambulance, either suffering an overdose—or worse. I lose sleep over the possibility I'll be asked to identify him at the morgue."

His voice broke on the last word and he squeezed his eyes tightly shut. Shelby sat forward and put her hand on his forearm, but remained silent. A long moment later, he opened his eyes and lifted his head to stare at her. She almost gasped at the anguish she saw.

"I don't want that to happen to us and our kids, Shelby. I know we haven't talked about any of this stuff, but it's important you know how I feel. I'm in love with you. I know you're the one. I want to spend the rest of my life with you. We're both from big families, but I don't want that for myself. The thought of any more than one or two children makes me feel panicked. My chest goes tight and I can't breathe. I feel like I'm suffocating. It seems extreme, but that's the way I feel."

She stared at him in shock. She'd always wanted a heap of kids. From her earliest memories, when she knew what babies were all about, she dreamed of having at least five or six. To her, a large number of children was the very definition of a family. She couldn't imagine stopping at one or two. She opened her mouth to protest, but Samuel beat her to it.

"While I'm being honest, I want to tell you something else. I understand you love your job and you worked so hard to get there, but if we're ever blessed with children, even one or two, I want you to be a stay-at-home mom."

A wave of shock rushed through her and she stared back at him in disbelief. Firstly that he was talking forever and quickly on the heels of that he was saying that he wanted her to give up her career. It was the twenty-first century. Women didn't have to stay home. They were entitled to scale the heights in their chosen career path. The fact that Samuel was a doctor and would always earn more than she did was beside the point.

She opened her mouth to voice her protest, but one look at the lingering pain in his eyes and she closed it again. This wasn't the time to get into an argument. There'd be time enough later for them to have a full and frank discussion. She only hoped he'd be reasonable. She wasn't sure what she'd do if his stance remained the same.

———

Jared Buchanan paced the confined space in

front of his desk. Glancing at his watch for the hundredth time, he cursed under his breath. His witness was late.

"What's the matter, Detective?"

Spinning on his heel, he came face to face with his boss. The superintendent looked a decade older than his fifty-two years. The job had a way of doing that. Jared grimaced and forced the thought from his mind.

"A witness has come forward in relation to the Bondi murders. She was meant to be here forty-five minutes ago and now she's not answering her phone."

The super frowned. "Shit. You mean to tell me that, so far, not one of your leads have panned out and now the only self-professed witness has gone AWOL. I need you to find her, Jared. I'm taking heat from the media, the commissioner, even the Minister of Police has weighed in. We have three dead bodies in Bondi. People are demanding to know what's going on. They want the perp found, Jared, and they want it like, yesterday. Do you understand?"

Jared's gaze remained steady. "Yes, sir. I understand. I'm doing the best I can."

"Then you need to do better."

Jared inclined his head in acknowledgement. After another hard glare, his boss continued across the squad room to his office and closed the door behind him. Jared breathed a silent sigh of relief. With another muffled expletive, he pulled out his phone and punched in the numbers of his witness.

Like it had the last ten times, the call went straight through to voicemail. Either the woman's battery was dead or she'd switched off her phone. Jared hoped for her sake it was the battery. This was the first eyewitness to come forward over the space of three murders. He wasn't about to let her disappear into the ether.

With a disgruntled sigh, he threw himself backwards in his seat and dragged his keyboard toward him. He might as well read over the press release the police media liaison staff had drafted. He'd managed to get the TV networks to agree to run another story. They were going to release photos of the victims' personal effects that had gone missing.

Through Instagram photos and Facebook posts, as well as speaking with the families, Jared had discovered some of the items the victims wore on the evening of their deaths hadn't been found at the crime scene. It was Jared's guess that the perpetrator had filched something from each of them and kept it as a trophy. It was a common occurrence among serial killers and with three deaths in four weeks, this was being treated as such.

The thought that some madman with a gripe against gay men was still out there, possibly planning another kill, made Jared's blood run cold. A surge of impatience rushed through him and he cursed again at the witness who'd failed to show. She didn't know how important she was to his investigation. The smallest morsel of information could be enough to blow the case wide. He needed to find her and when he did, she wouldn't be leaving his sight.

———————

Shelby gave a desultory knock on the front door of her parents' house and then let herself in. Nerves in her stomach clamored for attention, but she resolutely ignored them. She'd called ahead to make sure her mother was home and was both relieved and nervous when her mother assured her she was. Shelby had no way of knowing if her father had clued her mother in to the discovery of the contents of the den. The next few moments were going to be uncomfortable at best.

As usual, she found her mother in the kitchen wearing an apron and frowning down at an open recipe book on the wide granite counter.

"Momma! How are you? I haven't seen you since the wedding." Shelby kissed her mother on the cheek and then stepped back to survey her.

Despite the fact her mother was in her early fifties, time had treated her well. Taller than average, she was also well-proportioned. She was probably a little heavier in the hips, but she'd given birth to nine children. She was entitled to some lingering effects.

The fact was, Shelby's mom worked hard to keep herself trim and healthy. She might have been known for her cooking, but she was disciplined when it came to sampling the wares. She still took Pilates and yoga classes at least three times a week and was part of a regular walking group.

"How are you, Shelby? You're looking a little pale. Are you sure you're eating right? How's Samuel? I did enjoy meeting him. He's very cute. Everyone was talking about the two of you!" She winked and smiled.

Shelby laughed. "I'm sure my aunts were beside themselves with the possibilities. Have they booked the church yet?"

Her mother chuckled. "If they haven't, I'm sure they've checked the availability."

"Poor Samuel!" Shelby replied, not feeling the least bit sympathetic. "I wonder if he has any idea what it's like being part of a big Greek family."

"Let's hope he's brave enough to find out," her mother replied in a voice filled with sly innuendo.

Shelby refused to be baited. Even though Samuel had indicated he was keen for a long-term relationship, he'd also put everything into disarray by telling her he didn't want a large family and expected her to be a stay-at-home mom. She was hopeful they might be able to come to some sort of compromise, but that discussion had yet to occur and there was no guarantee he'd change his mind. It was troubling, to say the least, and she wasn't about to share her concerns with her mother. Not when there were far more pressing issues to deal with.

"What brings you over here, Shelby? Don't get me wrong, it's nice to see you, but you don't usually drop in like this. Is everything all right? It's not you and Samuel, is it? Don't tell me you had a fight."

Shelby forced a smile. "No, Momma, we didn't have a fight. It doesn't have anything to do with Samuel." She paused and then plunged in headlong. "I-I met with Daddy yesterday."

Her mother frowned. "What do you mean, you met with him? At his office?"

Shelby compressed her lips. It was obvious her father had said nothing to his wife. This was going to be even harder than she thought. She drew in a deep breath, eager to get it over with.

"Yes, Momma. I went to his office. I wanted to talk to him about his den." *There, she'd said it.*

Every speck of color disappeared from her mother's cheeks. It was like an artist had brushed her face with whitewash. She looked like she was about to be sick. At the same time, shock and panic flashed in her eyes and the sight of it nearly brought Shelby undone. She kept telling herself that the only thing that had come as a surprise to her mother was that Shelby knew about her daddy's proclivities. Knowing that helped her stand her ground and she waited for her mother to come to terms with her announcement.

"H-how? W-when?" her mother finally stammered and Shelby was relieved that her father had spoken the truth.

"Athena went into the basement. She called me."

Helen Gianopoulos let out a wail of distress and brought her hands up to cover her face. "Athena? She knows, too? Who else knows? Who else have you told?"

"No one else in the family knows. It's not

something I wanted to publicize. Daddy told me you've known for the best part of twenty years. Is that true?"

Her mother's shoulders slumped on a heavy sigh. She turned away from the counter. She picked up a wooden spoon still covered in cookie dough and then set it down again. She opened the fridge and peered inside and then closed the door without taking anything out. With her back to Shelby, she put her hands on her hips and stared out the window, into the small courtyard where she grew herbs in brightly colored pots and where her father used to go to have a cigarette—back when he smoked.

Finally, her mother spoke. "We'd been married fourteen years when I discovered your father liked men. It was right after John was born. I found some...things. I confronted your father about them. He admitted he was gay."

Shelby frowned. "But what about you? He'd been with you all those years. You'd obviously been intimate. You had nine children. I assume Daddy's the father."

"Yes, of course he is. He managed to perform his husbandly duties often enough for all of you to be conceived. It wasn't that we were intimate all that often, more that I was extremely fertile and he got the timing right."

Her lips twisted into a grimace. "I didn't realize he paid such close attention to my cycle. He knew the optimum time to conceive a child. He made sure he took advantage of that. He was always so thrilled when I told him I was pregnant. I naïvely thought it was because he was pleased he was going to become a father again. Little did I know it was because he knew the pressure was off him for a while."

Shelby shook her head in confusion. "So you only had sex when you weren't pregnant? Is that what you're saying?"

Her mother nodded, still facing the window. "Yes, that's pretty much how it worked, Shelby. Your daddy told me he didn't feel right about sleeping with me while I was carrying our baby."

"Didn't you find that strange?"

"A little, but you have to remember, we married young. I was a virgin on our wedding night like most good girls my age. I had no experience with men, of what happened in the bedroom. I came from an era where that kind of thing wasn't talked about, or if it was, it was referred to in such vague terms, no one had a clue what was going on.

"Over the years, as society changed and sex became more openly discussed in women's magazines and then amongst women themselves, I realized it wasn't normal for my husband to only have sex with me at certain times of the month and only when I wasn't pregnant. I also realized it was meant to be enjoyable and that it usually lasted more than a few minutes."

She shook her head slowly back and forth. While Shelby couldn't see her expression, her mother's voice turned distant.

"I had no idea a woman could have an orgasm, or that it was possible to crave your husband's touch. Sex between your father and me was almost clinical—a means to an end—the getting of a child. When I found out your father was gay, everything suddenly made sense."

Shelby's face burned with embarrassment. There were certain things children should never know about their parents and in normal circumstances, she'd never dream of giving voice to the kind of questions that could illicit such answers. Unfortunately, there was nothing normal about this situation and she had no choice. It was important to her peace of mind for her to understand. After this conversation was done, she'd never speak of it again.

"Why did you put up with it, Momma? Why didn't you leave? Your husband was gay. That little detail kind of negated the marriage contract. I think most people would have understood."

Her mother sighed heavily and slowly turned around to face her. Shelby expected to see sadness and resignation. She was surprised at the anger that flashed in her mother's eyes.

"Why would I leave him? We lived a very comfortable life. I had plenty of money, good friends, a beautiful house overlooking the beach, my children. I would have lost it all if I left him. Times hadn't changed so much back then that the courts would have favored me with a generous settlement. There was also the risk I'd lose the kids. I consulted a lawyer. Your father was already an important presence among the legal fraternity. He had powerful friends. I was advised to sit tight and keep my mouth shut." She eyed Shelby defiantly. "And so I did."

"But—"

Her mother waved away her protest. "Don't worry, Shelby, I did all right. Despite the fact that we both knew your father would trounce me in a courtroom, he felt guilty enough that he acceded to all of my requests. Number one on my list was that he keep his dirty little secret to himself. He promised never to tell another soul. He agreed to be discreet with his lovers. He also agreed never to touch me again."

Shelby stared at her mother and thought about all the sacrifices she'd made. She'd given up a chance at happiness; at sharing a life with a man she loved and who loved her back; at having a fulfilling sex life. And for what? A nice home, a comfortable existence, her children by her side.

"Would it have made a difference if Daddy hadn't been wealthy?" she asked, needing to know the answer.

Her mother held her gaze. "What does that matter?"

"It matters, Momma. You told me one of the reasons you stayed was because Daddy could provide you with a comfortable life. What if that hadn't been the case?"

"If you mean would I have stayed for the sake of my children alone, I guess the answer is yes. But we'll never know because he was wealthy. There's no changing that. You have to understand, Shelby. Things were different back then. Being a single mom was frowned upon. There was very little government support. I had no skills. I'd virtually left school and gotten married. All I knew was how to cook and clean and keep house and see to the needs of my children. I guess I could have secured work as a nanny or a chef, or even a housekeeper, but what was I going to do with my kids? The money I earned from those kinds of jobs would hardly have put food on the table, let alone cover the rent, the utilities, the school fees.

"So, your father and I came to an agreement. It suited his purposes, too. He was a prosperous, well-respected lawyer. He had a lot to lose. A blow like that to his reputation could have been fatal. He didn't want to take the risk."

She sighed quietly, her anger all but dissipated. "It wasn't ideal, Shelby. Far from it. But we made it work and it's worked quite well for us all these years. The nine of you were oblivious to your father's double life and that's the way we wanted it. And we've been happy as a family, haven't we?"

Shelby shook her head helplessly. "Yes, of course we have, but none of us had any idea! How could we have been happy if we'd known the two of you were living a lie? You must have been miserable all these years, and Daddy, too. He's had to keep an important part of who he is a secret for most of his life. The knowledge couldn't have made him happy."

"Your father made his choices a long, long time ago, Shelby. Nobody forced him into marriage. He could have found the courage to resist the pressure from his family. He could have left his village and moved to a city. Somewhere with millions of people where he would have been just another lost soul. He could have lived life openly as a gay man and nobody need ever to have known.

"But he didn't have that courage. When it came to the crunch, he was weak. So, he happened upon me—a pretty, innocent village girl—and he got down on bended knee."

Her expression hardened. Bitterness flashed in her eyes. "He *stole* from me, Shelby. He stole from me any chance I had of being happy, of living a normal life and that's why I'll never leave him. He'll pay every day of his life, literally and figuratively. I have access to whatever money I want and he lives out his shame between the four walls of our basement. It's the way it's always going to be."

Shelby's shoulders slumped on a sad sigh. For twenty-seven years, she'd been under the impression that her parents were happy. Okay, they weren't exactly demonstrative with each other like a lot of other Greek families were, but she'd put that down to the fact they simply didn't like to show their affection in public. There was nothing wrong with that. Some people were more "out there" than others. She never dreamed the real reason was because they couldn't stand each other's touch.

The discovery was devastating. She'd never be able to look at them the same way again and yet, she was expected to carry on as usual. She *wanted* to carry on as usual. She didn't want any of her other siblings to know.

There was nothing she could do to help Athena. There was no undoing what her sister knew and had seen, but Shelby was still firmly of the opinion that this aspect of her parent's lives shouldn't be spoken about again, by any of them. On that score, she and her parents agreed. The secret would go with them to the grave.

"I... I don't know what to say, Momma. I'm sorry. I'm sorry for both of you. I wish your secret had remained that way. You were right in that respect. *I* would have been better off not knowing. You don't have to worry about me telling my brothers and sisters. Let them keep their illusions that you and Daddy are happily married. I wish I could."

Her mother closed the distance between them and hugged her close. "Oh, Shelby! Honey, I never wanted you to find out. It's the reason why I insisted your father keep it a secret. You deserved to have a father you respected, looked up to, went to for advice. Nothing has changed in that regard. Despite everything, he's still your dad."

"Yes, of course," she choked as emotion tightened her chest. She wished she could agree with her mother's comments, but the truth was, she'd never look at her father in the same way again. He'd fallen from his pedestal and never again would he rise to such heights. Yes, he was still her father and that would never change, but everything else about their relationship had been irrevocably altered. And that's just the way it was.

Chapter 12

Dear Diary,

So, the secret I've kept hidden for so long has finally been revealed. I didn't mean for it to happen and I can't say that I'm relieved, but in some ways, it makes things easier. I feel like somehow I've found a confidante. Shelby and I have always been close. Now that she knows, I hope our relationship can deepen; we can share like we've never shared before. I look forward to it.

Samuel heard the key turn in the lock and his heart leaped in anticipation. He'd been rostered for a day off and had spent the time mulling over recipe books and then shopping for the ingredients. He'd given Shelby a key to his condo more than a fortnight ago and she now spent at least half of her nights with him. He wished it were every night, but she wanted to take things slow. The irony of that wasn't lost on him.

Rinsing his hands in the sink, he wiped them on the tea towel. Tossing it onto the kitchen counter, he turned in time to greet her with a kiss.

"Well, hello, Shelby Gianopoulos. You smell terrific!"

She wrinkled her nose. "There's something wrong with your sense of smell, Doctor Munro. I've been knee-deep in birthing mothers all day. I'm sure I have just as many body fluids on me as the bed linens."

He pulled a face. "Gross."

She smiled. "You love it! I bet you miss it every day you're away."

He grinned. Already she knew him so well. He threw his arms up in surrender. "Okay," he admitted. "I do. Just a little bit. What can I say? I love my job."

She kissed him on the cheek. "I'm going to take a quick shower." And with that, she disappeared in the direction of the bedroom.

Samuel went back to the kitchen and returned his attention to the pot on the stove. The lamb shanks had been slow-cooking for five hours. The meat would be so tender, it would fall off the bones. He'd flavored it with his favorite herbs and spices, including a healthy dash of good quality red wine and he couldn't wait to enjoy it with Shelby.

The creamy potato mash and mushy peas were ready, as was the home-baked apple pie. He'd made sure to buy some of Maggie Beer's

Vanilla Bean and Wattleseed Ice Cream—her favorite.

"*Mm*, something smells good," Shelby commented as she walked back into the room. She was dressed in his robe and had a towel wrapped around her hair. Her face was freshly scrubbed of makeup. She looked fantastic. His body stirred. With a concerted effort, he forced his thoughts away from taking her in his arms and focused on dinner instead.

"I cooked," he said simply.

Her eyes glinted in amusement. "Is there anything you can't do?"

"I'm not too good at fixing cars...or even changing tires, for that matter. You might need to go to a garage for that."

She linked her arms around his neck and kissed him on the mouth. "If that's your only shortcoming, I think I can live with it."

He stared at her in surprise and his heart picked up its pace. It was the first time she'd mentioned their future since the conversation they'd had a fortnight ago when he'd spilled his guts about his family. Not wanting to read more into her simple comment than she might have intended, he chose his words with care.

"I could get used to seeing you over the breakfast table every morning." He watched her closely, waiting for the moment when his words sank in. It didn't take long.

Within seconds, her eyes widened and her expression turned serious. "Are you asking me to move in?"

His gaze remained steady on hers. "Yes, I am. Would you like to?" He held his breath, waiting for her answer.

For a long time, she said nothing and his heart nearly pounded out of his chest. Then she stepped back and looked around her and finally, back at him. "Your place is to die for and you're not so bad, either. What's not to like?"

He eased his breath out and the slightest hint of hope trickled through his veins. "Is that a yes?"

She blew out her breath and once again, the humor in her eyes faded. "It's a maybe. I'm an old-fashioned kind of girl. I've always believed in marriage. Besides, we haven't talked about the whole having-kids and staying-at-home thing, yet. I think we should sort that out. It's an important issue and I don't want to push it to one side because it's too hard and then have to deal with it later, when both of us have so much more to lose."

She paused and reached for his hands and squeezed them. "I like you, Samuel. In fact, I'm pretty much already in love with you. You're the kind of guy I always dreamed about, but we're both well aware marriage isn't for the faint of heart and it would be marriage or nothing, for me. I'm not willing to live with you and share your life, your ups and downs, your hopes and dreams, bear your children, wash your underwear and not have a ring on my finger. Does that scare you?"

Elation spread through him and he grinned widely. "Not in the least. I've always intended to marry. If you ask me, this living together thing is a cop out. You either want to be with that person through the good and the bad for as long as you both shall live, or you don't. That's what marriage means to me. A lifelong commitment."

Coming up on her tiptoes, she pressed another kiss on his lips. "You're the sweetest man a girl could hope for. Now, let's talk about our future children and what they mean to my career."

Over mouthwatering lamb shanks, potato mash and mushy peas, they discussed the subject from all angles. By the time Samuel served the apple pie and ice cream, they'd come to an agreement. If they were lucky enough to have kids, they would welcome them with love. They would try for two, three at the most. Shelby would stay at home for the first year. After that, if she wanted to return to work part time, Samuel would fill in the gaps.

"You never know," Shelby said around a mouthful of pie, "I might be more than happy to stay at home, especially when the kids are young. My mother was always there when I arrived home from school. It was nice. We shared our day, ate cookies and milk, agonized over homework. I felt safe and secure and cared for. I was nearly ten before I realized not every kid had it so good."

Samuel thought of his own childhood and grimaced. "You have that right. My home life couldn't have been more different, but the longer I think about it, the more I realize I might enjoy being a stay-at-home dad. It's something I've never imagined, but I can see how worthwhile it would make me feel, being there for our kids, helping them out in a real and practical sense, not just being someone who earns the money and who walks out the door in the morning and walks back in again late at night. I want more than that."

Shelby got up and came around to his side of the table. Sitting on his lap, she draped her arms around his neck and kissed him. "I think we've sorted out what could have been a major issue. See how easy it was?"

His arms tightened around her. "It was only easy because of you. You're so easy to talk to—calm and cool and collected. It's refreshing. My parents used to deal with conflict by ignoring it. They'd walk around each other in stony silence for weeks. Finally, they'd have a mighty row. We all knew to stay out of the way until it was over. Quite often during those times I'd head out with my surfboard and escape into the waves. It was good therapy."

Shelby's expression filled with sadness and Samuel's heart clenched. This woman felt sympathy for his upbringing. She was sorry for the childhood he'd endured. Her tender heart only endeared her to him even more. He couldn't wait for them to become husband and wife.

Lifting his head, he captured her lips and kissed her with all the love and tenderness he felt way down inside. She returned his kiss, opening her mouth to deepen it. Her tongue stole inside and tangled with his and need burned through his veins.

His hand drifted down and slid under the pink T-shirt she'd changed into right before dinner. The soft cotton fabric teased the back of his hand as he cupped her breast. She hadn't bothered with a bra and her skin was warm and silky beneath his fingers. He found her nipple and tweaked it. The little nub puckered beneath his touch, filling him with satisfaction.

He moved his hand to palm her hip and press her more fully into his lap. His cock was hard and pulsed with need. The feel of her ass against him was both heaven and hell. He wanted her. Running his hand up the side of her ribcage, he cupped her other breast. She made little breathy noises of desire.

"Let's go somewhere a little more comfortable," he murmured against her lips. She nodded and slid off his lap.

He bent to sweep her up in his arms and with a little gasp, she clung to him with her arms around his neck. He padded barefoot down the hallway and deposited her on his wide bed. He'd left the curtains open and for a moment, they took the time to gaze out at the night sky. Tiny stars that were miles away sparkled like diamonds in the dark. A full moon illuminated a silvery path across the waves. The dark shadows of ships blurred the horizon. The scene was one of mystery and magic all at once.

"You really do have a great place," Shelby murmured.

"*We* have a great place," he corrected.

Joining her on the bed, he leaned across and kissed her. Slow and sensuous, he took his time tasting, teasing, discovering. He nibbled his way across her cheek and to her ear. Tracing the outline of the delicate whorls, he was pleased when she moaned and shivered. Moving lower, he nuzzled her neck and all the time, his hand squeezed and massaged her breast. She moved restlessly against him.

"Samuel, I—"

"*Shh*," he interrupted, kissing her once again. "There's no rush. Just so you know, I'm going to take all the time I want."

And with that, he found her lips again and drank her in. Long and deep, their lips stayed fused until both of them were gasping for breath. He released her mouth and kissed his way down her T-shirt, lifting the fabric up as he went. Tugging the shirt over her head, he stared down at her nakedness.

Every time he saw her, he was blown away by her beauty. Full, round breasts stood proudly, begging for his touch. Her nipples were a pale shade of dusty rose and were pebbled hard with wanting. He bent his head and took one of them into his mouth and suckled her like a baby.

"*Mm*," she moaned and closed her eyes, giving herself over to the sensations. He moved to the other breast and honored it with the same attention.

Ignoring the burning need in his groin, he kissed his way over her stomach. He dipped his tongue into her belly button and her muscles contracted. Moving lower still, he took hold of the waistband of her shorts and eased them over her hips. It was only then that he realized she wasn't wearing panties.

"No panties?" he murmured, flicking her a look and smiling at her embarrassment. He loved that she was a grown woman who wasn't new to the love game and yet she still had an innocent shyness about her that made him want her all the more.

Exposing her womanhood to his gaze, he buried his face between her legs. Breathing in her unique, sweet scent, he loved her all over again. His tongue delved between her soft folds and tasted her dewiness. Sliding deeper, he found her center and slid his tongue in and out.

Her hands came down to grasp his head and he reveled in the way she clung to him. Wordless murmurs of encouragement and need fell in disjointed breaths and gasps from her lips.

"Do you like that?" he growled.

"Yes," she gasped. "It feels insane. Nobody's ever done that to me before."

He smiled and licked her again. It wasn't until she was begging for him to take her that he ceased loving her with his tongue and lips. Shucking off his clothes in record time, he settled between her thighs. His cock was rock hard and throbbed with need. He was going to explode if he didn't have her, but despite the agony, he sheathed himself and then slid into her wetness slowly.

One excruciating inch at a time, he savored the feeling of her heat around him. Knowing how much she cared for him made it even more exquisite. He moved slowly, thrusting all the way in and then withdrawing until only the tip of his cock was inside. Over and over, he teased her and held his own relief out of reach.

It was madness, it was torment, he could hardly bear the suffering, but it wasn't until she cried out in surrender and shuddered beneath him that he allowed himself full rein. Moving faster, he plunged in and out of her, running the race of his life. She clung to his shoulders, her head flung back against the pillows.

Need built like an inferno inside him until he was moments away from the summit. He thrust into her harder and faster and finally shouted out his release. His chest pounded like he'd run a marathon, but never in his life had he felt better. Satisfaction, contentment, peace... She was his soul mate, his friend, his confidante. She was the woman he'd love until the end of time.

———————

Shelby stirred beneath the weight of Samuel's arm. She'd gone to sleep snuggled against him, but sometime during the night, he'd turned on his back and flung his arm across her chest. She pushed it gently away and climbed out of bed. With the aid of the moonlight, she made her away across the room.

After using the bathroom, she padded out into the kitchen in search of a glass of water. The widescreen TV mounted on the wall of the living room flickered in the darkness. She grinned. They'd left the dinner table in such a hurry, they'd forgotten to switch it off. She looked around for the remote and found it amongst some papers on the coffee table.

Turning back to the television, her attention was caught by the late night news. The news anchor announced the leading story and her heart skipped a beat.

"Police are still searching for clues in relation to the murder of three men in three separate attacks along the cliffs north of Bondi. The area is a well-known meeting spot for homosexuals and the police believe the victims' sexual orientation was the motivation for the killings. Several personal items belonging to the victims have been reported as missing. They include a gold and onyx ring, a Sydney Kings team jersey and a Melbourne Storm football cap. Police are appealing to anyone who might have information regarding these murders, or know the whereabouts of these items. Please call Detective Sergeant Jared Buchanan at the Bondi Police Station or Crime Stoppers on 1800 333 000 if you know anything that might assist in this investigation."

Shelby stared at the items displayed on the screen. The Storm football cap was the same as the one she'd seen in her father's office a fortnight ago. It had to be a coincidence. There was no way her father was involved in murder. The idea was preposterous. *Perhaps it was one of his clients?* After all, her dad had told her it had been given to him. Then she thought for a minute and shook her head. She was being utterly ridiculous to think there might be a connection. There were thousands of Storm caps just like that one. It didn't mean the cap in her father's office had anything to do with the cliff-top killings.

Determined to forget about it, she used the remote to switch off the television and then padded to the kitchen. Pouring herself a glass of water out of the jug kept in the fridge, she headed back to Samuel.

———————

Jared heard the sound of phones ringing and allowed himself a surge of hope. Since the news story on the missing items had aired the night before, they'd been ringing off the hook. A taskforce had been put together to help deal with all of the calls. Already, officers were speaking to potential tipsters and witnesses and recording their information. What was even better, he'd managed to locate his mystery witness.

After numerous messages and cursing the woman high and low, Maureen Nelson had finally called him.

"What happened to you?" he asked without preamble. "I waited at the station for hours. You never showed."

"I'm sorry. My phone battery died. It's taken me this long to scrape together the money to buy a new one. I had no other way of contacting you."

Jared bit back a curse, trying hard to hold on to his patience. "You could have come into the station. There was no need to call beforehand."

"I live all the way out at Mount Druitt, mate. I wasn't going to pay for the ride in and risk you not being here when I showed. What do you think I am, made of money? I don't know what all the fuss is about, anyway. A couple of guys got killed. So what? It happens out here all the time."

Jared bit his lip and forced himself to count to three. "All right, I'm sorry, Maureen. I understand why you didn't come in earlier, but I do need to talk to you. We have very few leads. You might be our only chance. And in case you didn't know, the body count's now at three. We need to catch a break before anyone else falls victim to this madman."

He cleared his throat and continued. "When we spoke on the phone a fortnight ago, you told me you thought you might have passed the killer on his way down. I'm still waiting for you to provide me with the details and my patience is wearing thin. I don't need to tell you, Maureen, how important you are to our investigation. We need to get together as soon as possible. How can I make this easier for you?"

"You can pay for my train fare. That would be a start."

"I can do one better than that. Give me your address and I'll come out and see you. It will save you the trip in."

"No, that's not a good idea," she replied hurriedly. "I move around a bit and I don't live on my own. It would be best if I come and see you."

Jared bit back a curse and held on to his patience with his fingernails. It wasn't unusual for people who lived on the fringes not to want the police making home visits, but he didn't give a shit about what petty illegal activity her roommates might be up to. It was probably dope and while he didn't condone any kind of criminal behavior, right now, his priority was finding a killer.

"All right," he conceded. "We'll do it your way. But forget about the train. Call a cab and tell them we'll cover the fare once you arrive at the station. That way you should get here before like...midnight."

The woman cackled on the other end of the phone. *"Hee, hee.* I like you, Detective. You've got a sense of humor. Most cops don't. Tell me, are you cute?"

Jared bit back a groan. This woman was doing his head in. Her evidence had better be worth it.

"I'm whatever you want me to be, Maureen. Now, get your ass in a cab and get over here. Don't forget to ask for Detective Buchanan."

"Oh, I won't. You can bet your balls on it." With a final chuckle, she ended the call.

It was almost three hours since he'd spoken to her and he could barely contain his impatience. The phone at his elbow rang and he snatched it up.

"Detective Buchanan, I have a woman by the name of Maureen Nelson down here. She says she has an appointment."

The general duties officer manning the reception sounded so dubious, Jared could only guess what the woman looked like. Still, her appearance was of little consequence. He needed to hear what she had to say. He was counting on her making a difference to his investigation.

"I'll be right down," he said.

Taking the stairs two at a time, he opened the door that secured the main part of the station from the waiting room. A woman wearing a stained blouse and knee-length shorts that stretched over her protruding stomach and did nothing to disguise her skinny legs stared at the domestic abuse posters and other public notices that papered the wall. With unkempt, straggly brown hair that looked like it hadn't been washed for decades and with a face that looked like life had dealt her a few harsh knocks, it was hard to judge her age. If he had to guess, he'd put her in her late twenties, but she could have been younger. She looked up as he entered.

"Maureen Nelson?"

"You must be Detective Buchanan. You're even cuter than I imagined."

She hefted her bulk toward him and held out her hand. Dirt encrusted her arms. He caught a whiff of body odor that almost made him gag, but he shook her hand without flinching and then turned to the officer behind the counter.

"Roger, there's a cabbie outside waiting for payment. Can you see to it?"

"Of course, Detective. Right away."

"Thanks." He turned back to his witness. "Let's go, Maureen. It's time for you and me to have a little talk."

He settled her into one of the interview rooms and asked her if she wanted a cold drink.

"What's on offer?" she asked, eyeing him curiously.

"The usual stuff. Coke, Fanta, Sprite. There's a vending machine down the hall."

She nodded. "I'll have a Coke, thanks."

He left the room and returned a short time later with the can. Handing it to her, he settled himself across from her in the only other chair. He put his elbows on the desk and stared at her.

"I want you to tell me about the night of November twelfth. You said you were walking along the path up on the cliffs of North Bondi. What time was it?"

Maureen took a mouthful of Coke and promptly burped. Without excusing herself, she answered. "I don't have a watch, but it must have been about one in the morning."

"Why do you say that?"

"I had a fight with my boyfriend. We were drinking in a hotel not far from Bondi Beach. He got nasty. Refused me a smoke, so I left before I did something stupid, like mouthing off at him. My momma always said I had a mouth. Anyway, it had just gone midnight when I walked out of the bar. I sat on a park bench for a bit, trying to clear my head. I finally decided to go for a walk. I love the beach. We don't get much surf out at Mount Druitt." She shot him a wry smile and he laughed.

"You're right about that," he murmured. Mount Druitt was as far inland as he could imagine. He nodded for her to continue.

"I figure it would have been about an hour

since I left Paulie," she said. "Paulie's my boyfriend."

Jared shot her a dubious look. "Mount Druitt's a long way from Bondi. What were you doing here?"

She shrugged. "Paulie's family are from over this way. He said he wanted to visit his old man. Wanted to ask him for money, most likely. Anyway, that's why we were here."

Jared noted the information on the legal pad in front of him. "How much had you been drinking?"

"I'd had a couple of Schooners, maybe three. I had a bit of a buzz on, but I was feeling all right. At least, I was until Paulie turned mean."

"So you started along the Federation Walk at Bondi Beach, headed north. Is that right?"

"I don't know what it's called, but yeah, I headed along the sidewalk. The beach was on my right."

"It was pretty dark that night, Maureen. What did you use for light?"

"There was a good moon that helped out, but I used the light on my phone."

"Lucky you had your battery charged," he murmured.

She chuckled. "Yeah, it was, wasn't it?"

Jared scribbled a couple more notes. "All right, Maureen, tell me what you saw when you were walking along the cliffs."

She picked up the can of Coke and tilted it to her lips. He watched her swallow. Once again, she let out a loud burp before setting the can back down.

"I was walking along, minding my own business, thinking about Paulie and how nasty he'd been.

We'd been together five or six months, long enough for him to stop being nice. And he has. Stopped being nice, I mean. It was all right in the early days, back when there was plenty of gear. He'd—"

"Maureen, can we just get on with it?"

"All right, all right! Hold your horses! I'm getting there!"

Jared only just managed to suppress an eye roll.

"I was heading up the hill, minding my own business, when I thought I heard a noise. It sounded like someone crying out. I thought I heard the sound of a dull kind of thumping and then there was another grunt or two. I wasn't sure if I'd heard right. The surf was loud in my ears, but when I saw the story on the news about the bloke who'd been murdered the same night I was there, I thought maybe I had heard something."

Jared's heart rate picked up its pace, but he kept his voice low and casual. "Tell me what else you heard."

She scrunched up her face. "Well, that's about it. But not long after, I passed a bloke along the path, heading in the opposite direction."

Jared sat forward. "How do you know it was a man?"

Maureen shrugged. "I don't. It was too dark to see his face. It was just an impression I got. He was big and tall, much taller than me. Even taller than Paulie."

"How tall is Paulie?"

"About as tall as you, Detective."

Jared nodded and noted the unidentified

person as more than six feet tall. "Did you notice anything else?"

"Not really. His face was in shadow, but he definitely had short hair. It was dark hair, I think, but it was hard to tell. I only saw him for a moment."

"So this person was coming down the hill toward you, away from North Bondi, is that correct?"

"Yes."

"And how close to the vicinity of the crime scene was it? I take it you saw the area cordoned off with the police tape, on the news?"

"Yeah, I saw it. That's when I got to wondering whether the man I saw had anything to do with it. It was around the same time and not far from where the police said the bloke was killed."

Jared nodded and made some more notes. He could hardly contain his excitement. Though his eyewitness left a lot to be desired, right now her evidence was the best he had.

"Did you notice anything else about this person?"

She rolled her eyes. "You already asked me that."

He ignored the attitude and replied in a voice that remained calm and steady, "Sometimes you remember things later that you hadn't thought about before."

She chuckled and nodded. "You know what, Detective, you're right. There is one more thing I remember. He smelled nice."

"Who?"

"The bloke I passed on the cliff. He smelled nice, like he wore some kind of expensive cologne. It was a little sweet for a bloke, if you ask me, but whatever floats your boat. No doubt he paid a fortune for it."

Jared noted the comment on his writing pad. "Can you take a guess how old this person was?"

"It was dark, Detective, and I only saw him for a moment. He was walking toward me on the path and then we passed. I didn't know at the time he was a murderer or I would have paid a little more attention: memorized his features; asked him his name and cell phone number. You know, that kind of thing."

Once again, Jared counted silently to three. The woman was beyond trying, but she was the best and only witness he had. He'd humor her if it was the last thing he did.

"Try your best, Maureen. A guess. Did he walk like a young man, or an older one? How did he dress? Nice clothes, or not so nice? Did he have facial hair?"

"Whoa, Detective! One question at a time! I already told you his face was in shadow. I don't think he wore a beard, but I couldn't be certain. He walked like a man, big strides, you know, but now that I think about it, I don't think he was young like me and Paulie. He didn't bounce with energy. He moved more like he was in a hurry, but not really. Does that make sense?"

Jared suppressed a sigh. Maureen's information was better than nothing, but he couldn't help but wish she had other details to offer. Still, what she'd given him was more than he'd had an hour ago and for that he was grateful.

"Do you remember anything about his clothing?" Jared asked again.

Maureen shook her head. "No, just that it was dark colored and I think he wore trousers. I don't remember seeing any bare legs."

"Did he speak to you?"

"No. I saw him coming toward me along the path. He had something in his hand. I was a little bit wary, given the time of night, but I didn't think too much of it. I've been out walking at night before. Sometimes, you come across unrestrained dogs. You never know if they're friend or foe." She shrugged. "I've carried a stick with me at times."

Jared scribbled some more notes and then looked up at her. "That's good, Maureen. That's really good. I really appreciate everything you've done. Thanks for coming in. You've been a real help."

She acknowledged his comments with a nod. "That's all right, Detective. It was worth coming in from Mount Druitt to meet you. Are you married?"

He smiled. "No, Maureen, I'm not married."

"Seeing anyone?"

"No, but you are. Paulie, remember? Your boyfriend?"

She grimaced. "Yeah, Paulie. My boyfriend."

Jared felt a surge of sympathy. She was a rough diamond and he was sure she had a heart of gold. He hadn't been lying when he told her how grateful he was that she'd come forward. He only hoped that the information she'd given him would bear fruit.

CHAPTER 13

Dear Diary,

I find the daily news so interesting. There's always something terrible happening in the world. A war, an earthquake, an act of terrorism. The news reader is always so serious and solemn, and rightly so. There's so much to be afraid of, so much that can go wrong. It's a wonder any of us sleep well at night, knowing what might lie ahead. Me, I sleep like the dead.

Shelby let herself into the house she shared with her siblings. Tossing her keys and handbag on the table in the hall, she called out as she made her way further into the house.

"Hello, family. Is anyone home?" She was met with silence.

It was hardly surprising. It was only four-thirty in the afternoon. She'd come straight from work after her shift. Over the past month, she'd been spending so much time at Samuel's house, she needed a fresh supply of clothes. She hadn't quite got to the point where she'd throw in a load of washing in the condo on the beach. It seemed too presumptuous, too intimate—which was plain silly, considering everything else they'd done.

Heading into the living room, she came to a halt. Dimitri was sprawled out asleep on the couch. The TV was on with the sound muted. He was dressed in one of his expensive suits, including his jacket and tie. Concerned for his wellbeing, she rushed forward.

"Dimi! Can you hear me? Are you all right?" Taking hold of his lapels, she gave him a shake. He came awake slowly and stared at her through bleary eyes. She swallowed her surprise.

"Dimitri! Are you okay? What are you doing here?"

He blinked a few times and his eyes slowly focused. He squinted up at her. "What are *you* doing here? I thought you'd moved out."

She flushed and poked out her tongue. Okay, so she'd been spending a lot of nights with Samuel. That didn't mean she'd left the home she shared with her siblings. Pushing his legs out of the way, she took a seat beside him on the couch.

"This isn't about me, Dimi. I'm not the one behaving strangely. I'm usually home at this time of day. You're not. And you look like you've pulled an all-nighter. What's going on?"

Her brother sighed and sank back against the couch, his head lolling on the headrest. Another surge of alarm went through Shelby. This was so unlike him. He was usually so focused, especially during the week. Normally he'd be at his office, grinding out affidavits. *What was going on?* She put the question to him again.

He looked at her and the sadness and resignation on his face startled her. "Dimi, talk to me. Please."

"I can't do it anymore, Shelby. I can't keep on living a lie. It's killing me."

Comprehension dawned and she drew in a deep breath and then blew it out slowly on a sigh. "Okay, I get that. Have you talked to anyone about it? Apart from me?"

"Like who? A shrink?"

"Yes, or maybe a good friend. Someone who'd understand."

He sighed again and shook his head. "No. What would I say? Nobody knows I've been hiding that I'm gay. My mates keep setting me up on blind dates, Dad keeps pushing me toward marriage. It's driving me insane, Shelby, and I don't know what to do about it."

At the mention of their father, Shelby paused. *Should she tell Dimitri about her discovery?* She'd promised her mom and dad she'd stay silent; that the best way forward was to keep the secret that had been protected for so many years. Her promise hadn't been given in response to any loyalty to her parents, it was more the urge to protect the rest of her siblings from the shock and disillusionment she and Athena had suffered.

No, Dimitri was struggling enough. She wouldn't

add to his pain by revealing something so shocking. He might never get over it. She'd never look at her parents the same way again. It wasn't fair to drag the rest of the family into this. She touched his arm.

"Dimi, have you talked to Daddy about it? He might understand more than you think."

Dimitri turned to her with a look of disbelief. "You're kidding? After everything I've told you about him. It's like a broken record, Shelby. You have no idea. He comes into my office on the pretense of seeking my advice, or clarification on a case and within moments, the conversation is steered toward his need for grandchildren and seeing the Gianopoulos family name continue down the line.

"It's got to the point that I shut the door to my office and pretend I'm seeing clients. I used to love my job. These days I can barely stand to go in there, knowing sooner or later throughout the day, Dad will appear with another less-than-subtle reminder that I'm letting the family down."

Shelby reached for his hand and squeezed it in wordless comfort. "Well, if you can't talk to Daddy, what about Momma? She doesn't feel quite so strongly about you getting married and carrying on the family name and she's your mother. She loves you." Shelby thought about the secret her mom had endured for so many years and then added, "She's been through a lot in her time. She might just understand. It's worth giving it a go, don't you think?"

Dimitri frowned. "Tell Mom? What makes you

think Mom would understand? She's lived a sheltered life. Dad's protected her from the worst society has to offer. She probably doesn't even know gays are normal people, like everyone else. I'd disgust and horrify her if I told her."

Shelby opened her mouth to protest and then closed it again. If she didn't want to raise Dimitri's suspicions or his hopes, she had to choose her words with care.

"Remember the part about the fact she's your mother?" she said gently. "Momma will love you, no matter what. And you don't give her enough credit. She knows more about the world than you think. She might have spent most of her life cooking and keeping house, but she's not stupid. She watches the news and reads the papers and checks out the gossip mags. I think you'd be surprised by how worldly our mother is."

Dimitri stared at her, a mixture of hope and terror on his face. "Do you think so? Do you think she'd understand?"

Shelby shrugged. "I'm not saying she wouldn't be shocked and maybe a little bit sad, but she loves you, Dimi. This secret inside you is eating you up. You can't go on like this. Tell Momma, get it out there and the rest will take care of itself."

"And what if it doesn't?" Dimitri whispered, his expression tortured.

"I can't promise anything, Dimi. I wish I could. But life doesn't come with guarantees. I guess that's part of the fun. We never quite know how things will turn out, but sometimes, we need to be prepared and take the risk. Without risk, there's no gain."

She took both of his hands in hers and squeezed them hard. "What do you have to lose? You're miserable like this. Who knows? Come out to Momma and the rest of the family and things might be better than you imagined."

"Then again, they might not," Dimitri added sadly.

"True, but like I said, nothing ventured, nothing gained. You've already said you can't live like this. The way I see, it, you don't have much choice."

A tiny smile of relief and gratitude made its way into her brother's eyes. "When did you get to be so wise?" he asked.

She grinned. "There's a lot about me you don't know."

His smile widened. "Really? Like what?"

Shelby pretended to think. She put a finger to her lips. "Like, I think I'm in love with Samuel."

Dimitri rolled his eyes. "Tell me something I don't know."

"Really?" she asked, surprised.

"Of course. It's as plain as the nose on your face. Every time you mention his name, your face lights up. It's like those corny chick flicks, only in your case it's real."

Heat crept up her face and she lowered her gaze. It was nice to have validation from her big brother.

"When are you moving in with him?" Dimitri's question broke into her thoughts. She frowned.

"What makes you think I'm going to move in with him?"

Once again, her brother gave her an eye roll.

"He loves you and you love him. Besides, you spend nearly all your spare time there. Wouldn't it be easier?"

Shelby shook her head. "I don't want to move in with him until we're married."

Dimitri laughed. "Really? That's a bit old-fashioned."

"I guess in most peoples' eyes it is and no doubt it's totally uncool, but that's the way I am. Besides, what's the hurry? I'm sure Aunty Maria, Aunty Sophia and Aunty Irene think I should be making a beeline for the church and even Uncle Theo might think so, but for me, finding a life partner isn't all about a headlong dash to the altar.

"I might have wanted a date for Elena's wedding in order to stave off the usual barrage of sympathetic platitudes and sorrowful looks, but that doesn't mean I'm in a hurry to settle down. I want to be courted like in the old days; to be picked up from work; to go on dates. I want to have fun times as boyfriend and girlfriend. What's wrong with that?"

Dimitri laughed outright. "Boyfriend and girlfriend? You're kidding me. You're twenty-seven, Shelby. No one your age uses those terms anymore."

She shot him a look of pure stubbornness. "Why not? Why don't we use those terms anymore? Why do we have to be someone's partner? Why have the words boyfriend and girlfriend gone out of style?"

"It's because people used to get married a lot younger. It's fine to have a boyfriend or girlfriend if you're like nineteen or twenty. Once you get past a certain age, those terms sound weird."

"So I'm supposed to be someone's partner or spouse. Is that what you're saying? Are they the only choices left?"

"Yeah, I guess so. What are you getting so worked up about? They're only words."

"No, Dimitri," she argued, wanting him to understand. "They're not just words. They represent so much more. To me, the word "partner" means something less than full commitment—like if you knew you were going to love each other until the day you died, you'd be willing to get married and then they'd be your spouse."

She shook her head slowly. "When did living together before marriage or even without marriage in the cards, become so acceptable? How did that come about? It's almost like marriage is an afterthought these days, and in many cases, not even that. It's taken so much of the magic out of it, out of forging a life together. It's like marriage is completely out of vogue and that's so sad."

Dimitri regarded her thoughtfully. "Yeah, sis, I think you're right. I'm not sure how it happened, but for a lot of people, marriage doesn't rate and it's not just people like me, gay men who can't legally marry here. There are a lot of people foregoing the bindings of marriage."

He shrugged. "Is it a good thing, or bad? I guess we'll have to wait and see. Wish I had a snapshot of society in fifty years to see where we'll end up."

Shelby fell back against the couch and sighed. "It's a sad state of affairs, Dimi. To me, marriage represents a public declaration, a vow of lifelong love and commitment, stability, security, safety, being with someone who always has your back. There's something special and incredibly uplifting about knowing someone who was once a stranger has chosen *you* to be with them for the rest of their life."

Dimitri reached across and chucked her gently under the chin. "You watch too many movies, Shelby. Real life isn't like that. There are no fairytale endings."

Shelby looked at him. "I'm sad you're so disillusioned, big brother. You're way too young for that."

"I am what I am." He shrugged. The smile failed to reach his eyes.

She smiled despondently back at him. "Ain't that the truth."

———————

Alexei twisted the thick gold band around his finger and frowned. It felt so foreign and unfamiliar. He wished he had the courage to leave it at home. He'd found it in his den, lying on the pillow. Immediately, he thought of Rodriguez and cursed the fact he hadn't insisted the man turn in his key to the side door that led to the basement. He'd have to change the locks.

He hadn't heard from his ex-lover for more than

a fortnight until now. The ring was just the start of it. Rodriguez had sent him a text only that morning and said he was on his way into the city to see him. Alexei couldn't hold back a groan of disbelief. In all the months they'd seen each other, Rodriguez had never approached him at work. They'd had an unspoken agreement that their relationship would stay confined to crowded gay bars on the darker side of town and to the warm delights that awaited them in the basement. Rodriguez understood that and had abided faithfully by the rules. Until now.

Alexei sighed. He twisted the ring again and not for the first time wondered if he'd done the right thing. He missed Rodriguez dreadfully. The sight of the ring on his pillow had filled him with so much joy, he'd had to blink back tears. Perhaps they could make it work, after all? Perhaps he could persuade his Latin lover that any relationship between them was better than no relationship at all? Would Rodriguez be willing to take up where they'd left off, secrecy and all? Alexei could only live in hope.

Shelby strode across the polished marble flooring that spanned the wide entryway to her father's offices. Nerves jangled in her belly at the thought of what she was going to do. She had no intention of breaking Dimitri's confidence, but neither could she sit back and watch him fall into a depression so deep he might never climb out of it.

Pressing the button at the bank of elevators that would take her up to the fifteenth floor, she waited impatiently. At last, the elevator *dinged* and the stainless steel doors slid open. Stepping around a departing occupant, she strode inside and hit the button for level fifteen. Like the last time, she hadn't called ahead. She didn't want to give her father a reason not to see her. She only hoped he wasn't in court or with clients, or had some other legitimate excuse.

"Shelby! How are you today? I wasn't expecting to see you again quite so soon."

Shelby smiled at her father's secretary. "Hi, Jennifer. I'm fine. Is my father in?"

"Yes, he is. I'll just let him know you're here. Is he expecting you?"

"No, but I'm sure he'll be happy to see me."

The secretary turned away and picked up the receiver of the telephone that sat on her polished wood-and-glass desk. The firm's name of Harton & Wentworth was carved into the front.

"He asked me to send you in," Jennifer murmured and pushed away from her chair. Coming around to where Shelby stood, the woman walked down a corridor and came to a halt outside her father's office. With a gentle knock on the door, she opened it and indicated for Shelby to enter. Murmuring her thanks, Shelby stepped inside.

"Hi, Daddy. How are you doing?"

Her dad shot her a look of wariness mixed with

surprise. "Shelby! What are you doing here? I thought we'd said all we needed to say."

"You're right, Daddy and I promise I won't ever talk about that again. That's not the reason I'm here." She paused and gathered her courage. "It's about Dimitri."

Her father frowned. "Where is he? The girls in his office told me he left hours ago. It's barely five-thirty. He'll never make partner that way. Who does he think he is?"

"Calm down, Daddy. It's not like that. Dimitri has always loved working here and he has no intention of shirking his responsibilities to the firm. It's just that, right now, he doesn't feel like he has a choice."

"What the hell are you talking about, Shelby? You're not making sense."

Holding onto her courage, she drew in a deep breath and took a seat in the high-backed leather chair that stood opposite her father's desk. She eyed him steadily.

"It's like this, Daddy. Dimitri talked to me about...some things he's concerned about. Important things. Things that are affecting his ability to work, and more. I'm not going to break his confidence. He doesn't even know I'm here, but you need to talk to him, or at least, lay off him about getting married."

Her father's frown deepened and his tone remained abrupt. "What are you talking about?"

"He told me you're on his back all the time about finding a girl and settling down. He's had enough of it and to tell you the truth, Daddy, I'm not sure that he'll ever be ready for that."

There, she'd said it. Kind of.

Her father moved closer until he stood towering over her. His expression was fierce. She imagined it was his courtroom face, when he was staring down an adversary. The image wasn't comforting.

"What are you saying, Shelby? For God's sake, just spit it out."

"Nothing, Daddy. I've probably said too much already." She pushed back her chair and stood and moved a little further away before turning back to face him. "Just do me a favor; talk to him. Okay?"

For the longest time, her father didn't answer. When he finally did, his tone was much more amenable and she couldn't prevent a sigh of relief.

"Okay. I'll talk to him. I want to find out what's going on. His billable hours have been down for months and sinking faster than the *Titanic*. Some of the partners are asking questions, wondering if he's their guy. He needs to sort out whatever shit's going through his brain and focus on his work if he's to have any chance of a partnership."

"Thank you, Daddy. That's all I ask. Just talk to him. And promise me you'll listen."

"I thought you just said you only wanted me to talk to him. You didn't say anything about listening."

A smile tugged at the corners of her father's mouth and Shelby returned his grin. Closing the distance between them, she put her arms around him and gave him a hug.

"You come across all fierce and scary, but you're not like that at all," she said.

His smile widened and he winked. "Don't tell the prosecutor that."

Stepping back, a flash of light caught her eye. She looked at her father's right hand and noticed a thick gold band sporting a large onyx stone on his finger. Something niggled at the back of her memory. She frowned.

"Where did you get that?" she asked, pointing at the ring.

He frowned and appeared momentarily disconcerted. "What, this?" he replied, holding up his hand.

"Yes. I've never seen you wearing it before."

Her father looked uncomfortable. "It's... It's a gift from...your mother. Yes, apparently she came across it a few weeks ago and thought of me. She said it was an early Christmas present." He shrugged. "It's been a long time since she gave me anything, Christmas or otherwise. I wasn't going to complain."

"Why would you complain? It's beautiful."

"Yes, I guess, but it's not really my style. It's a little...flamboyant. I'd prefer something more discreet."

At the mention of his desire for discretion, Shelby was reminded of his den in the basement and what went on there. A moment later, she remembered where she'd seen the ring and gasped.

"Did Momma tell you where she bought it?"

"No. I assumed it was from one of her favorite jewelry stores. Why?"

Shelby pondered whether she should say

anything. It was ridiculous to draw a connection between a ring and a spate of murders, but the ring wasn't the only odd gift her father had recently acquired. There was also the football cap.

But the cap had come from a client. At least, that's what her father had said. *Was he lying? Why would he do that?* Nothing made sense.

"Did you hear about those murders on the cliffs of North Bondi?" she asked.

Her father frowned at the change of subject. "Yes. Why do you ask?"

"They ran another story the other night. Did you see it? The police showed pictures of some missing personal items."

"No, I haven't caught the news all week."

"Apparently some things were stolen from the victims at the time of the attacks. There was a Sydney Kings team jersey, a Melbourne Storm cap and a gold and onyx ring—just like the one on your finger. The police were asking for information from anyone who might have seen the items or know their whereabouts."

Her father's eyes widened in shock and his face lost some of its color. "Are you *sure*?"

"Yes, Daddy. I'm certain. I saw the news report."

He shook his head slowly back and forth, as if in a daze. "But how could that be? How could I have two items matching the description of items stolen from murder scenes?" He murmured the words more to himself than to her, but Shelby's chest went tight. It seemed far too coincidental and yet, she refused to believe her father had anything to with the gruesome attacks.

"It must be just a fluke," she said, attempting a laugh. It fell flat. The bewildered expression on her father's face didn't change. "Besides, you got that cap from a client, remember?" she insisted. "The one who didn't know you root for the Sharks."

"Yes, that's right, only… It's not true."

Shelby's heart skipped a beat and she was flooded with confusion and sudden fear. "What do you mean, it's not true? You told me so yourself."

Her father sighed. Moving over to his desk, he sank wearily into his chair. "I know what I told you, Shelby. What I'm telling you now is that I didn't speak the truth."

"Daddy!" she cried in bewilderment. "What are you saying? Why would you lie?"

He grimaced and stared down at his desk, where his hands were clenched tight enough for the knuckles to show white. "I don't know. I didn't think it mattered."

"Then why are you telling me now?"

He was silent so long, she didn't think he was going to answer. Finally, he raised his head and stared at her. The fear on his face was almost palpable. "Because the person who gave me both the cap and the ring was Rodriguez Gomez, my former lover."

CHAPTER 14

Dear Diary,

I thought I could accept it, the joke my life had become. I thought I could ignore the fact my husband preferred men. I thought I could smile and laugh and drink coffee with my friends, all the time knowing that I lay down at night beside a man who'd been born without a soul.

As the years went on, the knowledge ate at me, like acid. The burden of keeping his terrible secret started playing with my head. It wasn't right, what he was—a scourge on society, a man who defied the teachings of the bible, who thought of nothing and no one but himself.

My bitterness grew and multiplied until it consumed me night and day. It's all I think about, all I pray about... Eradicating, once and for all, the filth that walk the streets; share our tables; swim in our oceans; play in our parks; that stroll with us side by side. It must be stopped and I'm the one to do it. Of this, I am certain. After all, I have God on my side.

Alexei Gianopoulos sipped at the single malt whisky he'd poured into a crystal tumbler from the bottle he kept in the wet bar hidden in his office. The alcohol was usually reserved for important clients, but tonight, he needed a dose of its reassuring strength.

Shelby had departed hours ago, but her words kept going around and around in his head. He was still shocked at the knowledge his ex-lover had given him gifts that were the same as the ones stolen from gay men who had been brutally slain. Obviously, they weren't the ones belonging to the victims, but still, the similarities had shaken him.

What was Rodriguez up to? What did the gifts mean? Was he trying to send Alexei a message? If so, what? To think he'd seriously contemplated inviting the man back into his life and that he was actually wearing the ring... He'd only put it on because Rodriguez had threatened to show up at his office. He was beyond relieved the man hadn't made good on his promise.

The police were calling the murders hate crimes. It appeared the only motivating factor connecting them was the fact all three victims had been gay men. The thought unsettled him. Those few weren't the only gay men in Bondi.

He fingered the ring on his right hand and a surge of nausea flooded his stomach. Rodriguez had threatened suicide and had followed that with a threat against Alexei's life. *Could Rodriguez be behind the brutal deaths on the cliff tops?*

He thought back to the time, nearly two months earlier, when he'd told Rodriguez it was over. It had happened right before the first murder... His nervousness grew.

Then there was the Melbourne Storm football cap. Rodriguez knew Alexei rooted for the Cronulla Sharks. They'd even gone to a game together. Alexei had taken a few of his kids, passing Rodriguez off to them as a friend. And yet, the man had gifted him with a cap from the opposition. He still didn't know what to make of it.

Was Rodriguez being deliberately spiteful, or was there something more sinister behind his actions? It wasn't until Shelby asked him how he'd come by it that he'd thought about the cap again. And now he was wearing yet another unexpected gift from his former lover. It was so strange. The whole thing was beyond unsettling.

With a sigh, he took another sip of his drink and resolved to speak with Rodriguez about all of it. As much as he dreaded the thought, the sooner the discussion happened, the better.

Helen Gianopoulos felt for the light switch in the darkness and flicked it on. With a heavy tread, she descended the stairs that led to her husband's den. Though she detested what the basement represented, she routinely found herself surrounded by its four walls. Today was no different.

She looked at the unmade double bed. The black satin sheets that hung half on the floor were stained. Her mouth tightened with disgust.

Her husband had constructed a private entrance where his friends could enter from behind the garden wall. It meant that she and her children were never subjected to knowing when there were visitors, but the sheets on the bed said it all.

Alexei had never asked her to launder the linens, but who else was going to do it? A housekeeper came in once a week to tidy upstairs, but nobody entered the den. It was the way both of them wanted it. They'd promised each other they'd keep the secret and that meant Helen was the only one who could do the job and as much as she detested it, being in that room—knowing what went on—helped to fuel her hate.

Everywhere she looked she was bombarded with images of filth and degradation. The pile of photos, the magazines, the videos—all lying around in clear sight. Even the pictures on the walls depicted disgusting sex acts between men. Alexei was scoffing at her, shoving it in her face. Other than him and the men he entertained, she was the only one who came down here. He'd left those things out in full view to anger her. She was sure of it.

If only he knew how furious it made her, how his actions caused her anger to spiral out of control. It hadn't always been that way, but more and more the beast inside her demanded retribution and she was finally giving in to its wild call...

———————————

The new mother cuddled her baby against her

and murmured against the infant's soft, downy hair. Shelby couldn't hear the words, but the image of mother and baby made her smile. She loved the aftermath of a successful birth, when the new mom and baby met properly for the first time. There was something so special and magical about it.

Now that she'd found Samuel, having a family of her own would become a reality. Not as many children as she'd hoped for, but even one or two would be loved and cherished. And she might even get lucky and have a multiple birth. If it happened on baby number two, she'd be the happiest woman in the world.

She smiled to herself at the thought. It was possible. Multiple births ran in Samuel's family. Everyone knew the hereditary link increased the odds. She'd always wanted to be a mother. She was sure she'd make a good one. That was something else to look forward to, another stage in her life.

Despite the recent revelations about the relationship between her momma and daddy, they'd both been good parents. She couldn't fault them there. In fact, she admired their ability to stick together for the sake of their children when they could have just as easily done the opposite. It went to show how much they loved their kids, that they were prepared to make such sacrifices.

Still, she couldn't shake her growing sense of dread. First, the discovery of her father's den, the lies and deception that had gone on for decades—on both sides. Then there was the football cap and now, the ring—given to her father by his lover. She didn't want to think about it. But the secrets were piling up, overwhelming her. Even her beloved brother, Dimitri, had been carrying around a big secret.

What was going on? Her perfect family was falling apart around her ears and there was nothing she could do about it. The thought saddened her beyond measure.

Paul Munro was desperate. Pacing up and down the sidewalk that ran along the shop fronts of popular Bondi stores and cafés. He tried to get a grip on himself. He hadn't had a fix for more than forty-eight hours and he was beginning to lose control. His head thumped; his heart pounded; his temper was razor-edged and all the time, he kept thinking about how his high had wound down. He needed to score—and fast—before he did something stupid.

He thought about Maureen and wondered where the fuck she was. She used to be able to score gear, even after she stopped using. She used to look out for him. She used to want to keep him happy. But he hadn't seen her since she'd told him she was the star witness in a murder.

"You're fucking kidding yourself, Maureen." He'd laughed. "And you think I'm the one off my brain! Ha! You're delusional. What have you been on? When did you start using again?"

She'd stared at him with a hurt expression and had told him, in no uncertain terms, to fuck off. She'd headed out in the opposite direction, toward the bus station. It was the last time he'd seen her. It was a shame. She usually had a little money. Enough to get by. Enough to see him through for a while. *Now where would he find the money he needed to score?*

He'd already tried his parents. First his father and then his mother. Neither had helped him out. All they'd done was lecture him about cleaning up his act, going back to rehab, *blah, blah, blah.* It was bullshit. He'd tried rehab. It hadn't worked. In fact, he'd scored some gear while he was in there. Rehab. A place to get clean. What a joke.

He guessed there was always Sam. His oldest brother had a heart kinder than most. Out of all his siblings, Sam was the one most likely to help him. The last time they'd spoken, it had gotten nasty, but that had been months ago. Paul was hopeful this time, Sam would come good for him. His brother couldn't stay mad at him forever. He loved him. Besides, he was a doctor. Out of everyone, Sam understood Paul's addiction the best.

Tugging the phone his mother had given him out of the pocket of his dirty jeans, he sent his brother a text.

Hi Sam, have u got time 2 meet me? I'm sorry about last time. It was all my fault. I really need 2 c u. I love u. Call me back. Jim Bob xx

He signed it "Jim Bob" on purpose, hoping it would melt his brother's resistance. It was a longstanding joke. As the fourth son, Paul had often been called Jim Bob by his family in a nod to an old TV show they'd watched when they were kids. *The Waltons* first aired in the seventies, well before any of the Munro kids were born, but his mom had managed to find the DVDs. They'd all enjoyed watching the stories and drama unfold around the fictional Walton family.

The show was set in rural America during the Great Depression and later, during World War II. Somehow, despite all of their trials and tribulations, the Waltons managed to stick together, support each other, and see the hard times through. The show had always left him feeling good until he got old enough to realize it was pure Hollywood bullshit. That kind of perfect family didn't exist.

He stared down at the screen of his phone and willed it to ring. When it beeped with an incoming text message, he jumped. *It was from Sam!* He couldn't believe it. Despite his hopes, he hadn't been sure his brother would respond. But he had, and that was an excellent sign. Soon, all would be well. Paul squinted to read the message. It didn't take him long.

OK.

Staring at the letters, he could hardly stem his elation. This time, Sam would come through for him. He'd give him money. Paul was sure of it. After sending off another quick message about meeting him at the Surf Club on Bondi Beach, Paul shoved the phone back in his pocket. Looking down at the filth on his hands, he grimaced.

He needed to clean himself up a bit if he wanted to convince Sam the money wasn't going to be spent on drugs. With that thought in mind, he hurried across the beach to the beckoning water. He couldn't get the smile off his face.

———————

Samuel stared down at his phone and re-read his brother's text. He had no idea why he'd agreed to meet with him. Paul would be looking for money. It was the only reason he ever contacted him. The last time, Samuel had said no. It had almost killed him, but he'd done it. *Could he be that strong again?*

His parents had stopped giving Paul money weeks ago. Everyone in the family knew he was using it to buy drugs, but still, it was a tough call. As he'd explained to Shelby, as far as Samuel was concerned, his parents were partly responsible for Paul's addiction. It wasn't fair of them to wipe their hands of him now when the problem had gotten so out of hand. It was a cop-out and it wasn't what parents were supposed to do.

Samuel compressed his lips tightly together as a wave of guilt surged through him. He wasn't being fair. His parents had spent thousands of dollars on rehab facilities. The best that money could buy. None of it had done any good. Paul was the problem. He didn't *want* to get well and no amount of rehab was going to help him until he wanted that for himself. It was as simple as that.

"Who's that?" Shelby asked, coming into the room.

Samuel didn't realize he was still staring at his phone until she indicated it with a movement of her head. He debated in silence what to tell her. She already knew about Paul and the fact he'd gone off the rails and Samuel had made it clear he wasn't supporting his brother's drug habit by giving him cash, but still, this was his younger brother. *Was he strong enough to turn his back on Paul again? And if he reached out to help his brother, would Shelby understand?* He wished he knew the answer.

No, better to keep the meeting a secret until he knew the outcome and whether he'd managed to stay strong. It was always possible Paul had gotten help and cleaned himself up. Not likely, but possible. *Maybe he just wanted to see him, like he said?*

There would be plenty of time for Shelby to meet his family, including Paul. This probably wasn't the best time.

"Samuel?"

Shelby's voice had sharpened and he realized he still hadn't answered her. Twisting around from his spot on the couch, he offered her an offhand smile.

"No one important, just an old friend I haven't seen for a long while."

"Someone from college?"

"Um, yeah. He wants to catch up this afternoon. Do you mind? He's only in town for the night."

She shook her head. "No, of course not. You could ask him over for dinner. I'd be happy to cook."

Samuel thought fast. "I'm not sure he has time for dinner. We might just catch a quick drink down near the beach."

She nodded. "Okay."

Hating that he'd lied to her, he got up and came around to where she stood and put his arms around her. Pulling her close, he kissed her on the cheek. "I won't be long."

"Hey, stay as long as you like. If it's been that long since you've seen him, I'm sure you have a lot to catch up on."

"That's true. And thanks, I'll bring back some of that vanilla bean and wattleseed ice cream you like. We can eat it after dinner."

She pressed a kiss on his lips. "You're so sweet. That sounds great. Have fun."

Samuel kept his smile firmly in place. Fun was the last thing this meeting was going to be.

————————

When Samuel headed for the shower, Shelby made a beeline for his phone. It wasn't that she didn't trust him, but there was something strange going on. The whole time he'd been talking to her about his so-called long lost friend, he hadn't once looked her in the eye. It felt weird and was so unlike him, she couldn't help feeling he wasn't telling her the truth.

Scrolling through his text messages, she came to the most recent ones. They had been sent from an unknown number. She read the message and frowned. It read like it was coming from someone a whole lot closer than an old friend: *I love you.*

What was *that* about? Weird, definitely weird.

She scrolled down further and discovered they were meeting outside the Bondi Surf Club. It wasn't the kind of place you went for a drink. This was getting stranger and stranger.

Why would Samuel say he was meeting a college friend for a drink when it was clear that a) they were way closer than friends and b) they weren't going to the Bondi Surf Club for a drink? It didn't make sense.

With a growing feeling of dread, she thought about what could be going on. *Who was Samuel meeting and why?* She was certain he wasn't telling her the truth. That begged the question: Why would he lie? She was determined to find out. She'd had enough of lies and deception to last her a lifetime. She wasn't going to stand for it in the man who might one day be her husband. With her mind made up, she set the phone back down where he'd left it and hurried from the room.

CHAPTER 15

Paul stood across the street from the surf club and tried to find the courage to walk forward. Despite his swim in the cool, clear water, sweat ran down his face. As his desperation reached fever pitch, he could barely refrain from screaming. He needed to get high and he needed it fast. If he didn't get high, he'd die.

The thought sobered him. *What the fuck was he doing?* The way he was feeling, if Sam didn't come through with some money, he'd march right into the convenience store and hold up the cashier with a knife. He kept one handy, tucked into the waistband of his shorts. He never knew when he might need it; when he might be forced to defend himself against other lowlifes.

And that's what he was. A lowlife. A no-good, loser drug addict who was throwing away his life. Just like his parents had said. Just like Sam had said.

Sam. His hero. The only person Paul looked up to. Sam would know how to help him. He was a doctor. All Paul had to do was ask for it. Could he do it? Could he try again to get clean? He'd tried so many times before and had failed. What if this time was more of the same?

He stared down at his bare feet, still stained with ingrained dirt. The truth was, he'd never really tried to get better. He'd never wanted to get clean before. He liked being high. He liked the feeling of being on top of the world, where nothing mattered and life was good. It was when he was sober that things got tough; that he'd be jolted back into reality. That was the hard part. Getting high and staying that way was easy. But he was now twenty-seven. Way old enough to know better, to want more than a quick fix.

His family wanted to help him. He knew they did. His parents might be committed to their careers, but underneath, they did still love their kids. And Sam. He loved him most of all.

Paul thought about the things he'd said to him the last time they'd been together. He'd asked for money, of course, and when Sam refused, things had turned ugly. Paul had spoken ugly words of bitterness and hate, but it was Paul the drug addict who'd spoken. Jim Bob had curled up in horror inside, cringing.

Was it too late to make amends? Was it too much to ask Sam to forgive him, to help him one more time? He didn't know, but as he focused on the surf club building across from him and saw the familiar outline of his brother, he knew he was about to find out.

———————

Samuel checked his watch and cursed under his breath. He'd arrived at the Bondi Surf Club at the appointed time, but Paul wasn't there. His brother had sounded so genuine in his text, like he really wanted to see him, but so far, he was nowhere to be seen.

Had he made the trip down for nothing? One thing he was glad of was that he hadn't said anything to Shelby about it. The thought of having to tell her his brother had stood him up after begging Samuel to meet made him squirm with embarrassment.

"Sam! You came!"

Samuel spun on his heel. He hadn't heard anyone approach. A moment later, Paul threw his arms around him and hugged him hard. Samuel didn't bother suppressing his smile. No matter what choices Paul had made and what rocky roads he'd traveled, he was still Samuel's kid brother and always would be.

"Jim Bob!" he said, deliberately using the endearing nickname from their youth. "How are you, mate?"

Paul grinned. His teeth were stained yellow and showed clear signs of neglect. Samuel wondered how long it had been since he'd used a toothbrush. His hair was damp, like he'd recently showered, but that didn't compute with the filth and ingrained dirt that stained his clothes. Samuel guessed his brother had shucked down to his underwear and gone for a swim. His brother's next words confirmed it.

"The water's good. You been in today?"

Samuel shook his head. "No, I've been at work since midnight. I got home and went to bed. I not long got up."

Paul chuckled. "Sleep when you're dead, Sam. That's what they say."

Samuel nodded and examined his brother closely. His longish, light-brown hair hung in thick ropes around his face, stiff with salt and grime. Stubble covered his cheeks. His eyes were as blue as ever, but there was a restlessness in them. Every time Samuel made eye contact, his brother looked away.

"How have you been, Jim Bob?" Samuel asked quietly.

The laughter disappeared from Paul's eyes. His expression sobered. "You know, big brother. I've been all right."

"Where are you living these days?"

Paul looked away and shrugged. "Here and there. The weather's good for outdoor living this time of year."

His attempt at a smile failed. Samuel's chest tightened. He hated the fact his brother had come to this. It was so unnecessary. He had a family, people who loved him. Okay, his parents might have been a little remiss in their duties, but they were good people who'd tried their best to help. They'd been just as devastated as Samuel to discover Paul had gotten into drugs.

"You can always go home, Jim Bob," Samuel said.

Paul looked at him. Tears glinted in his eyes. The sight of them broke Samuel's heart.

"How can I go home like this?" Paul asked him. "Look at me! I'm an addict. I've got no fixed place of abode. I hang out with other addicts, losers with nothing more to look forward to than their next hit. I'm one of them, Sam. How can I go home?"

Samuel stepped forward and grasped his brother by the arms. "Listen to me, Jim Bob. Mom and Dad love you. You're their son. There's always a place at home. You'll have to go back to rehab, get yourself cleaned up—but, hell, do you really want to keep living like this? You're not even thirty. You have your whole life ahead of you! And you're wasting it."

He gave his brother a little shake. His voice increased in volume, reflecting his frustration. "Don't you get it? There's no second chances here. You can't turn around in your forties and admit you fucked up and could I please have my twenties back? It doesn't work that way. You need to make every day count like it was your last. By God, one of these days it will be."

The tears flowed freely down his brother's cheeks. Samuel's heart clenched. He hated to see Paul in such a state, but this called for some tough love.

"You're right, Sam, of course you're right. But I

don't know what to do! I'm hot and cold and shaky, my heart's pounding, screaming for another hit. My brain keeps telling me that as long as I find some gear and get it into my veins, everything'll be all right. I can't fight it, Sam, even if I wanted to. I just can't."

Samuel pushed at his brother again, this time a little more forcefully. "Bullshit. Don't try that shit on me. You can fight it if you want to. You've been to rehab. You know there are trained professionals ready and willing to help. It's just that you don't want their help. You don't want to get clean. Don't tell me you're not strong enough. I won't buy it."

Samuel's breath came fast. He took a step away from his brother and did his best to get his temper under control. He hadn't meant to lay it all on Paul like that, but the guy had read him all wrong. The truth was, his brother had come here expecting sympathy and Samuel was all out.

He didn't regret his outburst. It was time the gloves were taken off. His parents had tried the soft and loving approach. It had gotten them nowhere. Samuel didn't pretend to have all the answers, but he was desperate to try something, anything that might break through his brother's haze of drugs and addiction and resonate deep inside.

He looked over at Paul. His brother was bent over at the waist and was wheezing like he'd run the fifteen-hundred meters at a sprint. Tears continued to run down his cheeks. With a sigh of resignation, Samuel closed the distance.

He touched his brother on the shoulder. "I'm sorry, Jim Bob. I shouldn't have said those things."

Paul came upright slowly and lifted his tear-stained face up to Samuel's. The desolation in their blue depths broke Samuel's heart.

"No, mate, you had every right to talk to me like that," Paul choked. "I'm an asshole, a loser. I'm fucking up my life. I don't even know why." He looked down at himself. "I hate living like this, like a loser who has nobody that cares." He swiped at his nose with the back of his hand and drew in a shaky breath. "I came here to ask you for money, but what I really need is your help. Help me, Sammie. Please, help me."

Paul's sobs overwhelmed him. Without a moment's hesitation, Samuel drew him into his arms. Holding his brother tightly, he murmured words of comfort against Paul's ear. The smell that emanated from his brother's body almost made Samuel gag, but he tightened his hold and ignored it, hoping that in some way he could imbue his brother with the strength he needed to face what was to come.

It was a long while later that Paul pulled slightly away. Samuel stared at him. "I want to help you, Jim Bob. We all do. But you have to let us and you have to want to help yourself. We can't do it on our own. You have to want this as much as us. More, even. Do you understand?"

Paul nodded. Once again, his eyes glinted with tears. "Yes, Sammie. I understand. And thank you for giving me another chance."

Samuel smiled. "Hey, this is just the beginning.

There are a lot of tough times ahead. You're going to hate me, I'm sure, long before you thank me again."

Paul grinned back at him and for a moment, Samuel caught a glimpse of the boy his brother used to be. His chest tightened with emotion. He'd do everything in his power to bring that boy back. Failure was no longer an option.

Finding his soul mate in Shelby only brought home to him how important love and family were. He wanted his brother to experience the same emotion, the same sense of belonging, the same security, the same contentment and Paul would never get there on his own.

Pulling his brother close for another hug, Samuel pressed a kiss to his brother's cheek. He'd bring Paul back from the brink if it killed him.

Shelby blinked in shock. She stood far enough away from Samuel and his companion that she couldn't hear what was being said, but she had a clear vision of what they did. The first time Samuel stepped forward and hugged the man, she'd been a little taken aback. The hug went on for a very long time. Finally, Samuel had stepped back and the two of them had continued their discussion. A short time later, they were hugging again and this time, Samuel leaned over and kissed him. Okay, it wasn't on the mouth, but even from a distance she could detect a level of tenderness. It was obvious Samuel cared for this man, this friend from college.

All of a sudden, Shelby gasped. Ian Broderick had told her Samuel was gay and that it had started while they were at college. She'd believed Samuel when he denied the allegations and she'd never questioned his sexuality when they made love, but what if she was wrong? What if his desire to get married was all an elaborate façade, the same way it had been for her father? All for appearances...

She'd been oblivious to the truth about her father's sexuality for nearly three decades and she'd spent more than two of those decades living under the same roof. She barely knew Samuel. They'd known each other for less than two months.

When she'd confronted him about Ian's allegations, she'd taken his denial at face value, accepting his word. *But how did she know for sure he was telling the truth?* The fact that he had a reputation for being a womanizer and that they'd made love didn't count. After all, her daddy managed to father nine children. Having sex with a woman didn't automatically cancel the gay issue out.

Unconsciously, she made a sound of distress in the back of her throat and immediately pushed her fist against her mouth. She was sure they couldn't hear her against the rush of the ocean and she was well concealed against the wall of the Surf Club, but still, she didn't want to be caught spying. It was going to be hard enough to come to terms with what she'd seen and decide what she was going to do about it without Samuel discovering her presence. Besides, she'd seen enough.

Retreating slowly back the way she'd come, Shelby headed to Samuel's condo. Though it was the last place she wanted to be, she didn't want to raise his suspicions. He'd expect her to be there when he returned. Until she knew how she was going to handle this, she'd pretend nothing was amiss. It would take all of her acting skills, but she was determined to pull it off.

———

Alexei poured himself another glass of whisky from the supply he kept in his den. His hand shook slightly as he brought the glass to his lips. His last conversation with Shelby had been going around and around in his head and the more he thought about what she'd told him, the more agitated he became.

He'd taken the time to search the Internet for stories on the recent gay killings. The media were calling the perpetrator the Cliff-top Killer. It hadn't surprised him to discover Shelby had told the truth. A Melbourne Storm football cap, a gold and onyx ring and a Sydney Kings basketball jersey had been missing at the crime scenes. One personal item had been taken from each victim. The police were calling them trophies. The killer stole something from his victims and kept it, probably reliving the thrill of the murder every time he looked at it.

It was sickening and he refused to contemplate for even a second that his former lover might have something to do with it. For all his faults and failings, Rodriguez was a lover, not a fighter. His talk of killing himself and Alexei was just that—talk. Alexei would bet his life on it. But what was with the unsettling gifts? Did he really think they were a way to win Alexei back? The truth was, they filled him with dread.

Was Rodriguez spiteful enough to buy him the very same gifts that had been stolen from the victims of the Cliff-top Killer, knowing the murders had taken place in his neighborhood? And if so, why? What did he hope to gain?

Alexei had left a message for his ex-lover and was waiting to hear from him. He hoped the man would call back soon. This not knowing what was going on was creeping him out. Moving restlessly, he paced beside the floor-to-ceiling bookshelf. A small, red package wedged between two books caught his eye. Walking over to it, he set down his glass and pulled the box out.

The bright gift wrapping glinted in the light. A white-and-red ribbon was tied around the box. Curious, Alexei tugged on the end and the ribbon slipped from its hold. Sliding his finger beneath the paper, he tore it off and opened the box. He gasped.

Nestled inside among silver tissue paper was an exquisite, handmade chocolate heart. The swirls and flurries were intricate and formed two perfect letters in the center: **A. & R.** *Alexei and Rodriguez.* He'd never seen anything more beautiful.

The sound of footsteps in the stairwell arrested his attention. Hurriedly, he shoved the lid on and put the box back where he'd found it and picked up his glass. His gaze darted around the room. It was clean and tidy, with all evidence of his extracurricular activities carefully hidden away. Belatedly, he noticed the bed had been made with fresh sheets. His wife must have been down earlier.

The thought had only just registered when she appeared around the corner. He set his drink down on the dresser and swallowed to alleviate his nerves.

"Helen! What are you doing down here? I thought you'd gone to bed."

"I never go to bed before nine." Her lips twisted. "After thirty-two years of marriage, you should know that."

He nodded in acknowledgement and then picked up his drink. She eyed it distastefully. "Would you like one?" he asked.

She snorted. "When have I ever drunk with you, Alexei?"

"We shared a glass of champagne at our wedding," he ventured.

There was a wild, unfocused look in her eyes that made him nervous. He hurriedly took a mouthful of whisky. The alcohol burned a pleasant path down his throat and he breathed a quiet sigh. He wasn't sure what was wrong with his wife. She looked a little on edge.

"So, what did you get up to today?" he asked, striving for normal.

She shrugged and looked around the room. "This and that. I cleaned up your mess and changed your sheets. I disinfected your bathroom, so it's all good for your next little romp."

Her eyes narrowed on his. Her expression was filled with such malice, it stole his breath. *When had she become so angry, so spiteful about his pastime?* It wasn't like she hadn't lived with it for many years.

"What's the matter, Helen?" he asked in a mollifying tone.

She rounded on him, her eyes blazing. "Why do you think *I'm* the one with the problem, Alexei? *You're* the one who likes to sleep with men. You're disgusting! You sicken me! You shouldn't be allowed to walk on God's green earth. It isn't right. It never was. I should have told you from the start. Well, it's not too late to make amends. Don't you worry about that."

A trickle of fear flowed through him, raising the hair on his arms. He stared at her and tried hard not to let it show. "W-what do you mean? What are you going to do?"

She laughed, but it was more of a cackling sound. "It's not what I'm *going* to do, Alexei. It's what I've already done. Three down and many more to go. I won't stop until I've eradicated each and every one of you."

"What are you talking about?"

"This, Alexei!"

With a flourish, she drew something from behind

her back. He hadn't noticed it in her hands until then. He peered at the jersey. Dark purple and gold... Sydney Kings...a number inscribed on the front. Darker stains marked the fabric. *Was that blood?* His heart kicked into overdrive.

"W-what is it, Helen?" His voice sounded tremulous.

She laughed again. "It's a Sydney Kings jersey, Alexei. It belonged to my second victim. Simon McLean was his name. I didn't know that at the time, of course. I thought you would have guessed by now, seeing as I left two gifts for you. Don't you watch the news?"

Alexei's feet were cemented to the floor. He stared at his wife in shock and horror, hardly comprehending what she said. "*You?* You're the one responsible for those horrible killings up on the hill?"

"Yes, and I'm pretty proud of myself, too. Everyone knows it's where men like you go to hook up. It was the perfect place to lie in wait. I snuck up on them when they were totally unaware and clobbered them fair and mighty over the head. Of course, I had to make sure they were dead. A few more blows, a little more suffering... It's no more than what they deserved."

Alexei shook his head, shock still ricocheting through his veins. His wife had just confessed to killing three men. It wasn't Rodriguez at all. *What the hell was going on?*

His brain felt like it was filled with thick fog. His feet refused to move. He had to get out of there, call the police. He had to pretend her words hadn't affected him, keep her talking, sharing the gruesome details. It would disarm her, put her off the scent. If he didn't want to end up her fourth victim, he needed to make sure she believed wholeheartedly he understood where she was coming from.

"You left me the ring and cap as keepsakes," he said in the mildest tone he could manage.

She smiled and moved closer. He did his best not to flinch. With the bloodied jersey mere inches away from his face, she patted his cheek.

"Yes, I wanted to send you a warning. I was through with all of this. For too long, I've allowed this filth to happen, right under my very own roof. Well, no longer, Alexei. Your despicable escapades are coming to an end." Her eyes narrowed menacingly. "I meant what I said, dear husband. I'm going to rid this earth of that scum, one man at a time. All I can say is, watch your back."

Fear erupted in his gut and poured through his veins like acid. "You wouldn't!" he sputtered, aghast at how wrong he'd been.

She smiled coldly and the sight of it iced his blood. "Just try me."

CHAPTER 16

Dear Diary,

Well, that was fun. I've waited a long time to see that expression on Alexei's face. All the time, he's been under the impression that he was the one with the power. Well, we'll see about that.

He nearly wet his pants when he realized what I'd done. To be honest, I thought he would have worked it out weeks ago. It's not like he didn't know the way I felt about him and his den. Did he think I'd sit back quietly and endure such humiliation forever? Not on your life.

Samuel let himself into his condo and tossed the keys onto the counter. Tugging open the fridge, he pulled out a beer and popped the top. Taking a couple of grateful swallows, he sighed heavily.

He'd left Paul in the company of his parents.

They were glad to see him and had welcomed him in, despite the wariness in his father's eyes. Samuel understood his reaction. They'd all been there before. This wasn't the first time Paul had come home, crying for help. But turning their backs on him wasn't a solution. He was their brother and son. And maybe, just maybe he'd make it through this time and come out the other side. They all lived in hope.

He looked around him and for the first time noticed the place was quiet. He wondered where Shelby was. There were no leftovers on the table, no dishes in the sink. It was late. She must have eaten. He should have called her and told her what had happened, but she thought he was meeting a college friend. He'd have to explain why he'd lied to her and he hadn't felt up to it at the time. He wandered down the hallway in search of her.

"Shelby? Are you here?"

A muffled sound behind the bedroom door caught his attention. Leaning against the panel, he turned the doorknob and switched on the light. Shelby lay face down on the bed among the pillows. She was crying. In concern, he hurried to her side.

"Shelby? Honey, what's the matter?" She tensed and then slowly turned to face him. Her face was blotched red with tears.

Another surge of concern rushed through him. "Talk to me, honey. What happened?"

She stared up at him in silence, as if debating what to say. He urged her again. "You're upset about something. I'd like to know. I can't help you if you don't tell me."

Fresh tears welled in her eyes. She opened her mouth and then closed it and then opened it up again.

"I… I wasn't going to say anything. But I waited and waited for you to return. I cooked dinner, but it went cold on the stove. Eventually, I tossed it out and then went off to bed. I saw you, Samuel. I *saw* you."

He frowned down at her. She wasn't making sense. "What do you mean?"

"I saw you down at the Surf Club. I saw you…with that man. You've been with him, haven't you? It's ten o'clock at night. You've been with him all this time."

Her words shocked him, but no more so than her accusatory tone. He'd been with his brother. *Did she really think…?* And then he remembered she didn't know it was Paul and her attitude made more sense. Still, his anger boiled just beneath the surface.

"Tell me what you think you saw, Shelby," he said, forcing himself to keep his voice calm.

She pushed herself up and stared him down. "I saw you hugging and kissing him. It was obvious that you cared. You're gay, aren't you? Just like my father."

Despite his best efforts, his anger found its head. "You have no idea what you saw and I'm nothing like your father," he replied coldly. She flinched, but he wasn't finished.

"You think I've been having an illicit encounter with a former lover. Is that it?"

She held his gaze. Defiance shone in her eyes.

"Answer me!" he shouted. He needed to hear her say it, confirm that she thought the very worst of him.

"Yes."

He shook his head in bewilderment. "Do you even know me at all?" He turned away, shaking his head, upset and mad all at once. *How could she think that of him?* After all they'd shared. It was beyond him.

When he spoke again, his voice was quieter, although his anger and hurt still raged inside. "I think you should go. I'll call a cab. Leave your key."

Shelby stared at him in shock. "Samuel, I think we should talk about this. At the very least, you could explain."

"Explain?" he shot back. "What's there to say? You've already made up your mind. Now, please, just go. I'd like to be alone."

"But—"

"*Go!*" he yelled and saw her jump. Her fear tore him apart. Unable to stay in the room a moment longer, he ripped the door open and left.

Shelby paid the cab driver and wearily climbed out of the taxi. It was going on for eleven-thirty and the late hour, coupled with her crying jag, had left her exhausted. Dragging her feet, she made her way up the front path to the house she shared with her siblings.

The place was in darkness, like she expected at that time of night. Opening the door, she let herself in, trying to be as quiet as possible. Tiptoeing down the hallway, she was guided only by memory and moonlight.

"Is that you, Shelby?"

She squeaked and peered around the corner. Dimitri lay on the couch in the living room in a half-sitting position, like he was on the verge of getting up.

"Dimitri, you frightened me half to death! What are you doing out here?"

He reached over and switched on a lamp that stood on a low table beside the couch. "I couldn't sleep. What are you doing? I thought you were staying with Samuel."

She grimaced and all of a sudden, emotion tightened her throat. "I was," she choked.

In the dimness, she saw Dimitri frown in concern. "Shelby, what is it? Did you two have a fight?"

She nodded. Tears welled up in her eyes. She thought she'd done with crying. Obviously, she was wrong.

Dimitri patted the couch beside him. "Here, come and sit down and tell poor old Dimitri all about it."

She offered him a wobbly smile. "You're neither poor nor old."

He shrugged unrepentantly. "I'm older than you. It automatically makes me wiser, right? Now, quit your complaining and come over here. I want to know what happened to make you cry."

With another sigh, Shelby made her way over to

her brother and threw herself down on the couch. Dimitri put an arm around her shoulders and gave her a squeeze. "Start at the beginning."

"Well, there once was this boy called Samuel."

Dimitri rolled his eyes and Shelby giggled. It felt good to laugh. Snuggling in against her brother's side, she recounted what had happened.

"Who do you think he was meeting?" Dimitri asked when she'd finished.

"He told me it was a college friend. I have no reason to think he'd lie. Then again, he might have been lying through our entire relationship, just like Daddy."

Dimitri frowned the same moment Shelby realized what she'd said.

"What do you mean, 'just like Daddy'?" he asked.

She thought fast. "I...I just meant... You know, Daddy's always talking things up, pretending he's a hotshot lawyer. I mean, he can't possibly have won all those cases. Surely, he doesn't think we believe him."

Dimitri stared at her. "Dad *is* a hotshot lawyer and yes, his success rate is the best in the firm." He twisted until he was facing her, his expression stern. "Now, why the hell don't you tell me what you *really* meant?"

Shelby fidgeted and refused to meet his gaze. She'd promised her parents their secret would stay with her.

"Shelby..."

Dimitri's voice held a note of warning. A moment later, he was tickling her mercilessly. She squealed and squirmed and tried to get away, but his superior strength won out. Gasping for breath, she finally surrendered.

"Okay, okay! Would you quit it! We're going to wake everyone up."

He shrugged unapologetically and waited with an expectant gaze. Biting her lip, Shelby played for more time, but Dimitri was having none of it.

"Tell me, Shelby, or I'll tickle you again." The set of his jaw told her it wasn't an idle threat.

"I can't," she said. "I promised."

"Promised who?"

"Daddy and Momma."

"Oh, so Mom knows, too."

"Yes."

"You know you're going to have to tell me. I'm the oldest kid in this family. I deserve to know."

"You deserve nothing."

"Brat."

They fell silent. A moment later, Dimitri tried again. "It's obviously important, Shelby. Does it concern me?"

She looked at him and shook her head. "No, not really."

He pounced. "Oh, so it does concern me. In that case, you're not leaving this couch until you tell me."

Shelby thought about it. *Would it be so terrible if he knew?* He was carrying a secret of his own. Perhaps knowing their father was also gay might help him come out, at least to his family? She glanced at him. He stared at her with a mutinous expression. She knew he'd carry out his threat. With another sigh, she told him.

Dimitri leaped off the couch, his face pale with shock. "*What? Dad's gay? You have to be kidding!*"

Shelby shook her head. She understood his reaction. She'd felt the same way. "No, I'm not."

"And Mom's known all these years?"

"Yes."

Dimitri wandered dazedly back and forth in front of her, obviously trying to process what she'd said. She remained silent for a while, giving him time to come to terms with her revelations.

"It's the reason I urged you to talk to them. Daddy or Momma, or both," she finally said. "After what they've been through, I think they'd understand and accept that you're gay. You could live your life openly, the way you want to, and Daddy would stop throwing you at girls."

A tiny smile lifted the corners of Dimitri's lips. "There is that." He moved to lean up against the TV cabinet that was filled with books, DVDs and photo frames. "I still can't believe it. How didn't we know? We lived there for years. It was happening in front of our noses."

"I don't know, Dimi. I've asked myself the same questions. It's seems impossible that we didn't have some inkling, but I guess we weren't looking for it, either. On the surface, Momma and Daddy seem happily married—well, as happy as most couples, I guess. There certainly didn't seem to be any underlying tension or arguments that never got resolved. If someone asked me, I'd tell them we grew up in a happy home. Now I think about what was going on and I just shake my head in disbelief."

Once again, Dimitri prowled around the room, picking up random objects and setting them down again without looking at them. "No wonder you wanted me to come out to them," he murmured. "Their secret is way bigger than mine."

"You're right. Having a gay son is nothing compared to the façade they've been living all their lives. You should tell them. You could tell them both together."

"No, I'd rather tell Mom first. She's had a long time to get used to Dad. She'll probably take it better. Then I'll tell Dad."

"All right, suit yourself. I'm just glad you're going to come clean. You can stop losing sleep over it, go back to work and enjoy your life again."

"I might even bring home a boyfriend." He winked.

Shelby picked up a cushion off the couch and threw it at him. He laughed and caught it easily before coming back to sit beside her.

"We still haven't sorted out what you're going to do about Samuel. You love him, right?"

"Yes, with all my heart," she admitted quietly.

"And he loves you," Dimitri added.

"Yes. At least, he used to."

"Good. Well, here's what you're going to do. You're going to go over there tomorrow and apologize for jumping to wild conclusions and ask him to talk about it. Just because you saw him getting up close and personal with a guy, doesn't mean he's gay. And if he is, well, I guess you're better off finding out now, correct?"

She nodded and swallowed a sigh. Dimitri was right. She owed Samuel a chance to explain when both of them were in a mood to listen and if he was gay, she'd best find out soon, before any more hearts got broken.

"What if he doesn't want to talk?" she asked, suddenly paralyzed at the thought.

"Then there's not much you can do about it, but I wouldn't worry too much about that. After all, who can resist Shelby Gianopoulos?"

He leaned over and pulled her into his arms for a hug. She relaxed against him, enjoying the feeling of security she always felt whenever she was with him. He was her big brother. He looked out for her, just like she looked out for him. They were family and family was important.

Samuel was also her family—or very near to it. She'd offer an apology and discuss what had happened. She only hoped he'd be willing to explain.

CHAPTER 17

Alexei pushed the papers around his desk aimlessly and wondered what to do. It was eleven the next morning and he still hadn't called the police. He'd come in to work early, intent on doing the right thing, but hours later, he was still undecided and it was eating away at him.

His wife had admitted to multiple murders and he was vacillating over calling the police. She was a cold-blooded killer who was determined to kill again and she'd as much as said he would be targeted. It was ludicrous to even contemplate keeping quiet and yet, so far, that's exactly what he'd done. He hadn't even called his children.

At the thought of his offspring, he thought of Shelby. She knew more about this than most. Out of all of his children, she'd be the least one shocked. *No, that wasn't fair.* Shelby would be as stunned as he'd been to discover Helen was a murderer.

He stirred uncomfortably in his seat and his hand hovered over the phone. He should just dial the police; tell them the story; get it over with. They'd no doubt come and interview him and then attend his home. Helen would be arrested, dragged off in handcuffs. The neighbors would be aghast, gossiping behind their hands. It would be splashed all over the news and social media. Both his career and Dimitri's would be over. It wouldn't matter that he was a senior partner and Dimitri well on the way to being one. They would never again hold their head up in Sydney society. They'd be lucky if they ever practiced law again. Who wanted a criminal lawyer to defend them when the man's own wife was rotting in jail?

Helen's decisions and actions would ruin them. Life would never be the same again. He'd have to move, probably out of the city, to some backwater town where nobody had ever heard of him or his crazy wife who'd made it her life's ambition to murder gay men.

It was all fucked up and would be that way from the moment he picked up the phone. *But otherwise, what was he to do about it?* He couldn't pretend she hadn't told him that she'd murdered three innocent men. And that there'd be more. By staying silent, he was guilty too, and silence was as good as condoning her actions. That thought was completely unacceptable.

With the thoughts going around and around inside his head, he sighed heavily and finally picked up the phone. When it was answered on the third ring, he gulped in relief.

Shelby had barely touched the "send" button on her phone when it rang in her hand. Her heart leaped. Taking Dimitri's advice to heart, she'd texted Samuel, hoping he was available and ready to talk. *Had he been thinking of her, too? Was he sorry about their fight?*

She barely glanced at the screen before answering the call. "Samuel, I just sent you a message. I—"

"I'm sorry, Shelby. It's your father. Where are you?"

She frowned in confusion. "Oh, Daddy. It's you. I was expecting someone else. Why are you calling?" she finally remembered to ask.

"I need to talk to you, Shelby. Where are you?"

"I'm at home. I don't work until this afternoon. What do you need to talk about? Can't we do it over the phone?"

"I'd rather do it in person. Do you have time to drop by?"

"At the office?" she asked.

"Yes. Is that okay?"

Shelby thought of the plans she'd made to head over to Samuel's condo and have a heart to heart. She could probably swing by her father's office in the city first and then continue on over to Bondi. As long as the discussion with her father didn't go on for too long, she should have plenty of time to fit both of them in before she had to be home to get ready for work. With a bit of luck, Samuel might also be rostered on the evening shift and she could catch up with him again on her break. She was working on the assumption things would work out between them and by the time night fell, they'd be together, reassuring each other of their love, and back on track.

"Um, yes, I guess so. I'll drop by as soon as I'm dressed."

"Dressed? Shelby, it's gone eleven."

"I had a late night, Daddy," she said dryly. "Give me half an hour."

"Great."

Her father sounded relieved and once again, she frowned. "Is everything all right, Daddy?"

He took his time answering. Shelby's concern ratcheted up a notch.

"I'm fine, honey," he eventually replied. "It's not me. It's your mother."

Her heart skipped a beat. "Momma? What's wrong with her?"

"I... I don't want to talk to you about it over the phone, Shelby. Come in to my office. We'll talk here."

"Just tell me she's all right," she pleaded. "She hasn't been taken to hospital, has she? It isn't a heart attack?"

"No, nothing like that."

Her father sounded so definite, Shelby relaxed a little. She could handle anything other than to be told her mother had suffered a heart attack. It was so unlikely, given how fit and healthy she was, but still... People who looked fit and healthy on the outside weren't always that way on the inside. Helen Gianopoulos wouldn't be the first fit and healthy-looking person to have her heart give out.

In record time, Shelby dressed and caught a train into the city. She made it to her daddy's building a little after eleven-thirty. Dressed in a tailored, short-sleeve blouse and a clean pair of cut-off denim shorts, she smiled at Jennifer and asked to see him.

"He's on the phone, Shelby," her father's secretary replied. "I'm sure he won't be too long. Take a seat. I'll let you know when he's free."

Shelby murmured her thanks and took a seat on the architecturally designed two-seater that looked more comfortable than it was. Flicking through the latest edition of *Vogue*, she tried not to think about why her father had asked her to come. Something to do with her mother, but it wasn't a health issue. For the life of her, she couldn't think of anything else.

"Your dad will see you now, Shelby."

Once again, Shelby murmured her thanks then stood and walked the short distance down the hall. She put her hand up to knock on the door that led to his office, but the panel opened beneath her knuckles. Her father stood on the other side.

"Daddy! How are you? I came as quickly as I could. What's going on?"

He ushered her into the room and gave her a

brief hug. "Thanks for coming, Shelby. I didn't know who else to call."

She stared at him and a lump of dread settled into her stomach. "What do you mean, you didn't know who else to call?" she asked cautiously. "What's happened, Daddy?"

As she watched, the color slowly leached out of his face until he looked pale and old and gray. Her alarm increased. *What was going on?* Her father was acting most peculiar and he still hadn't told her what had triggered his strange call. Suddenly impatient, she urged him once again.

"Daddy, I'm meeting Samuel shortly. Can you please just tell me what's so important you couldn't discuss it over the phone? I've made a special trip into the city because you asked me to and now that I'm here, you can't bring yourself to speak to me. I—"

"Your mother confessed to me last night that she killed those three men on the cliffs of Bondi."

Shelby stared at him in stunned amazement. If he'd told her he'd booked a one-way ticket to the red planet, she couldn't have been more shocked.

"I beg your pardon? I don't think I heard you right," she replied and tried on a smile. Her lips felt dry and taut and with the echoes of what he'd just said reverberating in her head...she couldn't pull off any kind of smile.

"You heard me right," her daddy said quietly.

Shelby shook her head. "Hang on, I thought you just said Momma confessed to killing those poor men on the cliffs near North Bondi."

"Yes, that's what I said."

She scoffed in disbelief. "That can't be right. Momma might be a lot of things, but she's definitely not a killer."

Her father sighed and rubbed a hand tiredly across his face. "You're not listening, Shelby. Your mother confessed. She showed me the bloody shirt. Literally. It was a Sydney Kings team jersey, like they reported in the news and it was covered in blood. How would she get such a thing if she didn't have something to do with it?"

All of a sudden, Shelby felt lightheaded. She felt around for something to hold onto and found the back of a chair. Her fingers tightened around it in a death grip. Blood pounded in her ears, making it hard for her to hear. She saw her father's lips moving, but only made out a few of the words.

"Gold...onyx...Melbourne...cap."

"I thought you said you got those things from your...male friend?" she accused.

"I thought I did. He... He told me he'd left me a gift. When I found the cap and ring, I thought they were from him. But now I know different. It wasn't him at all. It was your mother. It was her all along."

"Are you saying Momma took those things off the murder victims and *gave them to you?*" Shelby was appalled at the thought.

"She killed them, Shelby! At least, that's what she said. Never in my life would I have thought her capable of it, but what do you want me to say? She confessed to killing them. She showed me the bloody shirt. She said she was on a mission to rid the world of homosexuals, one gay man at a time. She even threatened *me*. I—"

Shelby tuned out. She had a sudden frantic thought of Dimitri. He'd left home not long before she did, with a promise to talk to their mom. He'd headed off to the train station whistling and with a bounce to his step that Shelby hadn't seen for a long time. Now, the thought of him breaking the news to their mom that he was gay filled her with dread.

"Where's Momma?" she asked.

"I don't know, I guess she's at home. She didn't mention to me she had any appointments. Then again, we haven't been sharing each other's diaries a lot lately. Why do you ask?"

"Dimitri's on his way over there. He's going to tell her he's gay."

"*What?*"

The shock on her father's face might have been laughable if the situation hadn't been so serious. From what her daddy had said, her mother was unstable, perhaps even insane. She'd murdered three innocent people, all because they were gay. Who knew what she might do if Dimitri confessed to being gay, too.

"Dimitri's gay, Daddy. He has been for a long time—probably forever. It's the reason he's not interested in girls and why he gets annoyed with you every time you discuss them. He's on his way home right now to come out to Momma. He thought she might be more understanding than you."

"You're right, I don't understand!" her father

bellowed, looking hurt and confused and angry all at once.

"Daddy, this is not the time for your theatrics. We'll talk about it later. Right now, I need to call Dimitri and tell him not to say anything to Momma. Whether she killed those men or not, to tell you she did is way past weird. There's something wrong with her. I don't know whether she's insane or delusional or, God heavens, if she's actually telling the truth, but I do know we need to get Dimi out of there while we can."

"Yes, of course," her father replied in a tone slightly less angry.

Shelby picked up her handbag and riffled through it for her phone. "I'll call Dimi. You call the police."

"The police?"

Her head snapped up in surprise. She stared at him. "Yes, Daddy. The police. They need to become involved. You're going to hate the publicity, but we can't deal with this on our own. What if Momma *did* kill those people? We can't pretend she never said anything. She could kill again. Let the police handle it. They're the professionals. They're used to this kind of thing."

Her father shook his head, frowning. "But the media will have a field day. I can't take the risk—"

"Just do it!" she cried and scrolled frantically through her contacts for Dimitri's number.

She glanced over at her father and saw him pick up his phone. A little of the tension went out of her. And then her call to her brother went through to his voicemail and the ache in her stomach intensified. Leaving a brief message for him to keep his mouth shut until he'd spoken to her, she ended the call.

"I'm heading over there," she said and started across the office for the door.

Her father nodded and pointed to the phone which he now held up to his ear. She gave him a thumbs-up and left, all the time, praying Dimitri was safe.

Rodriguez Gomez listened to the voicemail message left by Alexei for the fifth time. He smiled with contentment. Alexei wanted to meet with him, to talk. A surge of excitement flooded Rodriguez's veins and he nearly jumped out of his seat. The woman next to him on the bus threw him the evil eye and he forced himself to settle down again.

Alexei wanted to talk to him urgently and this time of the day, that meant at his office. Things didn't get any better! Rodriguez had never been allowed anywhere near Alexei's place of work. It was off limits, like so many other public places. But that was all about to change. Alexei was finally ready to declare to the world they were in love! Rodriguez couldn't believe it! He'd even worn his favorite purple trousers and silky lime-green shirt for the occasion. Alexei loved that shirt. And Rodriguez loved Alexei.

The bus came to a halt at Martin Place.

Rodriguez jumped off and made a beeline for his lover's building. Impatiently, he threaded his way through the throngs of people enjoying an early lunch. He passed the fountain and thought about how the water rushed in time with the joy that raced through his veins. Soon, very soon, the whole world would know Alexei Gianpoulos was his.

The building that housed his lover's office towered above him. His heart leaped with excitement. With joyful strides, he entered the elevator and pressed the button for the fifteenth floor. With every passing second, his anticipation grew. The moment he'd been waiting for was about to happen. The elevator *dinged* and the doors slid open and all at once, he found himself in a wide open office space furnished with a single reception desk and a small couch. He went up to the woman who sat behind the counter.

"Excuse me, I'm here for Alexei Gianopoulos."

The woman looked over her glasses at him and frowned. "Do you have an appointment?"

"No. Yes. That is, Alexei needs to speak to me."

The woman continued to regard him with a stern expression on her face. "I see. And you are...?"

"Rodriguez," he supplied with a wide smile. "Rodriguez Gomez."

She lowered her gaze and picked up a phone and spoke quietly into the hand piece. A moment later, she ended the call and looked back up at him.

"I'm sorry, Mr Gomez. Mr Gianopoulos has

declined to see you at this time. Perhaps you could make another appointment?"

Rodriguez frowned in confusion. "Declined to see me? No! He can't do that! He sent me a message. He told me he wanted to talk to me!"

The woman remained unmoved. "That might be so, Mr Gomez, but I'm sorry, you'll have to do it some other time. Right now, Mr Gianopoulos is busy."

Rodriguez stared at her in incomprehension. *This couldn't be happening!* Pain and anger surged through him. He refused to allow Alexei to ruin this day. He moved closer to the receptionist and leaned over the counter as far as he could go.

"You tell your boss to get his ass out here or I'll kick up such a din, he'll wish to God he'd done as I said."

The woman's eyes widened, but she didn't move.

"Pick up that phone and call him!" Rodriguez yelled, his temper getting the better of him. *"Now!"*

———————

Jared Buchanan re-read Maureen Nelson's statement for the umpteenth time, trying to pinpoint something he might have missed. The crime scene photos from all three murders were spread out on the desk in front of him. Maureen was sure the person she'd passed on the path immediately below where the murders had taken place was a man, but she was basing this presumption purely on the physical size of the person she'd seen. It was equally possible the person could have been a woman, albeit a large one.

The fact that the first blows all came from behind was significant. It meant that it was more likely the perpetrator hadn't engaged the victims in conversation, or anything else. It was like the perp had lain in wait for someone to come along and then had pounced.

A woman killer fit this scenario better. The area was a well-known meeting place for gay men. A woman would stand out, be remembered, especially at that time of the night. A man could have simply pretended to be there for sex, like the victims presumably were. A man, engaged in conversation with the victims, wouldn't have had to come up from behind. They could have simply taken the victims by surprise in the middle of a faux sexual act, catching them off guard.

But Jared had no proof either way and that was really pissing him off. He clenched his fists and tightened his jaw with irritation. The phone at his elbow rang. He absently picked it up.

"Bondi Detectives. This is Detective Sergeant Buchanan speaking."

"Is this the detective handling the investigation of the Cliff-top Killer?"

The voice was surprisingly calm. Jared immediately tensed. "Yes, what can I do for you?"

There was silence on the other end. Finally, he heard a heavy sigh. "My name is Alexei Gianopoulos. I'm a senior partner at Harton and

Wentworth. I think my wife might be the person you're looking for."

Jared held his cool, even as his heart rate took off at a gallop. The police received prank calls all the time. This one might be no different. He refused to get excited until he knew all the facts and even then, he'd want hard evidence.

"What makes you say that, Mr Gianopoulos?"

"She has the trophies, the things you were looking for."

Jared's excitement increased. Dragging a pen and a pad toward him, he began to scribble some notes.

"Can you come to the station, Mr Gianopoulos?"

"No, I need to get home. I'm afraid my wife might do something stupid. You see, my son—"

The man broke off. Jared frowned. "What about your son?"

"Look, don't worry about my son. You need to look into Helen, my wife. I think she's dangerous."

"I really need to take a statement from you, Mr Gianopoulos. If you can't come to the station, perhaps I can meet you at home."

Jared heard another heavy sigh in his ear. "All right, I guess that's the way it has to be. I'll see you there."

After giving Jared his details, the man ended the call. Jared stared at the phone in his hand in bemusement. The caller had sounded elderly. Surely it wasn't possible an elderly woman had caused the trauma to his victims? Then again, perhaps the wife was significantly younger. It was always a possibility.

Knowing there was nothing to be done but to go and attend the home in Bondi, Jared picked up his keys, informed his boss where he was going and asked one of the other detectives to ride along. Ten minutes later, they were on the road.

No sooner had Alexei hung up the phone and it rang again. He picked it up and answered it.

"Yes, Jennifer?"

"I'm sorry, sir. I have a man by the name of Rodriguez Gomez out here. He says you wanted to see him."

Alexei was filled with a surge of nerves and apprehension. *Rodriguez was here! At his office! What the hell was he going to do?* When he'd left the message for him, he'd expected the man to call him, not turn up at his place of work. *Shit.* The day was going to hell faster than he could keep up. One thing he knew, he didn't have time to deal with Rodriguez.

"Tell him I'm busy, Jennifer. He'll need to make another appointment."

"All right, sir."

Hanging up the phone, Alexei pushed away from his desk and began to pace his office. His gut was filled with dread and an increasing sense of foreboding. He needed to get home and ascertain that Dimitri was all right. He needed to be there when the police arrived.

A commotion outside his door caught his

attention. Straining to hear through the sound of his blood rushing through his ears, he heard Rodriguez yelling. *Great. Just what he needed. A scene outside his office.* Picking up his jacket and keys, with a sigh of resignation, he opened the door and headed out. Rodriguez spied him the moment he appeared in the hallway and came striding toward him.

"Alexei! There you are! I tried to tell that woman you wanted to see me."

From the corner of his eye, Alexei saw Jennifer push away from her chair and hurry in his direction. He held up his hand to ward Rodriguez off.

"I'm sorry, Rodriguez. You shouldn't have come here. I'm busy. Right now, I have a family emergency to attend to. If you don't mind—"

"I'm your family, too, Alexei! You can't keep shutting me out! I *love* you! I'd do anything for you! Don't you understand? I love you, Alexei! And I know you love me, too!"

Alexei froze. Jennifer's face filled with shock and horror. Rodriguez stared from one to the other, tears running down his face. With nowhere to turn and nothing to say, Alexei pushed past both of them without another word and escaped into the elevator, his face burning with humiliation.

Shelby tapped her finger impatiently against the glass window of the cab and wished for the tenth time that Dimitri would answer his phone. She'd even tried her mother's number, but it too went unanswered. She had no way of knowing if her mother were home or if Dimitri had even arrived. There was nothing for it but to go over there herself and pray she could prevent a catastrophe.

She clung to the hope her mother had been lying when she'd bragged to Shelby's father about killing those men. It didn't make an iota of sense and Shelby couldn't imagine her mother doing such a thing—not in her wildest dreams. No, her daddy must be mistaken, or else her momma had said it to seek attention. Why she'd use something so horrible and gruesome to make her point, Shelby didn't know.

Her phone buzzed, indicating a new text message. As the sound registered in her mind, she frantically scrambled through her handbag and pulled it out. She stared at the screen.

Samuel.

Her pulse leaped. In all the panic of the past little while, Samuel and their fight had skipped her mind. It seemed like a lifetime had passed since she'd texted him. *Had it only been a few hours?*

She read the text message and her heart melted.

I remember someone telling me once that if u truly love someone, u can forgive them anything. I love u more than I thought possible, Shelby. Let's talk.

She blinked back a sudden rush of tears. Too bad she was on her way to her parents' house to deal with God knows what. All she wanted to do was head straight for Samuel's place, clear up their misunderstanding and make things right again. *He still loved her!* She was flooded with relief and joy. She hurriedly typed a reply.

I love u 2. Would love 2 talk right now, but I'm on my way over 2 my parents' place in Bondi. A slight family emergency. I might b an hour or 2. R u home?

A few minutes later, she received a reply.

Yes. Is there anything I can do? Do u want me 2 come over?

She pondered the question. She had no idea what she'd find when she got there. It could be nothing, or she could walk in upon a shocked and devastated mother who could possibly turn violent and a brother who didn't know where to turn. Dimi definitely wouldn't be prepared for their mother to go off the deep end. Shelby had encouraged him to talk to the woman, to tell her he was gay. If there were even the slightest truth to her being involved in the hate crimes dogging their neighborhood, Dimi could be in real trouble.

Should she get Samuel involved in something that had the potential to turn so ugly? Would he stick around if her mother turned out to be a killer? Would she still want him if he didn't? Blowing her breath out between her lips in indecision, she finally sent off a reply.

Thx. That would b good.

After texting him the address details, she tossed her phone back into her handbag and counted the minutes until the cab arrived.

CHAPTER 18

Dimitri stared at his mother and awaited her reaction. This wasn't going at all well. Silently, he cursed Shelby for insisting his parents were in the mood to accept his sexuality. His mother had remained silent and stony-faced ever since he'd told her.

"Mom, say something. Please. I'm gay. It's not a death sentence."

"It's against the bible, Dimitri; against the teachings of Jesus; against everything you were ever taught. Why, Dimitri? *Why?*"

Her cry of anguish pierced his heart. He never meant for it to be like this. He never meant to hurt anyone. Hell, it had been easier living a lie, keeping the truth to himself. He should never have listened to Shelby.

"I'm sorry, Mom. I shouldn't have told you. I didn't mean to upset you. I thought you might understand. Given that Dad..."

Heat suffused his cheeks. His mother's gaze narrowed menacingly. He looked away.

"What about Dad?" she growled.

Dimitri stared at her in surprise and felt even more embarrassed. She wasn't going to make things easy. The sound of his phone ringing momentarily distracted him, but he ignored it and cleared his throat.

"Shelby told me about it...about Dad...and his den."

Anger blazed in his mother's eyes. He took a step backward. Even with the wide kitchen counter between them, he suddenly felt unsafe. He'd never seen that expression on her face before—so wild and fierce and angry. Shelby hadn't once indicated his mother detested his father's homosexuality. In fact, he'd gotten the distinct impression that she'd come to accept it over the years. She'd stuck by him, after all. That had to mean something. But from the look of fury on her face, she was anything but accepting.

"Shelby told you all about it, did she?" his mother said in a weird, sarcastic, sing-song voice.

He shrugged in confusion, at a loss to explain his mother's odd reaction. It was like she'd been taken over by some evil spirit, someone who looked like his mother, but behaved like a stranger.

"Yes, Mom. She did. And I thought you were okay about it. It's the reason I finally found the courage to tell you I'm gay. I thought you'd understand." His phone rang again and he swore under his breath. He didn't have time to deal with phone calls.

His mother's face swelled up with anger, turning

her cheeks crimson. With a hand on either side of the chopping board, she leaned over the counter.

"You thought I'd be okay with it, that I'd understand. Ha!" she scoffed mirthlessly. Without warning, she leaned even closer, until her face was inches away. He could hear the breath whistling between her teeth.

"Your father's a homosexual, an abomination against God and you thought I'd be *okay* with my oldest child telling me he's gay?"

This was a mistake. He should never have entertained the idea that his parents would understand. He cursed Shelby silently. *Wait until he caught up with her...* All of a sudden, he wanted to get away from there and try and forget the past humiliating moments, but his mother's narrowed gaze held him in place. Her breath sounded harsh in the stillness. She bared her teeth at him and he tensed in shock. It was like being close to a feral animal. One wrong move, and he'd be ripped to shreds.

Which was plain ridiculous. This was his mother, the woman who loved him and who he loved in return. She might be a little unhappy about his revelation, but he was sure she wouldn't do him harm. His gaze slid to the large butcher's knife that lay within reach on the chopping board. A pile of salad vegetables had been diced and sliced and sat in a bowl next to it. She must have been in the middle of preparing lunch before he stopped by.

The knowledge reassured him and he eased out a breath he hadn't realized he'd been holding. Preparing lunch was such a normal, everyday thing for her to do. She wasn't a raving lunatic who could turn on him at any minute. She was his mother and she'd just suffered an enormous shock. He could understand her going off the deep end for a bit. He'd done such a good job of concealing his secret, even his mother had been caught off guard. She just needed some time to get used to it. That's all it was.

"I'm sorry, Momma," he said.

He hadn't called her that in years, but it was a term he'd used as a child and he hoped it would remind her of the young boy he'd been and in some respects, still was. He loved her and needed her approval. *Who wanted to be at odds with their family, and least of all, their mother?* Certainly not him.

"Sorry? You're *sorry?*" she screamed. "How can you be sorry? If you were sorry, you would have married a nice Greek girl years ago, like I told you. You'd have three of four children and be living the dream, living the way God intended. I wouldn't have to go through the agony of knowing my son's headed straight for the fires of hell. It's bad enough knowing that's where your father's going. But he made his choices many years ago and I had nothing to do with that. He was that way inclined from the beginning, only, he hid it from me even longer than you."

She pulled at her hair and stared at him beseechingly, anguish and pain in her eyes. "Why did you have to tell me, Dimitri? Why couldn't you be more like him? I don't understand it. Now I have to get rid of you, too."

Dimitri regarded her in confusion, certain he'd misheard. "What are you talking about, Momma?"

Instead of replying, his mother took hold of the knife. Rounding the kitchen counter, she slowly advanced upon him. He backed away until he came up hard against the wall and still she came at him. His phone started ringing again and all of a sudden, he was desperate to answer it, but his mother's eyes gleamed with a light that seemed so evil, he stood rooted to the spot. He shivered in fear.

"What are you doing, Momma? Please, put the knife down."

"It's too late for that, Dimitri. You should never have opened your mouth. I was quite happy not knowing you share your father's disgusting predilection. But you had to go and spoil it and now I have to remove you from my life and from the lives of everyone else you might contaminate. For years, I've put up with this filth from your father, allowing it in my home, but not anymore and especially not from you."

She made a sudden move toward him and the knife flashed in her hands. The air whizzed past his face as she stabbed at him.

"*Fuck! Mom!* What the hell do you think you're doing? Stop it!"

He dodged a second attempt and debated his chances of taking the knife from her. She was as tall as him, maybe taller and weighed almost as much. Her rage had given her extra strength. When she came at him a third time and the blade only narrowly missed, his fear morphed into terror. He was going to be stabbed to death by his mother and there was nothing he could do about it.

Shelby tossed the driver a handful of bills and jumped out of the cab. Half-running up the driveway, she paused to catch her breath. The house was quiet and peaceful, like it always was. The pansies and petunias in the front garden were in full bloom, scenting the air with their sweet perfume. The midday sun was high in the sky and shone warmly on her face. If she didn't feel so taut inside, she'd take a moment to appreciate the perfect day.

Dimitri's Audi was parked outside the door of the double garage. Her heart skipped a beat. *He was here.* She could only assume her mother was, too, seeing as both garage doors were closed. It was her mother's usual practice to leave her side open if she went out. She looked around for her father's car, but it was nowhere in sight. Either he'd also parked in the garage, or she'd beaten him there.

Shelby wondered if Dimitri had received her messages and if he'd kept his mouth closed. In quiet desperation, she prayed that she'd walk in and find a scene no more contentious than her brother arguing with her mother over the secret herbs and spices that needed to go into the sausage, or some other such nonsense.

Easing open the front door, she held her breath. All was quiet. And then she heard a scream that raised the hairs on her arms and made everything inside her go cold.

———

Samuel took his foot off the accelerator and crawled forward, checking the house number of the address Shelby had given him over the phone. One mansion after another filled his vision. Bondi was an affluent suburb and there was some serious money invested on this street. He'd known her father was a prominent lawyer, but he had no idea she came from this kind of wealth. Still, untold riches didn't necessarily guarantee happiness. Just ask Paul Munro or Helen Gianopoulos.

The thought sobered him. He couldn't imagine discovering his father was gay and had been that way pretty much his entire life. He wondered how Shelby had been able to take the news so calmly. Okay, maybe not calmly, but she seemed to have accepted it a whole lot easier than he would have. He admired her for that.

He spied a shiny, black Audi R8 in the driveway and parked his Aston Martin behind it. The car couldn't belong to Shelby. He'd never seen her in a car like that. He assumed she'd taken public transport, like she usually did.

He'd teased her about it after he discovered

she owned a BMW Roadster, but she only laughed and said it was so difficult to get parking around Bondi Beach, that it was easier to leave her car at home.

He wondered who owned the Audi. No doubt it was one of the members of her family. She'd told him she was dealing with a family emergency and despite the negative connotations, he looked forward to meeting them. An emergency probably wasn't the best of circumstances to meet his future wife's family, but then again, Shelby wouldn't have told him to meet her here if the emergency were truly something she couldn't handle. He couldn't imagine her wanting him to meet her family for the first time under less-than-pleasant conditions.

Filled with curiosity, he set the park brake, switched off the ignition, unclipped his seatbelt and then climbed out of the car. With casual strides, he made his way up the wide cobblestone path that led to the front door.

———————

Alexei's gut clenched once again on the nerves that hadn't let up since Shelby had left his office. His promised phone call to the police was the least of his problems. Rodriguez had proclaimed his love to the world and by now, everyone at Harton & Wentworth would know about it. He'd never be able to show his face back there again.

He fought against the overwhelming devastation that filled him at the thought. For so long, his life had been perfect. Now, everything was falling apart. Every mile brought him closer to his home and the debacle he might or might not find. His charmed life would be laid bare for all to see, including the police. The tension and apprehension in his gut increased.

Had he done the right thing? What if his wife was innocent? He'd have made a spectacle of himself and his family for nothing. He only hoped the detective he'd spoken to would be discreet and question his wife with as little fanfare as possible. He clung to the possibility that she'd made the whole thing up and had somehow fabricated the evidence. That kept him moving forward.

Turning onto his street, he automatically turned his head to look at the view. The Pacific Ocean was spread out before him, sparkling blue, dancing in the sunshine. The beach was dotted with swimmers and further out, surfers bobbed up and down on the waves. It was a perfect spring day. He wondered how long it would stay that way.

Slowing his Mercedes S-Class coupe, he pulled into his driveway. Dimitri's Audi was parked in front of the garage, blocking the door. He still couldn't believe his oldest son was gay. All the times he'd pressured the boy to find a nice girl and settle down and he'd been forcing him in the same direction Alexei's life had taken. And look how that had worked out? He made a sound of despair in the back of his throat and switched off the ignition, forcing the thoughts from his mind.

Another vehicle was parked behind Dimitri's Audi. Alexei frowned. The silver Aston was unfamiliar. Shelby hadn't said anything about buying a new car. He wondered who owned it.

Taking a moment to gather himself, he stared down at his hands where they rested on the steering wheel. There was still no sign of the police, and for that he was grateful. It would give him time to speak with Helen and determine to the best of his ability whether she was really a cold-blooded killer or if she'd played him for a fool. He could almost hear her disbelieving laughter as he informed her he'd called the police. Given a choice, he preferred that the joke was on him. The alternative was simply unthinkable.

Jared glanced at his partner and raised a single eyebrow in silent query.

"Talk about ostentatious," Detective Oliver Stacks remarked, giving voice to Jared's thoughts.

Jared looked out the window of the unmarked squad car and did a quick calculation in his head of the net worth of the owners who resided behind the impressive walls of the grand manors that lined the street. Apparently Alexei Gianopoulos also lived here. It was obvious his criminal law business was thriving.

The wide, cobblestone driveway ended at two

double garage doors. Several hundred thousand dollars' worth of vehicles were parked outside. Jared pulled the squad car in behind a Mercedes. He could see their reflection in the other car's shiny, champagne-gold exterior.

"I wouldn't mind being their car dealer," Oliver murmured.

Jared silently agreed. Throwing off his seatbelt, he collected his jacket off the back seat. Stepping out of the car, he slid his jacket on and then turned back to his partner.

"Let's go and see what all the fuss is about."

Shelby crept down the hallway toward the kitchen, in the direction where the awful sound had come from. Her heart pounded and her palms were damp. She had no idea what she was going to find. She wished she could call Samuel and tell him to hurry along, but Dimitri might be in trouble and every second could make the difference.

"Momma! *Nooo!*"

The terrified scream made her jump and she took off at a run. She dashed into the kitchen, her breath coming fast. Her mother stood over Dimitri wielding a vicious-looking knife. He was already on the floor. Blood stained his shirt front. The knife came up and plunged into his chest again. Shelby screamed.

She wasn't aware that she'd moved, but all of

a sudden, her feet propelled her forward. She screamed again, and this time, the sound of it seemed to penetrate the angry haze that surrounded her mother.

"Momma! *Stop!* What are you *doing?*"

"Stay away, Shelby! This is between me and your brother. It has nothing to do with you. He's not my first and he won't be my last. This whole abomination was started by your father and it will end with him, too. You mark my words."

"I don't think so, Helen."

Shelby turned around and gasped at the sight of her father. She'd never been more relieved in her life. He stood in the doorway looking so calm and collected. She wondered how he could be like that when it was obvious her mother had gone insane. Dimitri was bleeding all over the floor and their mother was determined to finish him off.

A movement behind her father snagged her attention and she gasped again at the sight of Samuel. *Oh, God! He was here!* A witness to the madness. She would have died with embarrassment if the situation hadn't been so serious. She looked from her father to Samuel and relief won out.

At least there were people who could help her, help Dimitri. Together, they ought to be able to restrain her mother. Her father stepped forward and held out his hand to his wife, seeming to read Shelby's mind.

"Give me the knife, Helen. I don't know what the hell you think you're doing, but you're not helping anyone by hurting Dimitri."

"Like hell I'm going to give you the knife," her mother snarled. "I've started out on this journey and I mean to see it through. I'm pleased you arrived home early, Alexei. You've saved me the trouble of tracking you down. I waited so patiently for the other three."

She chuckled and it was filled with such evil, it sent shivers running down Shelby's spine. She stood rooted to the spot in horrified silence as her mother continued.

"Like a hunter waiting for prey, I stood silently in the darkness, my weapon at the ready. The first time it was a tire wrench, but it was too hard to dispose of. The next couple of times I got smarter and found a weapon on the cliff. A trusty tree branch did the trick and it was easier to get rid of. After I finished them off, I cut up the branch and put it in the green waste bin where it was taken away by the council."

Shelby stared at her mother in disbelief. She didn't recognize the woman who stood so close. She heard the words coming from her mother's mouth, but refused to comprehend. Her mother wasn't a monster. She was good and kind and generous. She always had time for her children, to talk through their disappointments and challenges. It had been that way for as long as Shelby could remember.

Where had that woman gone? Shelby couldn't come up with an answer. Her mind had blanked out, refused to work. Even breathing was a struggle.

Her mother's gaze suddenly narrowed on

Shelby's father. "I was just telling Dimitri, it's going to end with you, Alexei. I hope you're ready to descend to the fires of hell, because that's where you're going. God has spoken. There's no room in heaven for the likes of you. Or *you*."

She spun on her heel and stabbed the air with the knife in Dimitri's direction. Shelby cried out in fear.

"No, Momma! Leave him alone! Please, put the knife down."

"Put the fucking knife down, Helen," her father remonstrated, his voice harsh.

"Please, Mrs Gianopolous, you need to step back and put the knife down." The final plea came from Samuel.

He stepped even closer and Shelby blinked in horror. He was within arm's distance of her mother. The woman could spin back around and be on him in an instant. He'd never survive such a close-up attack. Her heart pounded. Sweat trickled into her eyes. Time stood still while her mother appeared to consider her options.

The faintest *click* reached Shelby's ears and a moment later, all hell broke loose. Two armed police officers stormed through the doorway, guns pointed at her mother.

"Drop the knife! *Now!*" one of the officers yelled.

Her mother's eyes widened momentarily in surprise and then she blinked and smiled. "Well, well, well. Who do we have here?" she asked, her conversational tone at odds with the wild light in her eyes.

"Drop the knife, lady," the other officer yelled.

"*Tut, tut, tut,* Officers. Go back to where you came from. I have everything under control here. You see, this is my family, my husband, my daughter, my son. The surfer is my daughter's boyfriend. As you can see, we're doing all right on our own. We don't need your interference, so get on with you."

The officers shot each other a quick glance before directing their attention back to Shelby's mom.

"Put the knife down, lady. I won't ask you again."

Once again, her mother smiled. "I think you've been watching far too much television, Officer. I don't have to do as you say. This is my home. I'm king of the castle and my husband is the queen." She giggled at her joke. Nobody joined in.

"I can do whatever I want," she continued. "Right now, I'm dealing with a problem and you're in the way. Now, you either leave while you still can, or accept the consequences."

The officers looked at her in amazement and Shelby understood how they felt. Her mother was out-and-out crazy. There wasn't the slightest bit of doubt. She hardly dared to move a muscle, lest her mother turn on her and do something unthinkable. She'd already attacked Dimitri. Shelby didn't want to be next.

"We're not going to ask you again, lady. Drop the knife or we'll be forced to subdue you," the older officer said.

Yet again, her mother chuckled. "Oh, officers!

You're so funny. You're going to subdue me! Hilarious!"

The officer who'd spoken made a move for the canister of pepper spray at his hip. At the same time, Shelby's mother lunged toward her father with the knife held high. She sliced the wicked looking blade through the air and her arm came arcing down.

Shelby watched in slow motion as the knife sliced through the air. It plunged into her father's chest. Seconds later, blood flowered across his shirtfront. Her father screamed in agony and Shelby's screams matched his.

The police officers drew their guns and a moment later, two sharp reports filled the air. Shelby screamed again. The smell of gunpowder burned her eyes, there was yelling everywhere. Samuel grabbed her around the shoulders and dragged her from the scene.

Gasping and crying, she tried hard to stop herself from going into shock. The carnage in the kitchen was forever burned into her mind. Her teeth were chattering, her stomach taut. Any moment, she thought she might be sick.

"Dimitri! Daddy!" she gasped and Samuel pulled her close.

"Stay here, okay?" he said. "I'm going to check on them."

She stared at him, barely comprehending, but before she could speak, he disappeared the way they'd come. Sirens sounded in the distance. She sank slowly to the floor.

CHAPTER 19

Dear Diary,

I had it all planned out. It was blessed by God. My plan to clean up His backyard. It was my job to eradicate this scourge from the earth. My actions were entirely selfless. I did it all for them—the good, God-fearing Christians who deserve to live in a better world.

I survived two bullet wounds from over-eager police officers. Stupid thugs. The good news is, I lived to tell the tale. The paramedics dismissed my injuries, saying I suffered no more than a couple of flesh wounds, but I know different. It was a miracle that I survived—nothing more, nothing less.

The prosecutor wants me to plead guilty. He's told my lawyer if I contest the charges and go to trial, I'll be found guilty and die in jail. Nothing's more certain, or so he says. I'm not so sure. Like I said, I have God on my side and God can do anything. Just ask Him.

Shelby sat beside the hospital bed and held her brother's hand. His injuries hadn't been life-threatening like her father's. The ICU staff were still restricting her father's visitors, so she chose to spend the long, idle hours with Dimitri. She didn't mind. Watching his chest rise and fall slowly and rhythmically brought her comfort. The two stab wounds he'd received to his shoulder and stomach missed everything vital, but he'd still lost quite a bit of blood and required surgery to repair damage to muscle, nerves and other tissue. The doctors had assured her he'd pull through, but she'd be relieved when he opened his eyes and acknowledged her presence.

The door to Dimitri's private hospital room opened and Shelby looked up. Samuel stood in the doorway, looking almost as disheveled as she felt. A rush of warmth and relief went through her at the sight of him. After everything that had happened, it was so good to have someone to lean on.

"Samuel, thank you for coming."

He came toward her and bent low to kiss her tenderly on the lips. "You've been here for hours. Why don't you let me sit with him for a while so you can take a break? The coffee downstairs is passable and you could grab a bite to eat. I would have brought something up with me, but I wasn't sure what you'd want." He glanced toward Dimitri who lay still and silent in the bed. "Has he woken yet?"

"No, but the doctors are happy about how things went. They say he's resting peacefully, rather than being unconscious. I guess that's a good thing."

"Of course, it is. He's a lucky guy."

She grimaced. "No, my daddy's the one who got lucky. If you hadn't been on hand to perform CPR, he would have died. The paramedics took ages to get there. He would have bled to death. He owes you his life. *I* owe you his life."

Samuel shrugged. "I did what anyone would have done. How is he, anyway? Still in the ICU?"

"Yes, they're keeping him there overnight, at least. They won't move him out until he regains consciousness. He lost a lot of blood. They gave him a transfusion. They're hopeful he'll pull through, but they're watching him closely. He had a heart attack in the back of the ambulance."

Samuel squeezed her hand comfortingly. "Yes, I heard. I made enquires before I came up here. He's under the care of the best heart specialist at the Sydney Harbour Hospital. He's going to be all right."

Shelby listened to Samuel's reassurances and was grateful for them. He was a doctor. He knew what he was talking about. She allowed herself the tiniest sigh of relief. Samuel dragged another chair up beside the bed and once again, reached for her hand.

"We haven't talked about what happened between us, Shelby, before your mom went crazy. Are you up to it?"

A rush of nerves filled her stomach, but she nodded. If they had any chance for a future, they needed to resolve the outstanding issues.

Tightening her hold on his hand, she drew in a deep breath and began.

"Let me start by saying how sorry I am for going off at you like that. I spoke rashly, without thought, without giving you a chance to explain. It wasn't fair."

Samuel regarded her somberly. "No, it wasn't. But you're not entirely to blame. I wasn't honest with you and I regret that."

She held his gaze. "That man you met, he wasn't a college friend, was he?"

"No, he wasn't."

She drew in a breath and forged on. "Okay. So, who was he?"

"Paul."

She frowned, searching her memory for a match. "Paul?"

"My brother."

If he'd said the man had been his dealer, Shelby couldn't be more surprised. She stared at him. "Your *brother*? But... The text was from someone called Jim Bob." She blushed and then admitted, "I read it while you were in the shower."

"Jim Bob's a nickname, something left over from our childhood."

Shelby accepted his explanation and then remembered something else. "I thought you said you weren't in contact with him, that you hadn't seen him for a long time."

"You're right. I did. But he texted me yesterday and asked if we could meet. He sounded...so lonely. I told you earlier how I've struggled with the choices he's made—hell, I *still* struggle with them—

but when it comes down to it, he's my brother. I can't turn my back on him. Never again." He drew in a breath and then blew it out on a sigh. "So, I agreed to meet with him."

She shook her head in confusion. "I don't understand, why didn't you tell me? Why make up some story about an old college friend?"

Samuel grimaced. "I don't know. I guess I didn't want you plying me with questions I wasn't ready to answer, especially after what I'd already told you about Paul. His life for the past decade or more has been so different than mine. He's a drug addict who lives on the streets. He has had no interest in getting clean. His friends are other addicts." Samuel shook his head. "I wasn't ready for you to meet him, but I needed to see him again. I hoped that maybe this time, he'd be ready to accept help, to do what he needed to do to get his life back on track." He paused and studied her. "It was arrogant of me, but that's what I thought. So I met with him, we talked, *really* talked and by the end of it, I'd convinced him to give rehab another go. He'd reached a critical point himself. He was ready for reason."

"Oh, Samuel!" she breathed, filled with a sense of amazement. "How wonderful."

Samuel smiled softly. "Yes, it is. And this time, I think he might just stick it out. He seemed more ready, more willing to make changes in his life."

"Where is he?" she asked.

"He's staying with Mom and Dad. They're

making the arrangements for him. Fortunately, they've managed to pull some strings. He'll go in next week."

"I'm glad," she said. "For all of you."

Samuel moved closer and took both her hands in his. "Shelby, the first time you accused me of being gay, I thought we'd discussed it and you accepted my explanation. Then you saw me with Paul and you immediately jumped to the same conclusion, despite everything I'd said."

Shelby squirmed with embarrassment. She was ashamed of how quickly she'd judged him, especially given everything they'd shared. She kept her gaze lowered to the floor.

"Shelby, look at me."

His quiet command had her lifting her head. She met his steady gaze.

"If we're ever going to make it, we need to trust each other. Without that, we have nothing. I'm not just talking about the gay thing. I'm talking about anything. We discussed your concern weeks ago. I was shocked when you raised it again in a different context. It's why I was so hurt and angry. It was obvious you hadn't believed me the first time."

"See, that's the thing," she replied. "I *did* believe you. At least, I thought I did. Then I saw you with Paul—who I thought was a college friend—and I went a little crazy. I remembered what Ian had said and I didn't know what to think. For weeks, I've been dealing with family secrets—first Dimitris' and then Daddy's. I guess my head was still in a bit of a spin. It's no excuse, but... They both had so many secrets, Samuel. I... I didn't want you to have secrets, too."

His expression flooded with understanding and tenderness filled his eyes. "It's all right, Shelby. I get it. I really do. Next time, though, if you're concerned I'm cheating on you with a man, can you please just talk to me about it?"

She laughed. Samuel cupped her cheek in his hand and kissed her softly on the lips. The love and tenderness in his touch sent a shard of need rushing through her. She opened her mouth and deepened the kiss. A noise from the direction of the bed brought her back to awareness. She broke off the kiss with a gasp as she realized exactly what it meant.

"Dimi!"

"Shelby? What happened? Where am I?"

He sounded dazed and groggy, but at least he was conscious. She stood and pushed her chair out of the way and moved to stand beside him. Taking his hand, she pressed a kiss against the warmth of his palm.

"Dimi! I'm so glad you're awake! I've been sitting here all afternoon."

His lips turned up into a small smile. "Sorry to keep you waiting."

She punched him lightly on the arm.

"Ouch!" he cried out in mock protest.

She couldn't stop grinning. "Dimi, you have no idea how worried I was. Even when the doctors assured me you were going to pull through. When I walked in the kitchen and saw you on the floor..."

Dimitri shuddered, as if reliving the memories, too. Shelby was immediately contrite. She'd been through nothing compared to her brother. She'd wait for him to get well again before discussing the awful scene with him again.

"What's going to happen to Mom?" Dimitri asked quietly.

"Dimi, we don't have to talk about this now. I... I shouldn't have said anything."

"No, I want to. I assume she's been arrested."

Shelby nodded. Samuel moved to put an arm around her shoulders. She was grateful for his show of support. She cleared her throat.

"It was mayhem there for a while. Momma was screaming the house down, Daddy was doing his best to calm the situation and you were bleeding all over the tiles. The next thing I realized, the police were there, yelling at Momma to put the knife down. She went berserk and stabbed Daddy... The police shot her, but she's all right. They treated her for minor injuries and then took her to the station. They sent a couple more detectives back to interview us. No doubt now you're awake, they'll want to speak with you, too."

"Is Dad all right?" Dimitri asked, his eyes shadowed.

Shelby assured him their father was going to be fine. Dimitri gave her a weak smile.

"I'm glad. He didn't deserve to go like that."

"No one does," Samuel said quietly. "It's a shame your mother didn't tell anyone how she was feeling. She could have gotten some help."

Both Shelby and Dimitri remained silent, each lost in their thoughts. As far as Shelby was concerned, the grudge their mother had borne against gay men went back decades. She wasn't sure any amount of therapy would have helped. It saddened her to think it, but she felt it deep in her bones. As if sensing her thoughts, Samuel tightened his arm about her shoulders.

"We might leave Dimitri to rest, honey," he said.

With a murmur of agreement, Shelby leaned over and kissed her brother on the cheek. "I'm so glad you're going to be all right, Dimi. And don't worry about Momma and Daddy. It will all work out one way or the other. Just think, now that you've come out, you can live your life however you want."

A frown marked his face. "What will all the others think?"

Shelby didn't pretend to misunderstand him. "Our brothers and sisters will get used to the idea and they'll love you just as much as ever. Just see how they've rallied around you now? The nurses had to restrict their visits to two at a time. They've been so worried. You're our big brother, Dimi. Nothing changes that."

Dimitri's eyes shone bright with tears and he hurriedly waved them off. "Go, the pair of you, before I turn into a blubbering mess."

With a fond smile and a wave of good-bye, they left the room, hand in hand.

Epilogue

Six months later

The first sounds of the wedding march being played by the strings and piano reached Shelby's ears. She turned to her father and reached for his arm, not feeling the slightest bit nervous. It was like she'd been waiting for this day her whole life and she was going to enjoy every minute. She guessed her calmness had a lot to do with the man who waited for her at the altar.

When someone was as sure as she was that she'd met her soul mate and was about to join with him as one, nerves didn't come into the equation. If anything, she was impatient to see it done. They'd waited as long as they had out of respect for the family and their mother. Her trial had come and gone and she'd been brought before the courts for sentencing.

In the end, she'd pleaded guilty by reason of insanity and it was probably the best outcome for all. She'd spend the next twenty years behind the high walls of a secure psychiatric facility. Still, knowing that her mother wasn't here at her wedding filled her with sadness. Momma would never attend a family gathering again—at least, not for a very long time.

"Are you all right, Shelby?" her father asked, peering at her with concern.

"Yes, Daddy. I was just thinking about Momma. I'm sorry it turned out this way."

"Me, too. I just wish she'd said something years ago, before her hate became all-consuming. I can't help but wonder if there was anything I could have done. I blame myself for not knowing how much our secrets were affecting her. I lived with her for more than three decades. If anyone could have known about it, I was the one."

"You can't blame yourself, Daddy. She was good at keeping secrets."

He looked at her sadly. "We both were."

As the music coming from inside the church began to swell, Shelby leaned over and kissed her dad against his cheek.

"Let's not think about it now, Daddy. Today is all about love and laughter and new beginnings. I love Samuel more than I ever thought possible and we've promised each other we'll never keep secrets."

"I'm glad you found someone special, Shelby. Samuel's a good man. I've seen the way he looks at you. You've done well for yourself and you've done your aunts and uncle proud. They're seated in the front row beside Dimitri and his partner. Cornelius has been keeping them occupied with amusing anecdotes of his life working as a male stripper. Last time I checked, your aunts had grins stretching from ear to ear."

Shelby smiled. "I'm so glad Dimitri found someone to make him happy and that the family have accepted his way of life."

Her father gave her an embarrassed smile. "I think the aunts and uncles were more shocked about me than your brother. I think it made it easier on him."

Shelby kissed him on the cheek. "Well, I'm just glad we can put all of that behind us and get on living our lives."

Her father nodded and held out his arm. "I agree. Let's get on with it, then."

As she entered the church to the strains of Pachabel's beautiful *Canon in D*, she gazed down the aisle to where Samuel stood. Paul and his other brothers stood beside him. In a few minutes, Samuel Munro would be her husband. To have and to hold, in sickness and in health, from this day forward. She couldn't wait.

Note to Readers

I do hope you have enjoyed reading Shelby and Samuel's story. If you've enjoyed this book, please feel free to leave a review for The Cliff-Top Killer at Goodreads and your favorite digital retailer. Every review is very much appreciated.

Receive a free book when you sign up for my newsletter at www.christaylorauthor.com.au. You will also receive news on upcoming stories, release dates, book launches and other snippets. I love to receive feedback from my readers. Please feel free to contact me at chris@christaylorauthor.com.au.

The Likeable Fraudster is the next book in the Sydney Harbour Hospital Series.

Here's a sneak peek:

Jake Alexander has it all. Young, single and good-looking, he's living the high life as a successful doctor running a Sydney Harbour Hospital medical practice with Shane Kirkbride and Kevin Johnson, his two best friends from college.

But then, Shane is found murdered in the back room of the clinic and the police are insistent the murder was an inside job. It's ludicrous to think that Jake or Kevin might be responsible, but the police have the two of them in their sights.

Kevin is let off the hook when he produces an alibi—he was out to dinner with his girlfriend and there are plenty of witnesses to back him up. Jake isn't so lucky. He has no one who can come forward and vouch for his whereabouts. The police turn up the heat.

Jake isn't surprised to discover Katrina West is Kevin's alibi. As Kevin's long term girlfriend, the pair are as good as joined at the hip. It pains Jake to admit it, but the two of them make a great couple and will no doubt one day marry. The thought depresses the hell out of him, but there's nothing he can do. His only hope is to get over his feelings for Kat and find a woman as perfect as she.

But as the police investigation becomes more pointed, Jake is flat out just trying to survive. Why won't they believe his protestations of innocence? Why is he the only one who believes they're wasting their time? Meanwhile, the person who did it might very well get away with murder...

The Likeable Fraudster will be released on 28 February, 2017 and is available for pre-order from your favorite digital retailer.

ABOUT THE AUTHOR

Chris Taylor grew up on a farm in north-west New South Wales, Australia. She always had a thirst for stories and recalls writing her first book at the ripe old age of eight. Always a lover of romance and happily-ever-afters, a career in criminal law sparked her interest in intrigue and suspense. For Chris to be able to combine romance with suspense in her books is a dream come true.

Chris is married to Linden and is the mother of five children. If not behind her computer, you can find her doing the school run, taxiing children to swimming lessons, football, ballet and cricket. In her spare time, Chris loves to read her favorite authors who include Richard North Patterson, Sandra Brown, Kathleen E Woodiwiss and Jude Devereaux.

You can find out more about Chris and sign up for her newsletter at her website:

http://www.christaylorauthor.com.au